PRAISE F

"Peering into the daily lives ... provide a thrill for readers . . ."

—*Booklist*

"[*Raven Lane*] sticks to your skin and makes you second-guess your assumptions."

—*Pique Newsmagazine*

"Amber Cowie has written an unputdownable suburban nightmare, which calls into question all our safe assumptions about what happens on the other side of the picket fence. *Raven Lane* will linger with you long after the final page."

—Blake Crouch, bestselling author of *Dark Matter*

"*Raven Lane* is a sexy, provocative thriller about devastating secrets and shocking behavior in one bohemian, suburban enclave. With timely themes and boundary-pushing revelations, *Raven Lane* starts with a bang and doesn't let up until the final jaw-dropping twist."

—Robyn Harding, international bestselling author of *Her Pretty Face*

"Beware! Enter the sexy, sordid affairs of *Raven Lane* with a clear schedule, because you won't be able to put this *hot* thriller down. Paired with your favorite vino or tea, you'll find the escape into this suspenseful page-turner full of delicious betrayals. Loved it. Clever. Unique. Hot. Devilish fun."

—Shannon Kirk, international bestselling author of *Method 15/33*, *In the Vines*, and *Gretchen*

"A fateful accident on an otherwise lovely summer evening opens a veritable menu of lust, lies, and buried secrets for restaurateur Esme; her husband, Benedict; and their neighbors. Atmospheric and edgy, *Raven Lane* serves up a satisfying tale of questionable choices and their unanticipated consequences."

—Linda Keir, author of *The Swing of Things* and *Drowning with Others*

"Nothing is quite as it seems on idyllic Raven Lane. Inside this carefully curated neighborhood, accomplished artists, writers, and musicians inhabit their beautiful modern homes and each other's lives, but something sinister lurks just beneath the surface. A terrible car accident unravels a litany of lies and betrayals as police begin to consider the possibility of a murder. This haunting thriller will keep you reading late into the night!"

—D. M. Pulley, author of *The Dead Key* and *No One's Home*

"Amber Cowie's *Raven Lane* is the sly, sexy, irresistible tale of a family—make that an entire neighborhood—that embraces self-deception as a means of daily survival. The result is a page-turning piece of fictional anthropology that illustrates the tragic differences between what we are, what we imagine we are, and what others want us to be. I'm sorry that it's over."

—Bryan Gruley, author of *Bleak Harbor*

"In *Raven Lane*, Amber Cowie delivers a deliciously discomfiting and compelling domestic suspense told from the intimate third-person point of view of Esme Werner, whose version of events appears increasingly questionable after a terrible accident on a balmy September evening shatters the delicate facade of a privileged neighborhood, revealing a salaciously toxic—and deadly—tangle of relationships below. For fans of domestic suspense with unreliable narrators, this tale of marriages and parenthood gone wrong hits the right notes."

—Loreth Anne White, bestselling author of *In the Dark*

"Another thought-provoking read from Amber Cowie. Raven Lane is a seemingly tight-knit community of close friends but which is shot through with misconceptions and murderous secrets. Interwoven into the tightly written plot is a book within a book, cleverly reflecting the goings-on in *Raven Lane*. Do we all have a monster within us? Keep turning those pages to find out."

—Imogen Clark, bestselling author of *Postcards from a Stranger* and *Where the Story Starts*

PRAISE FOR *RAPID FALLS*

"*Rapid Falls* is an ingenious thriller cleverly disguised as a straightforward story about two sisters coping with the aftermath of a tragedy. Just when I'd thought I'd figured it out, the novel twisted into something entirely different, leading to an ending worthy of Alfred Hitchcock. You aren't going to want to miss this remarkable novel."

—Karen McQuestion, bestselling author of *Hello Love*

"*Rapid Falls* flips the script of the family saga of tough love and simmering resentments so hard and fast I think I got vertigo. Dark, delicious, and utterly subversive . . . I leave you with a warning: this one packs a wallop."

—Emily Carpenter, author of *Every Single Secret*

"Blood is thicker than water, but in *Rapid Falls*, both are fraught with danger. Sibling rivalry, obsessive first love, and a tragedy that haunts a family: the suspense had me hooked, desperate to see what secrets would surface. But that's the trouble with sisters—how can you hide a dark heart from the person who knows you best?"

—Jo Furniss, bestselling author of *All the Little Children* and *The Trailing Spouse*

"In this smart, riveting thriller reminiscent of Patricia Highsmith's works, a dark alchemy of family secrets and sibling rivalry spins ever more wildly toward a shocking, diabolical ending. I couldn't put it down!"

—A. J. Banner, *USA Today* bestselling author of *The Twilight Wife*

"In *Rapid Falls*, two sisters are haunted by a prom night tragedy. One's life is spiraling out of control and one seems intact. But appearances can be deceiving. Cowie brings her readers to the edge of a cliff and then dares them to dive off—right into the rough and tumble that is Rapid Falls. Twisty and gripping."

—Catherine McKenzie, bestselling author of *Fractured* and *The Good Liar*

"In *Rapid Falls*, everyone is the good guy in their own story. Like a spider spinning a web, Ms. Cowie skillfully takes this notion and elevates it to a fantastically dark and dizzying place. Say goodbye to any preconceived ideas about sisterhood, the power of grudges, or happily ever after, because this book will sweep them away and leave you gasping for more."

—Eliza Maxwell, bestselling author of *The Unremembered Girl*

"Hypnotic and darkly twisted, *Rapid Falls* is the true definition of a page-turner. It's so compelling that you will not want to put it down. Cowie's smart storytelling and mesmerizing prose paint a stunning debut, making it one of my favorite psychological thrillers of the year."

—Kerry Lonsdale, Amazon Charts and *Wall Street Journal* bestselling author

"*Rapid Falls* is a deeply seductive psychological thriller about two sisters and the secrets they struggle to keep as their lives—and their lies—begin to unravel."

—Sheena Kamal, bestselling author of *The Lost Ones*

"Years after a tragic car accident, a young woman's 'perfect' life unravels one stunning revelation at a time as the events of that fateful night come back to haunt her. Amber Cowie's gut-wrenching thriller sends you reeling through drunken bonfires, small-town intrigues, and family secrets as a single betrayal alters the course for everyone involved. A page-turner from start to finish; you can't look away until the jaw-dropping conclusion."

—D. M. Pulley, bestselling author of *The Buried Book*

LOSS
LAKE

OTHER TITLES BY AMBER COWIE

Rapid Falls

Raven Lane

LOSS LAKE

AMBER COWIE

A NOVEL

LAKE UNION
PUBLISHING

Published by Lake Union Publishing, Seattle

www.apub.com

Amazon, the Amazon logo, and Lake Union Publishing are trademarks of Amazon.com, Inc., or its affiliates.

ISBN-13: 9781542042017
ISBN-10: 1542042011

Cover design by Shasti O'Leary Soudant

Printed in the United States of America

To Lucas.
I think you would have liked this one.

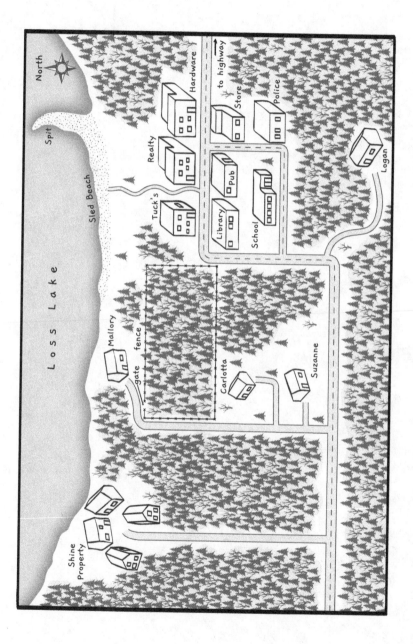

PART ONE

PART ONE

CHAPTER ONE

The lake seemed like an impossible ocean. Though it was nestled in the hollows of the northern mountains just as Mallory Dent had expected from its outline on her map, its endless expanse was nearly beyond her understanding now that it lay before her. As she drove toward it, the knots in her shoulders earned by hours behind the steering wheel untied. She had been anticipating the lake over the course of her thirteen-hundred-mile journey north. Now that she was here, she had a sense that it had been waiting for her too.

After another glance at the hand-drawn map her real estate agent had sent, she turned off the highway onto the main street of the town of McNamara, smiling at the friendly clapboard buildings that lined the road. The late-afternoon sun winked in the plate-glass windows like a jocular uncle as she passed. She breathed in deeply and tasted pine. The unseasonably warm fall weather was like a kiss of greeting. She hadn't expected it to feel so pleasant this far north. Or so familiar.

Twenty-seven hours before, when she had placed the last of her husband's belongings into a trash can beaded with precipitation, she had been chilled to the bone with the coming onslaught of the gray, wet Vancouver winter. As the afternoon sun beamed through her windows, the back of her neck was damp again but with sweat rather than cold rain. Her brown hair hung heavy, like an arm slung around her shoulders.

Tension continued to ebb from her body. Now that the feeling was dissipating, she realized how worried she had been about her decision to purchase a home in McNamara. For two months, she had been numb, her emotions nothing more than intellectual exercises, remote and curious, even while she planned the biggest move of her life. Though she'd known she was taking a risk when she bought a small ranch house sight unseen in the little town beside Loss Lake, fifty miles inland from the rugged northwest coast and more than a thousand miles north of Vancouver, she had told herself it was a gift to be so reckless. She was alone now. She could make her own mistakes. Graham was dead.

The thought of her husband clawed at her throat like a small animal. She swallowed hard, then tapped the brakes of her silver sedan at the only stoplight in town, which was inexplicably red despite hers being the only car in sight. The pause gave her the opportunity to look at her surroundings more closely.

To her right was an old-fashioned hardware store. Its display window was jammed with sun-faded plastic Adirondack chairs and beach balls. Rakes and leaf bags were piled haphazardly on the side, suggesting a contentious clashing of the seasons. Further evidence of the infiltration of autumn were the hand-drawn pictures of jack-o'-lanterns strung from the roof. Their jaunty expressions provided a sweet charm to the scene. Her cheeks flushed with unexpected pleasure, as if it had been her own child who had drawn the decisive yet wobbly lines on the paper pumpkins. The feeling was odd and unexpected. She and Graham had decided not to become parents when they had married ten years ago. As a forty-year-old widow, it was now both biologically and socially unlikely that would change. But the thought reinforced her deepest hope about her new life. In McNamara, anything was possible.

Beside the hardware store was a tiny real estate office. Mallory saw the name Betty Barber, the same woman who had sold her the house, painted on the sign dug into the small patch of immaculate white pebbles out front. It made sense. The town didn't seem large enough to need more than one person selling houses. Through the gap between the buildings, a trail wove its way toward the shining water of Loss Lake. Mallory had been told that the lake was man-made, unexpectedly caused by the failure of a dam farther upstream in the mid-1970s. Apparently, the water had flooded the valley like a tidal wave, trapping trees below the surface and submerging everything in its path. Despite what remained in its depths, the lake looked as picturesque as a postcard.

On the other side of the street, there was a small grocery store. The exterior of the building—light-brown shingles and big windows covered with flyers boasting sales and bargains—was nondescript, but something about the place seemed welcoming. She promised herself she would return to it soon. Never before had her time seemed such a luxurious, ample commodity. Without the encumbrances of school, work, and relationships, she could explore her new community at leisure. Graham's death had given her freedom in the worst possible way. She had to try to make the best of it despite the guilt that clung to her like sticky cobwebs.

The directions that Betty had provided indicated that her new house was located a few miles west on the same sandy shoreline that bordered the main street to the north. The light turned green, and she pressed the accelerator. She had never lived by herself, much less owned a home on her own, free and clear. She had moved from her parents' house into a college dorm, then found a shared residence with a few of her fellow nurses post graduation, where she had stayed until Graham had proposed. The idea of stepping into a house that was wholly hers was unimaginable. She unrolled her window, and the scent of the trees became stronger. Her body was absorbing pieces of this unfamiliar world with every breath. As the car rolled forward, the pressure of becoming someone new became more daunting than exciting.

"You can do this," Mallory murmured like a mantra. She recited the next steps of the directions in her mind. *Turn left at the gas station on the corner, then take the first right onto the dirt road.* Betty had told her to use a tree that had been struck by lightning as a landmark, which had seemed strange, but after about a mile on the bumpy road, she spotted the wizened trunk and branches that had been snarled and stunted by a storm. Betty was right. It was unmistakable even for a city girl like herself. She turned fast, and the back of her car swung out violently. As she righted the wheel, her heart was beating hard enough to feel in her fingertips. When her tires gripped the dusty road once more, Mallory's courage returned. Steadying the vehicle made her feel as bold as a race car driver. She had never driven on an unpaved road in her life, and the jolts beneath her wheels reminded her of what she had already overcome to get to this place.

She drove faster. The two buildings on the right-hand side of the road blurred in the corner of her eye as her car flew by. The road sloped down and then up, obscuring her view of the water she knew was in front of her. Her attention was drawn to the dense stretch of forest to her left that threatened to swallow up the road. The trees were tall and tight, a mix of green, red, and orange. In some places, their branches knit together like a sweater. Dappled sunshine flickered across the dirt road. The mischievous shadows disguised the hollows and ruts, forcing Mallory's eyes to adjust to the change in the light.

As she continued down the road, the forest rose up on the right-hand side of the road as well, forming a tunnel of bark and leaves. Strangely, the trees here were encompassed by a tall chain-link fence. From what she remembered of the map Betty had sent, Mallory knew this fence marked the southern edge of her hundred-acre property. One hundred acres of forest and beach. It was too huge to comprehend on a piece of paper, let alone stretching out in front of her. Mallory had grown up in Vancouver. Properties there were not measured in such vast terms, and prices were incomparable. The money from the sale of her and Graham's house had been enough to buy the house and property outright, making her the second largest landowner in McNamara, her real estate agent had trilled. Mallory had been sickened at the idea that Graham's death had resulted in her wealth. She pushed aside that fact as she passed tree after tree. Knowing that each of them belonged to her was surreal after a lifetime of limited urban lawns.

Seeing the forest in real life made the previous landowner's decision to install a chain-link fence more inscrutable. Its presence suggested that the network of plants, trees, and moss had to be caged like dangerous animals in a zoo, but the area seemed too wild to be contained by the unfriendly barrier. Uncultivated nature sprang from the ground all around her. Odder still was the fact that the metal links did not extend around the entire property—only the large, forested section between the neighboring house and her own—which indicated that the purpose of the fence wasn't security. The long stretch of shoreline that she owned was left unrestricted, leaving the northern access points to her home from the lake completely open. Instead, the placement suggested that it had been designed to keep something in rather than to ensure people stayed out. She made a note to ask Betty about it, feeling a pang of concern that other important items might also have slipped her notice. Since Graham had died, Mallory had sometimes found herself struggling to follow the thread of conversations. Several times, she had entered a room only to become bewildered by her purpose in being there. It worried her to think that the fog that clogged her thoughts might have also obscured her ability to understand details about her new home, but she willed the concern away. She was here now. She would learn what she needed to know.

The trees thinned a little on both sides of the road, and Mallory passed the northern perimeter of the fence. Ten feet farther up, as the map had promised, a driveway—her driveway!—appeared on the right. She turned onto it, feeling triumphant in her ability to find her way. Graham had always assumed the role of navigator in their relationship. She was pleased to realize that had been more a habit than a necessity. The road that led to her new home had been cleared to the width of two cars. The leafy trees that stood like soldiers on either side of it were also flirting with autumn, their broad leaves turning from green to the same vibrant hues of yellow, orange, and red she had noticed on the main road.

Then, as the dirt road crested to the level of the shore, the lake came into view once again. This time, the sight made her gasp. Though she had grown up beside the ocean, which nearly lapped against the sidewalks of Vancouver, Loss Lake seemed more vast and imposing. The gentle slope of the narrow lane shortened the foreground, making the lake blur into the deep-blue sky above it. The blended horizon of water and air seemed to go on forever. The late-day sunlight bounced off the surface like headlights approaching her on a dark highway. A light breeze picked up. The ripple of the waves reminded her of the way the piano keys had moved when her mother used to play.

Three days before, during their final dinner together, her mother had asked Mallory if she really believed uprooting herself and moving more than a thousand miles northwest was the right decision, especially so soon after her husband's death. Mallory knew the question was underscored by her mother's deep dread of change. She still lived in the same split-level suburban home she and Mallory's father had purchased shortly after their marriage. Mallory hadn't let her mother's anxiety nip at her heels. She was in motion. The goodbye dinner was a formality, one last thing to tick off her list. Mallory had already left her old life behind. One house was sold and the other bought. One person was alive and the other dead. It was time to go. She told her mother that she had been in limbo for nearly two months. She couldn't stay a minute longer in the house where Graham had died.

Her mother's eyes had shone as she murmured her understanding. As they embraced, Mallory could feel her mother relaxing. On some level, she knew her mother was happy to have her gone. Mallory was living proof of her mother's greatest fear. All her life, her mother had fretted about women left alone by the passing of their husbands. Having

Mallory safely ensconced in a home of her own more than a day's drive away meant that she didn't have to be reminded of her daughter's plight and her own to come. Someday, possibly soon, Mallory's father would end up succumbing to liver damage from his quiet alcoholism. As her mother kissed her cheek, she had asked Mallory to check in once a month. Mallory had agreed. She knew it was unlikely that they would speak much more than that.

Though she had made her decision quickly, moving to McNamara hadn't been as rash as her mother thought. Mallory's methodical training as a nurse was too ingrained for that. Before making her purchase, Mallory had assessed the small town. McNamara was small and remote—the closest community to it was a town of five thousand people called Turner about seventy-five miles away—but the tiny population of only three hundred and fifty-four people was close-knit and active. Mallory had seen an activity listed every month of the year on the online community calendar: festivals, Bake-Offs, and dances. The social media groups were active, and people were unusually kind to each other in the forums, often gently policing anyone who made negative posts or offhand comments that could be interpreted as insults. The lack of a hospital in town wasn't a deterrent to her, though it meant reentering her field would be challenging. Even after purchasing her new property, the sale of their home had left her with enough of a financial cushion that she didn't have to worry about finding work again anytime soon. It was possible that, with careful planning, she might never nurse again. But what had really sealed the deal for the small northern town was the lake that hugged the residential and commercial areas like a lover. In photographs, Mallory had been drawn to it. In real life, the effect was amplified beyond measure. Loss Lake may have been an accident, but it was mesmerizing. She unrolled her window another inch to hear the waves as she drove forward to her home and her future.

As the road jogged to the right, Mallory finally saw her brown-shingled one-level home. Like the lake, it looked exactly like the pictures Betty had emailed her but somehow entirely different in its three-dimensional reality. A tiny thrill ran down Mallory's spine, and she realized that a part of her had doubted it actually existed. The sale of her previous home had felt so onerous and time consuming, though it had been rapid compared to the usual time frame of real estate. There had been moments when Mallory believed she would never be able to leave the house in which she no longer belonged. To fill the time she'd rubbed her hands raw cleaning, but the air inside had still smelled sour, like something inside the walls had spoiled.

In contrast, the clean lines of the ranch house standing in front of the lake radiated strength and peace as they had in the digital images Mallory often pulled up on her laptop late at night after the purchase had been finalized. The house wasn't beautiful, but it looked solid and strong, like it could weather the blows of guilt and grief that Mallory had been forced to absorb during every one of the sixty-two nights since Graham had died. It was surrounded by a wide expanse of lawn and well-tended flower beds. The leaves of a cluster of fading marigolds were browning as fall began to take hold, but nothing could diminish the beauty of the property.

She winced as her back tire hit a particularly deep pothole, drawing her gaze away from the velvety water that made the scene as bucolic as a landscape painting. She pulled slowly into a level spot outside the front door, shifted to park, got out of the car, and stretched herself into a straight line. The movement reminded her of how her body had changed over the twelve months of Graham's illness. Though she had quit her job and done her best to nurse her husband by herself, the task had proved too much to handle alone. She had lost nearly as much weight as Graham by the end due to stress and lack of sleep. Back in Vancouver, her weight loss had made her feel insubstantial, as if her sadness were eating away at her the same way Graham's illness had at him. Here, it made her feel as light as the whispering breeze.

She marveled at the way the house had been built to encompass a view that hadn't existed yet. Prior to the flood in 1974, the large plate-glass window in the front that looked through an identically sized window in the back would have shown nothing more than a forest like the one behind her circled by the chain-link fence. Now, Mallory could peer through both windows to see the rolling water nudging at the small beach on the other side of the house. It made her new home seem hollow, nothing more than a darkened tunnel to the lake. She shook her head to rid it of the strange idea, and another thought rushed in. During their search for a home together, Graham had rejected a ranch house, calling it a shoebox for old people. She had acquiesced, and they had ended up with a two-story.

She let a deep breath lift her shoulders, sighed out the memory of her husband, then made her way to the house. She kicked a few small stones, causing them to roll out in front of her like tiny footmen paving the path to the front door. As Betty had directed, Mallory extracted a key from beneath the mat, still in awe of the fact that the practice was commonplace in McNamara, and slid it into the lock. Despite the rust that surrounded the aged lock, the key turned effortlessly.

She let the door swing open without stepping inside. Now that she was here, she wanted to savor her new house, unwrapping it as slowly as possible, the way she used to eat her candy bars as a child. She decided to unload the car first before exploring every room and spent the next half hour ferrying the dozen boxes and suitcases that contained what was left of her old life to the threshold of her new one. With each step, she grew more excited. After depositing a particularly heavy box on a stack inside the door, she thought she heard a high-pitched shriek on the wind. She stepped outside quickly to discern its source and paused, her body still, but the only sound was the rustle of dancing leaves. She continued with her task, and, finally, the house contained everything she had wanted to keep from her past.

She raised the fob and beeped her car locked. The electronic chirp sounded out of place among the bird calls and the waves. With a slow smile, she pressed the button again and unlocked her doors. Hearing the mechanisms release made her feel safe. According to Betty, McNamara was a place where locks weren't necessary.

Finally, it was time.

She edged past the tower of boxes, past the entryway closet on the left side of the narrow passage, and into the kitchen. The back window of the house faced directly north, and the beatific light from the low sun warmed the space. To the right of the kitchen were a back door and an open space for a dining room table. Beyond that was a large room sandwiched by the two large windows she had seen from outside. Mallory chuckled softly at the yellow shag carpet that covered the floor and the faux cedar planking that lined the walls. Though the glints of changing light from the water sparkling throughout the dated room were pretty enough to make the deep mustard color slightly less unpleasant, even the sun couldn't save the room from the tragedy of its original furnishings. The house hadn't been updated since it was built in the mid-1960s, and it showed. The air smelled of dust with a whiff of body odor, like an old sweater left in a drawer too long.

So many ways to make it your own, Betty had cooed over the phone.

Mallory had been unexpectedly moved by the clichéd pitch. Making something her own was a dream that she'd never realized she had until the real estate agent had suggested it. But her excitement had also troubled her. She had been married for so long. It was difficult to shift her place in the world from the collective to the individual without feeling the heaviness of guilt.

Now that she was here, however, the idea of redesigning a home with only herself in mind had become more inspiring than treacherous. It was another way the light of McNamara was able to pierce through the aftermath of Graham's dark death. She began taking an inventory of what she loved about the place and what she would change. The windows were incredible, and whoever had built the place had been forward-thinking enough to keep the living space open rather than create the boxed-in rooms of many houses of the era. Only the foyer was fully divided from the living room by a wall. The kitchen kept its sense of openness with a pass-through between the hanging cabinets and the counter.

She looked to the left. Past the kitchen, a long hallway led into the other half of the house. From the floor plan Betty had sent her, she knew that there were two large bedrooms at the end of the hall with a bathroom between them. As she began to make her way toward them, a sharp knock on the front door made her jump. Mallory bit her lip in uncertainty. *You can do this. It's likely a friendly neighbor,* she told herself as she moved toward it. *People here must know things almost before they happen.*

She swung the door open and saw a tall man with close-cropped sandy-blond hair. His hazel eyes turned gold as a sunbeam lit his face. He looked stern, almost aggressively masculine. *So not my type,* she thought before reversing course immediately. She didn't have a type. She was married. Except she wasn't. She spoke to cover her ping-ponging thoughts.

"Hello?"

It sounded more like a question than a greeting. Halfway through the word, she had registered that the man was in uniform. A police officer.

"Good afternoon, ma'am." His hard gaze swept her face, her body, and then flitted from box to box behind her before returning to make eye contact. "Sorry to bother you. I can see you've just arrived."

"I did, yes," Mallory said.

"Uh-huh," he said.

Mallory noticed a muscle jump along his straight jawline. It was shadowed with stubble salted with silver where the darker hair had faded. He looked to be in his midforties. Younger than Graham had been, but older than her.

"Are you the welcoming committee?" she asked weakly when the silence grew uncomfortable.

The officer closed his eyes, then rubbed under each of them in turn. On another person the gesture might have looked like swiping away tears, but this man didn't look like he cried often. Mallory guessed he was brushing away his own fatigue.

"No, ma'am. I wish I was. I'm Sergeant Joel Benson. I'm here to inform you of a death."

Her heartbeat faltered. Was McNamara really small enough to warrant a police officer delivering news like this to every household?

"That's awful. Who died?"

He eyed her carefully, and she realized how stupid her question had been. She had hardly been in town for more than five minutes. How could she possibly know the person? She covered her confusion by looking at the ranking stripes on his chest, then realized it might seem suspicious to avoid his eyes. She forced herself to reconnect with his gaze.

"Sorry. I'm sure you can't release the details."

His expression didn't change as he answered her. "Best we can tell it was a drowning, but they'll be sending a coroner up from Turner shortly."

"Oh my God," Mallory replied. Black spots crowded the edge of her vision. She took a deep breath to try to dispel them.

"Bad business, for sure," the sergeant said. "It was on that beach about a mile from the turnoff to town. You would have seen it on the way in."

Mallory blinked hard as she tried to figure out how to answer him. She had seen the beach. In fact, she had stopped there to stretch her legs. It didn't seem worth mentioning. "The one with the spit?"

The sergeant paused again, and his severe eyes grew thoughtful as he considered her wording. "Well, sure. We call it Sled Beach, because it used to be where everyone took out their toboggans, but I guess it is more of a spit now."

"A sledding hill? It's underwater," Mallory replied.

"Didn't used to be. Not before the dam burst."

"But surely you aren't old enough to remember that?"

His mouth quirked, but Mallory couldn't tell if it was a suppressed smile or a twitch of annoyance.

"No. That was about a year before I came along. It's the way everyone refers to it. I suppose people around here have a long memory."

Another question burst out of her before she realized she was going to ask it.

"Do you tell all the residents of McNamara when someone passes away?"

He paused again. Mallory thought she saw confusion crease his expression before it hardened again into a solemn gaze.

"No, of course not. But it's my legal duty to notify the landowner," he said.

"What do you mean?"

"Ma'am, the death occurred on your property. It's triggered a formal investigation. We need to rule out your negligence."

CHAPTER TWO

The space under her arms became unpleasantly clammy.

"Negligence?"

"Yes. Ma'am, maybe it's best for me to come in. We can discuss this inside."

It didn't sound like a suggestion. She stepped back to allow the sergeant to move past her into the house. She realized that it was odd for her to let him take the lead only as he turned sideways to squeeze past her unpacked boxes. Despite the leaning tower, he moved confidently. All her professional life, she had been trained to acquiesce to doctors. More recently, she had acted the same way when the paramedics answered her call after she had found Graham, breathless and tinged with blue, in the hospital bed they'd had installed in the main room. But it seemed wrong to begin her new life with the same behavior. She wanted to be different in McNamara than she had been in Vancouver.

She drew herself up to her full height of five foot five as she followed the sergeant. Once in the kitchen, she noticed that the cupboards were more orange than they had appeared in photos. She tried not to let the discrepancy between the images and reality underline the way the sergeant's arrival had changed her first nearly sacred moment in the house to something closer to profane. She fought the hopelessness that threatened to overcome her, but it was too late. The news of another death so close to her dulled the energy her earlier joy had given her. She struggled to remember the name of the sergeant but found it had been lost somewhere in her distracted thoughts. Once again, her mind was miles away from her.

The sergeant leaned against the side of the U-shaped counter farthest away from the living room as he spoke. Unlike her, he looked at ease. Now that he was out of the sunlight, his eyes had darkened to a shade close to cinnamon. She tried to mimic his relaxed posture on the counter across from him, but the handle of the drawer dug into her spine.

"I'm going to need to take down some details," the sergeant said, a spiral-bound notepad already in hand. She nodded despite the fact that his eyes were trained on the paper. "So you are Mrs. Mallory Dent. Recently widowed."

She was surprised that he already knew her name, but she reminded herself that news traveled fast in a town as small as McNamara.

"Yes, that is correct."

Her voice came out tighter than she had hoped. She swallowed hard to loosen the coiling muscles in her neck, recalling an urban legend that had circulated among her friends when she was a teenager about a woman who had broken her neck by turning it too quickly to the side. She willed herself to relax, sipping at the air like her yoga instructor used to recommend.

"Ma'am? Are you all right? You look pale. Must have been a long drive coming all the way from Vancouver."

Again, Mallory was uneasy that he knew where she was from. When had the drowning been discovered? How had he had time to ask questions about her?

The sergeant shifted his weight forward. Despite herself, Mallory flinched. A flash of sympathy tugged down the creases at the corners of his eyes before he turned and pulled open the door of a large supply closet to his right. As she watched in surprise, he took out two folding chairs before returning to the center of the kitchen and unfolding one for her with a squeak. The closeness of his body unnerved her almost as much as his knowledge of the contents of the closet, but he didn't seem to notice.

After he had placed the second chair opposite hers, he met her eyes again and indicated she should sit. He seemed to be making it clear that this was not a social call. Mallory settled on the seat, and the sergeant did the same. The space in the kitchen was limited, especially given the length of the man's legs. Their knees were only inches away from touching, which made Mallory feel more uncomfortable. She had not been alone with a man other than her husband for the last year. Before that, her contact with other men had been limited to other staff at the hospital where she used to work. Graham had been the first man she'd seriously dated, so it wasn't as though she had any history to draw on before him. Since Graham had died, she had kept her distance from other people both physically and emotionally. They'd had only a handful of close friends who had come for the funeral, then mercifully faded away from her, back into their own lives.

She took another deep breath but felt no less clouded by the disassociation that had been her default setting for months. She was present but far away. Aware but not absorbing. *This is a routine notification,* she thought. *You must remember what the sergeant says. It might be important later.*

"I apologize. It has been a long day, and this is very upsetting news. Yes, I am Mallory Dent. I bought this property . . ." She trailed off, unable to recall the date when she had signed the papers. Mallory's slow mind could summon only vague memories of insurance forms and homeowner reports.

The sergeant flipped to the previous page in his book. "September first. Just over a month ago. The property was empty and ready for occupation immediately. You moved quickly."

"You know a lot about me," Mallory said.

"Betty Barber filled me in. McNamara is a close-knit community, Mrs. Dent."

Mallory was oddly chastened at his words, as if it were she who was breaching protocol and not him.

"Of course."

"We do have rules, however. I'll need to see some identification from you."

"Sure," she said. "My purse is by the door."

She rose from her chair, feeling grateful for a moment on her own, fleeting as it was. Once he had looked over her license and taken down her cell phone number, he regarded her with curiosity.

"A big move for you."

Mallory agreed, though she wasn't sure it had been a question.

"I've lived here most of my life. I'm trying to wrap my head around a person who buys a property in a town they've never visited without ever seeing it."

Mallory's cheeks burned. "I saw photos."

"Did Betty give you a property map at least? Do you know how big your piece is?"

She hesitated before she said yes.

From the skeptical look on the sergeant's face, she sensed her answer had been unconvincing. She had looked over the document as carefully as she would have reviewed any medical chart, but now that he was staring at her, she couldn't recall much more than the fact that it was a rectangle. The specific demarcations and landmarks had flown from her mind in a way that she had never experienced before. Had the weight of grief crushed her ability to think straight?

"Okay, I need to show you something." The sergeant scrawled a rough sketch on a fresh sheet of paper from his notepad, using the main street of the town for reference. "I'm no cartographer, but this should give you a sense of where we are and where the accident happened."

As Mallory looked at his drawing, a few details returned to her from the map Betty Barber had sent. Her property was a rectangle with a long backside of shoreline. Her house, which the sergeant had marked with an *X*, was located close to the western edge of the property. The sergeant's drawing indicated that the chain-link fence she had seen circled the entirety of the wooded area, as Betty had noted. The rest of her property extended all the way behind the shops she had seen on Main Street, right to the highway, encompassing Sled Beach on the eastern side. Of course the small beach she had stopped at on the way in belonged to her. How could she not have realized that? She tried to cover her shame with a sigh and a smile.

"It has been a long day, Sergeant. I did receive a deed and a map. It's coming back to me now. I think it was just a shock to see you and to hear your news," she said.

"Yes, it was a shock to us all." He shifted back into his seat. "Did you stop anywhere along the way? Or push on through?"

She paused, knowing that her frequent withdrawal from the conversation must be making her seem odd, but she needed time to gather her thoughts. She worried that mentioning the fact she had stopped on the beach in question would make her seem involved in whatever had happened. Besides, the whole journey was becoming so fuzzy in her mind she wasn't sure she could trust herself to talk about it.

It had taken her two days to get to McNamara from Vancouver. After a frustratingly late start on the first morning due to her inability to locate her wallet, which she had sworn she left by the door the night before, she had been relieved to get into the car. As she drove, the busy streets of the city had become a major expressway that cut through fields recently devastated by the fall harvest. About five hours past Vancouver, the road narrowed again into a single-lane highway that wove and pitched through mountain passes already treacherous with ice and the threat of snow. Higher and higher she had climbed, stretching her jaw frequently to pop her ears, marveling that she had never seen the peaks she was passing by though they were less than a day's drive from the city where she had lived all her life.

When the mountains dived into a green valley and the hills around her began to purple like a bruise, she pulled over at a cheap motel after eight hours on the road. Its sign boasted "Cheap Beds and Cheap Eats," which seemed more like an insult than a promise, but she had been too tired to risk staying on the road after dark to search for another place. Besides, Mallory had heard that Prince George, the small city where she spent the night, was the major outpost for McNamara and all the tiny towns to the north that had flecked her map like the dark bugs that had fallen prey to the force of her windshield. It seemed sensible to get a feel for it.

She had been proud of her adventurous spirit as she slipped under the thin sheets, telling herself that a true traveler wouldn't worry about the greasy feel of the tan quilted comforter that lay on her shoulders. Sure enough, she slept well for the first time in weeks. She was finally free of the seemingly endless demands of her husband's death: the paperwork, cleaning, and planning. For a few hours, she didn't have to worry about the tasks and facts that kept sliding through her mind like wet sand through open fingers. Despite its flimsy walls and the rattle of footsteps outside her door, the cheap motel room seemed safe. She had finally shaken the sense that something was creeping up behind her.

After a quick breakfast of coffee and toast at the diner attached to the motel, she was back on the road at 7:00 a.m., driving straight north as the sun rose cautiously on the right side of her car, where a passenger would have sat if she had not been alone. She had passed through Turner in the late afternoon, roughly an hour and a half before arriving in McNamara. She wasn't sure what level of detail the sergeant required, so she summarized the journey as succinctly as possible.

"I stayed the night in Prince George," she said.

"Okay," he said, writing it down.

She felt like she had passed a verbal exam. It made her bold enough to ask a question of her own.

"Can you tell me anything about the drowning?"

He looked at her carefully, then seemed to reach a positive conclusion. "Sled Beach looks pretty enough, but that spot is deceiving. We had a storm this morning, and best guess is the high volume of water caused a rip current."

"Is that like a riptide?"

"Yes. Loss Lake is big enough to generate waves under the water that are strong enough to pull a person out into the deep. You've got to be careful here after a storm. The wind pushes a lot of water up on the beach, and, when it recedes, a strong current can be created. It's temporary, usually only lasts a day or so, but if a person's not aware of it, it can be fatal."

"And that's what you think happened today?"

He gave a slight shrug that seemed to be more of a dismissal than an answer.

"Like I said, the coroner is on her way, and she'll probably bring somebody with her to suss out the weather conditions. But yeah, that's my best guess. Wouldn't be the first time."

"That's awful."

"As far as the victim goes, we don't have an identification yet. No one local. Someone passing through on the highway. My deputy is running the plates now. Could have stopped to cool off on their way through. It's strange to take a dip in early October around these parts, but it's warm enough today. Did you hear or see anything unusual when you arrived? Might have been right around the time you pulled in."

"No, I didn't," she said.

"The wind was probably kicking up in the wrong direction for you to hear much back here," he said.

Suddenly, Mallory remembered the unusual sound on the wind. She felt sick.

"Wait. I did hear a noise as I was unloading. Oh God. Do you think that could have been the person calling for help?"

The sergeant's expression sharpened. "What did it sound like?"

Mallory closed her eyes and willed herself to remember. "It was high-pitched, like a child. A sudden shriek."

"Close by?"

"Yes," Mallory answered. "It sounded like it came from across the lawn, near the edge of the forest. But I could be wrong."

The sergeant shook his head. "I'll look into it, but that sounds more like a hawk."

"It didn't sound like any bird call I've ever heard."

"No, ma'am. What I meant was that it sounded a lot like the sound a bunny makes when a hawk dives. They often scream right before the talons sink in."

Mallory was embarrassed and unnerved. "Maybe."

"The truth is most drownings are silent. This one might not have been discovered at all if it wasn't for a dog walker who saw a shape far out in the water and reported it. That stretch of beach isn't too busy this time of year."

She was taken aback at his casual admission that other people used her property, but she tried not to show it. The last thing she wanted was to break a small-town custom before she understood how things were done in McNamara. Maybe private property didn't mean the same thing when people had so much to spare. The sergeant continued.

"We had to get the helicopter up in the air to try and track the body. That current pulls fast and hard into the middle of the lake. We got up just in time to see someone was out there, but they sank before we could throw down a line. We might never be able to recover the body unless it washes up on shore."

Mallory's stomach flipped at the idea of a body floating in the water behind her house. Her eyes were drawn to the window above the sink, where, beyond the glass, the wind had coaxed curls on the surface of the water. A band of clouds had begun to form on the horizon, edging its way closer in a line of gray and black. In the silence, the sergeant stood up and walked over to the counter that divided the kitchen and dining room. He leaned over to peer through the pass-through into the empty room.

"Is your furniture arriving later?" he asked.

Mallory was too unsettled to soften her response. "No."

The sergeant narrowed his eyes.

Mallory felt wrong-footed and tried to explain. "I didn't want to bring it with me. My furniture reminded me of . . . where my husband died."

The words came out before she had a chance to catch them, and she prepared herself for the familiar recoil that came when she spoke of her husband without using euphemisms. But instead of the fearful contempt that usually showed up, the sergeant's expression changed into an expression close to compassion.

"I see."

He held her eyes for a moment, then looked away. Mallory sensed he understood that her decision had been rooted in more than the complexities of shipping furniture. Graham's death had forced her to learn that grief wasn't only an emotional state. True sorrow carried a person to a remote place. Grief was the process of finding a way back. Only those who had experienced it seemed to understand. The sergeant seemed to be one of them. She wondered who he had lost.

"At least you have two chairs now," he said, gesturing to the metal folding chair she was sitting on with a hint of a smile.

"Were these left over from the last owner?" she said. "That was kind of them."

His friendly expression faded.

"No. Betty put them in here; she has to bring something into houses that are on the market for a while so she can dust the high corners. This place has been empty for a long time—close to ten years now. The previous owners wouldn't have left anything behind."

His expression darkened further, and she didn't dare ask why no one had lived here for so long. He changed the subject.

"Did you stop in on Carlotta on your way in? It's good to know your neighbors when you live alone. You never know when you might need some help."

Mallory rubbed her arms as a slight chill passed over her. She hadn't thought to introduce herself. Already, it seemed she had misunderstood the rules of a small town.

"Carlotta?"

"Carlotta Gray. Your nearest neighbor," he said. "You would have passed her house coming in."

"The librarian," Mallory said, pleased to remember a snippet of Betty's descriptions.

"Yes, that's her." He looked around the room. "It's nice to see someone living here again."

"It's good to be here," she said.

The sergeant drew in a quick breath, then brushed lint off his thighs.

"Listen, I'll be in touch if there's anything else I need. You're not planning on taking a swim today, are you?"

"No."

"Good. Like I said, this lake is unpredictable at this time of year. It's best to be as cautious as you can. This isn't the first time I have had to look into a death like this."

"Other drownings?"

The sergeant cleared his throat. For the first time in their conversation, he appeared less than self-assured.

"Yes. There have been other deaths."

How many dead bodies lay on the lake floor? she wondered. This time she didn't turn toward the lake, though she still sensed it kicking up behind her. She imagined the increasing force of the water beating against the shore like a drum.

"The lake sounds dangerous."

"All lakes are dangerous, ma'am. If anyone says anything else, take it with a grain of salt."

"What do you mean?"

The sergeant looked like he regretted mentioning anything at all. "It's all foolishness, but I suppose you're bound to hear it sooner or later. Logan Carruthers has been banging on about it enough. There's talk of a monster in the lake."

Mallory tried to figure out how to respond to the sergeant's words. The offhand reference to someone she had never met was confusing but nowhere near as jarring as the idea of a creature living in the water outside her home.

"A monster? Like in Loch Ness?"

She thought she heard the sergeant breathe out a curse word that was barely audible as he exhaled.

"Something like that. Some business owners use the legend to drum up business, especially around this time of year."

"Is fall particularly dangerous?"

"Some people will tell you that the deaths aren't a coincidence. October is the month the valley was flooded back in 1974, and the deaths have always occurred in October."

A twinge of apprehension struck, as if the lake might swell suddenly and engulf her. She reminded herself she was exhausted from two long days of travel and the long months of grieving and nursing that had come before. The sergeant couldn't be suggesting anything supernatural.

"Do you believe there's a monster here?"

The side of the sergeant's mouth twitched again, but, this time, Mallory was nearly certain it was a hidden smile.

"Lakes like this one are powerful. It's important to respect the forces around us. You strike me as a woman who understands that. Be careful on that beach back there, and I'll keep you posted if anything else comes up that you need to know about."

Mallory was strangely flattered. She thanked the sergeant as he left to go back to his patrol car, only realizing when she heard his car door slam that she had forgotten to ask his name again. She closed the door but stepped away before she could follow through on her urge to slide the dead bolt into place. Though her earlier enthusiasm for eschewing locks had lessened, and McNamara didn't feel quite as safe now as it had before, she wanted to trust in the town and the security she hoped it contained. She had spent too much of her life being scared.

She walked to the window that faced the lake. The fifty-foot stretch of sand along the lapping water seemed more ominous after the sergeant's visit. Mallory shivered and wished she had thought to pack a kettle. A cup of tea would settle her nerves and give her the energy she needed to unpack. She looked at her watch and realized the Main Street store would likely still be open. She took one more quick look at the lake before walking back toward the front door. It seemed like the right time to properly introduce herself to McNamara. Maybe getting to know the people here would help her feel less alone.

CHAPTER THREE

As she swung open the plate-glass door of Kylie's Korner Store, Mallory was engulfed in a fog of patchouli. On a shelf above her head to the left, a circle of embers glowed on a cone of incense. Behind it, a large statue of Buddha sat, incongruously adorned in a mesh-backed baseball hat with the words "Cash, Bass, or Ass: All Payments Accepted." Roughly a dozen identical snow globes were placed around the odd altar. Each of them contained a swimming creature that looked like a cross between a sea serpent and a slug. Its body was positioned in three ripples coming in and out of the painted base like a ribbon candy made of mud. Its color was wholly unappealing—the brownish gray of every paint in the box mixed together. The cartoonish depiction of the monster of Loss Lake mollified Mallory's earlier fears.

The tacky knickknacks were a sharp contrast to the gentle wails of Enya that flooded from the speakers as Mallory untangled a wire shopping cart from a line of its brethren and moved slowly down an empty aisle. Had she been with Graham, the juxtaposition of tchotchkes, New Age signifiers, and fishing gear might have made her laugh. Instead, her throat unexpectedly tightened with tears. She forced herself to swallow as she headed to the dairy cooler. Since his death, she had hidden her strange surges of emotion by rarely going out in public. In the city, it had been easy to meet all her needs without seeing another human. She had groceries delivered, food ordered in, and packages left on her doorstep. But in a small town, it was necessary to be exposed. She had thought it was what she wanted—a way to force herself out of her cocoon of isolation. Now, she wasn't so sure.

As Mallory stared at the half-empty shelves, tears rolled down her cheeks, which immediately became hot with shame at their presence. She distracted herself by thinking of an essay written by a German native who had been separated from her family and friends in West Germany by the signatures of postwar rulers. Days after immigrating to the US, the woman had also cried in a grocery store when she was confronted by the wealth of food on display. But the memory of the woman's sorrow only made her feel worse. Mallory wasn't a political refugee overwhelmed by the wealth of her new home. She was a spoiled urbanite who had made a terrible, hasty decision to try to outrun death, only to have it end up on her doorstep moments after arriving. She reached for a block of cheap cheddar nestled next to a slab of shrink-wrapped feta. As she deposited it into her cart, she smelled something even earthier than patchouli incense. A woman glided up to the spot beside her elbow.

"Oh, hon."

Before Mallory had time to register much more than a fluff of ginger-colored curls sprouting from the top of the woman's head, she was pulled into a soft, oddly comforting embrace. Her round curves snuggled against Mallory's torso like a body pillow, and something feathery brushed the back of her head. The tears Mallory had been fighting released in a shocking flood, and she began to cry without restraint. The woman held her as her body trembled with the emotion. When her sobbing ceased, the woman squeezed her for one more beat, then opened her arms and stepped backward. Mallory wiped her eyes as the woman regarded her approvingly. Her eyes were as green as the frills of kale she was holding.

"Your energy was all over the place when you walked in, hon. You can't bear this alone. You need to let it go."

Mallory made a noise that sounded like a laugh that hadn't fully formed. "Pardon?"

"You need a cup of tea and place to sit down. I'm Kylie Shine. You must be Mallory. But tea first, questions later. Caffeinated or spiritual?"

Mallory blinked at the young woman as she tried to understand the question. The whites of her eyes were as clear and luminescent as a pearl.

"Um, spiritual? I don't do well with caffeine in the afternoons."

She also wasn't sure how well she could handle whatever a spiritual brew might be, but she kept that to herself. Kylie beamed brightly enough to make Mallory feel that she had answered correctly, then sidled in front of her and gently pushed her cart to one side.

"Come with me. Your shopping can wait."

"What about the other customers?" Mallory asked, then realized they were the only two people in the store. Her cheeks flamed at having said the wrong thing again.

Kylie reached up and placed her hands on either side of Mallory's face. For a brief disorienting second, Mallory thought Kylie was about to kiss her. Instead, she broke into an enthusiastic grin.

"Don't worry about it," she said with a wink. "I own the place."

She turned on her heel and headed toward the back of the store. For the second time that day, Mallory found herself in a cloud of confusion incited by a McNamara native. She dutifully followed the small, round woman down the aisle to the back of the store. Kylie's curls circled her head like the fluff of a dandelion gone to seed. On closer examination, her hair held strands of red, dirty blonde, and caramel. Her skin was clear, almost shining with good health, and Mallory guessed she was somewhere between her early and mid thirties. Though her frame was wide, her clothes were wider, hanging off her body in swatches of flowing fabric, suggesting that she wanted to take up more space in the world than her body allowed. Mallory was drawn to the bright patterns like a butterfly to a flower. Kylie's patterned golden muslin blouse draped over a pair of loose, bright-orange pants. A rope tied in a complicated knot at the back seemed to be the only thing that was holding them up. Its silky woven strands cascaded from her hips nearly to the floor. Her wrists were wound with wooden beads with small threads dangling from them. The only indication that Kylie was at work was the apron wrapped around her large bosom, though it was tie-dyed in a raucous combination of gold, brown, and green.

At the back of the store, Mallory saw a small alcove behind two low coolers of produce. Kylie smoothly deposited the bunches of kale with a group of others before pushing through a waist-high gate, then holding it open so Mallory could enter. The space was furnished with two tables, four wooden chairs, and a pile of oversize throw pillows in predictably wild patterns. Mallory saw a bar to the side, which Kylie ducked behind. Several teapots, as well as an electric kettle, were poised for action on top of the counter.

"Make yourself at home, hon. Your spot will find you. This is a place for rest."

Mallory looked at the wild pillows strewn across the floor and wondered if the old running injury in her knee could handle the pressure it would require to settle on one. She opted for a large wooden chair instead. Once seated, she realized that the piece had been hand carved from a single block of wood and polished to the smoothness of fresh butter. Its strong, wide arms were the color of maple syrup catching the light as it poured out of a bottle. Its seat and high back seemed configured for her body. She traced one finger down the length of the arm, marveling at the surface, which was as cool as marble.

She looked up as Kylie arrived with another cheerful smile and a steaming cup of tea. Mallory returned the smile, though she suspected hers was not as bright, before raising the earthenware mug to her lips.

"Maca and turmeric latte with goat milk. Of course."

Mallory took a deep swallow before her nose registered the powerful smell of mold and dirt wafting from it. It took every ounce of strength she had not to spit out the foul-tasting liquid the moment it coated her tongue.

"It's, um, interesting."

Kylie laughed. "At first, it's a bitch to get down. Then you'll crave it."

Kylie took a swig from her own mug as Mallory set hers down on the arm of her chair without taking another sip.

"I can tell," she lied.

Kylie's sparkling eyes grew rounder as she leaned forward.

"Listen, Mallory. I can't imagine what you've been through. I thought you were going to be older when Betty told me about your husband. But you're so young!"

Betty Barber definitely made her rounds.

"I'm not that young," Mallory said. It wasn't intended to generate a denial from Kylie. Since Graham had died, Mallory had felt every day of her forty years deep in her bones. "But yes, it was a shock. I appreciate your sympathy."

Mallory took another sip of her drink to cover up the fact that she had no idea what else to say. She had grown unaccustomed to speaking to strangers at all, let alone weeping on their shoulders and confiding in them moments after first meeting. The musty liquid had not improved in flavor, but at least it provided her with something to do.

Kylie edged her way to the front of her seat eagerly as she spoke. "You know, grief gives us a window into the otherness. It's a devastating moment which forces us into a liminal period. By being so close to someone on the other side, you become suspended between death and life. In stasis."

Mallory found herself nodding, and Kylie bowed her head briefly before continuing.

"I'm glad you have finally arrived. McNamara is a powerful place. It's no wonder that you were brought here at this time. You are here to heal."

"I suppose," Mallory said, feeling uncomfortable. The sergeant had said something similar about the power of the lake, though she doubted he would echo Kylie's convictions about grieving. The idea that every citizen of McNamara held their town in such high regard was deeply easeful. If the residents were happy here, it was a good sign she had made the right decision. She wanted to love it the same way as they did. She tried another sip. This time, she couldn't hide her wince. "Do you have any sugar?"

"Goddess no." Kylie pinched her face in mock disgust. "We use raw honey. Straight from my bees out back."

Kylie beamed as she walked back to the counter and grabbed a brown clay pot with a wooden spoon leaning out. Her hair bounced as she moved. When she returned, she blew a curl out of her eyes. Mallory lifted the spoon and let the thick golden liquid pour off the edge into her cup. She took another small sip and found the concoction marginally improved.

"I can't imagine how traumatic it must have been to have Joel show up on your doorstep like that. What a way to see the town, your new home! After all you've been through," Kylie tutted.

"Joel?"

Kylie smiled. "Sorry, I mean Sergeant Benson. I suppose you met him in a more professional capacity, but I never think about him like that."

So Kylie had already heard about the drowning. Was there a group chat for the whole town?

"You know him?"

Kylie cocked her head. "Of course I do. He's my brother."

"Your brother is the sergeant?"

Kylie nodded solemnly, as if Mallory had noted something significant, then she smiled again. Mallory's face must have registered her confusion as she tried to work out the difference in their last names. Was Shine Kylie's married name?

"Don't worry about keeping it all straight. McNamara isn't like a big city. You'll get to know everyone soon enough. In the meantime, however, we need to stock your cupboards. I can't imagine you were able to bring much of anything in one carload from Vancouver."

"That would be great."

Mallory was grateful for the chance to leave her half-finished tea on the table without having to end her conversation with the intriguing woman. Despite Kylie's enthusiasm, she had experienced nothing to suggest that her body would ever seek out the drink again. She wished she were comfortable enough to ask more questions about the sergeant, but it was difficult to trust that she was presenting herself well these days. Her ability to focus blazed and sputtered like a candle in a drafty room. Besides, Kylie was right. McNamara was home to fewer than four hundred people. Nothing about them could stay a mystery for long. The best thing she could do was put the drowning and the sergeant out of her mind for now. She rose and followed the swishing of Kylie's clothing out the small gate and back into the store.

Kylie returned to the abandoned cart and began filling it with cans of beans and handfuls of fresh vegetables as she suggested recipes and meal preparation. Occasionally, Mallory sneaked in the essentials she required, congratulating herself on remembering a kettle when they reached the scant housewares department. Pushing the sludge out of her mind to remember what she had packed and what she had left behind took so much of her energy that she was only able to half listen to Kylie's words as the store owner acted as her personal shopper. Even more distracting was how unfamiliar the brands and products were on the shelves.

Instead of a selection of mint toothpaste, Kylie's Korner offered a choice of anise, charcoal, and orange-ginger. Rather than coffee, Mallory had to content herself with a suspiciously lumpy bag of chicory. Mallory felt guilty at the thought, but she wondered if she would have to drive back to Turner to fill her cupboards with the conventional items. Kylie stopped mid-aisle and turned backward. Her bright-green eyes flashed like an unexpected change of a traffic light.

"You do know to be careful, right?"

Mallory silently thanked the sergeant for filling her in on part of the local history. It was nice to finally understand a McNamara reference.

"The sergeant told me about the monster."

She spoke cautiously to avoid any suggestion of doubt. The sergeant had been clear that some people in the town were firm believers, and, judging by the snow globes, she suspected Kylie might be one of them. Kylie's eyebrows crowded toward each other, causing two vertical lines of disbelief to appear in the center of her forehead. She sighed out in exasperation. It made Mallory feel foolish to have mentioned the legend of Loss Lake.

"No, not the monster. That's my brother, not me. He's been scared of monsters since I told him that a killer rat was loose in our house and then hid our guinea pig under his bed."

"Joel?" He hadn't seemed worried when they had spoken. In fact, it was hard to imagine the strong-jawed man being fearful of much.

"No, no. My younger brother, Henry."

In spite of her renewed embarrassment at misunderstanding her new town, Mallory grinned and realized it was the closest she had come to laughing in days. Maybe weeks.

"That's a relief."

"Joel was probably just trying to warn you away from the kookier side of this town," Kylie said with no indication that she too might be included in this category. "This lake has seen its fair share of deaths, but I don't think it has anything to do with a monster."

Mallory smiled encouragingly, happy to see that Kylie's affinity for alternative foods didn't supersede logical explanations.

"If anything, the fact that the Turner Dam was directly above us on a ley line is more compelling—"

Mallory interrupted her before their connection as healthy skeptics was eroded. "How many deaths have there been?"

Kylie shrugged. "Lots. But this is a big lake. Didn't Betty tell you about this stuff?"

Mallory shook her head. Dread snaked through her at the idea of the bodies below the water and her worry about whether she had forgotten another important part of the conversation with her real estate agent. She couldn't recall a single conversation about death during the woman's high-speed chatter about which gas station in Turner had the cheapest fuel and where to buy winter tires.

"No. I'd love to hear more."

For the first time, Kylie looked uncomfortable. "Well, the first one people talk about was Alice Halloway back in October 1974, the year the dam broke. She was in her house right below the dam. It was a farmhouse, way far from town and the only one right in the path of the water. The place was north of your house. Mine too, actually. I live on the property beside you."

Mallory didn't have time to acknowledge the fact that they were neighbors. The thought of a house rapidly plunged underwater was too terrifying to ignore.

"Why didn't anyone tell her about the dam breaking?"

"Apparently, the water rushed from the dam like a wall. She didn't have time to get out. From what my dad told me, at least it was really fast."

"Oh my God," Mallory murmured. "That's awful." She swallowed hard as her earlier fear about the lake rising up to swallow her returned. The idea grew gruesome in her mind. Mallory saw water pouring in through the windows of her bedroom, soaking her comforter until it weighed more than an anchor.

Kylie's face was grim as she continued. "Yes, it was. After that, there were several more drownings in the lake, a few years apart. Boating accidents mainly."

"And they all happened in October?"

"So Joel told you that too." Kylie smiled to ward off Mallory's panic. "Don't worry, okay? McNamara is a safe town. People aren't always careful in water, and it's normal for there to be careless deaths like that. There's only been one person killed with a gun here, like, ever."

The muscles in Mallory's neck tensed up again, and Kylie bit her lip like she sensed she had said the wrong thing.

"What happened then?"

"I shouldn't have mentioned it," Kylie said, looking down. "I was talking about the hunting accident."

"In the woods?"

"Um, no. Oh, jeez. I thought you knew. It's what I meant about being careful."

"What happened?"

Kylie placed her hands back on the cart and gripped it like the handlebars of a bicycle she desperately wished she could use to escape the conversation. Her mouth pulled down at both edges. Mallory read the expression as deep sadness—the kind that had never been fully released. She laid her hand flat on top of one of Kylie's, which prompted her to continue.

"A bullet went wild from the woods near the lake and right through a window."

A pulse of grief came off her as Kylie continued speaking.

"They never found the hunter. Probably an out-of-towner who didn't understand what a stray bullet could do and how close they were to a residence. They likely didn't know they had hurt someone."

The other woman's eyes filled with sorrow, and Mallory wondered if Kylie had known the victim. She asked her next question gently, relieved to be comforting someone else for a change.

"I'm so sorry, Kylie. Did you know him?"

"Yes," she said. Her eyes were magnified by the tears pooling in them. "He was my brother."

"Oh, Kylie. I'm so sorry. What a terrible accident."

The other woman bowed her head. The movement caused a tear to slip from her eye in a single line down her cheek.

"Yes, it was."

Mallory and Kylie regarded each other for a moment, united by their shared losses. Then Kylie blinked and rubbed her eyes.

"We should probably get you on your way home. You must have a lot to do."

"I do." Mallory paused. She didn't want to pry, but the woman's earlier words made her wonder if there was something she should be doing to keep herself safe. "But why did you say that I should be careful?"

Kylie looked miserable.

"Because he was killed in your house."

CHAPTER FOUR

As they finished filling Mallory's cart, she was happy to let Kylie redirect their conversation back to the deep health benefits of a bean-focused diet while her own thoughts wandered. The information Kylie had passed on left Mallory feeling foggy-headed. Once again, the unprocessed emotions she had carried around with her since Graham's death descended like a thick veil. No wonder the house had remained empty for so long. Mallory knew it was difficult to sell a residence after a death had occurred within it. A few potential buyers of her own home had become leery after learning that Graham had passed away in the front room.

At the register, Mallory learned that the store could not accept credit cards. Kylie explained that everyone in McNamara ran a tab that they paid off in cash at the end of each month. Setting up her own seemed both deliciously old-fashioned and incredibly reassuring. She had climbed the first step to being accepted as a McNamara local.

As she exited the store with Kylie's call to come back soon echoing behind her, she noticed the building behind the grocery store was marked "Police Station." She wondered if Sergeant Benson was inside, searching to solve the mystery of the earlier drowning. Had he been able to determine the name of the victim? Though she expected the memory of his visit to fill her with trepidation, instead she experienced a flutter of reassurance as she thought of how closely connected he was to Kylie. For some reason, the knowledge of their relationship gave her a sense that the man would handle the investigation fairly. He too had lost someone close to him due to an odd twist of fate—an accident that no one could have predicted or prevented.

Once safely buckled into her car, she headed out of the parking lot to turn left. Her vehicle was the only one on the street, so she drove slowly to clear her head and take further notice of her surroundings. Already, the storefronts had begun to seem more familiar than foreign. Across the street from Kylie's, the cluttered hardware store window caught her attention once again, but this time, Mallory noticed that there were additional pieces less prominent than the bright deck chairs. Tucked into the far corner was a line of rifles forming a military salute to a mounted deer head that had garish orange vests hung from its antlers. She thought of the stray bullet that had sheared through the window in her house, and her neck tensed. She needed to talk to Betty Barber, she thought as she passed the woman's office, which was unfortunately closed. Wasn't it illegal not to disclose a violent death to a new buyer? She tried to recall how her Vancouver real estate agent had told those looking at her own home about Graham's death. Had she volunteered the information? Or waited to be asked? The memories were vague and indistinct, painted in oversaturated watercolors.

Her mind sped as quickly as the scenes of McNamara outside her car. Directly across from Betty's office, she saw a seedy-looking bar that she had missed earlier, with a small school located somewhat incongruently right behind it. On the corner at the end of the main street was a small brick building displaying an elegantly painted sign that declared it to be the town library. From her conversation with the sergeant, she now knew that it employed her closest neighbor, Carlotta, whom she decided she would try to meet tomorrow.

She turned onto the dirt road that would lead her home. To her left was a run-down trailer on the corner that she hadn't registered on her previous trip. The small building looked derelict enough to be abandoned, but there was a beat-up car parked outside. Its peeling painted sides and sagging bottom were precariously propped up on four rounds of wood, suggesting a previous flood. Mallory shuddered as she remembered the story Kylie had relayed about poor Alice Halloway, and she pressed the gas harder to get past the dilapidated trailer.

In contrast, down the road stood a pretty white-shingled cottage that apparently belonged to Carlotta. Its black roof and white exterior made it look like something out of a Beatrix Potter story. Unlike its closest neighbor, the little house appeared to be meticulously maintained. It sat in the center of a perfectly mowed swath of lawn. The bright-yellow door was flanked by two uniformly trimmed rosebushes, each of which had unfurled late-season yellow roses in nearly the same shade as the door. The lovely home briefly lifted her spirits, and Mallory's curiosity bubbled up at the thought of meeting the residents of both the perfect cottage and the falling-apart trailer. As Kylie had said, in a town this small, it was bound to happen sooner rather than later.

Unfortunately, her unease became heavier as she passed through the forest, then turned her car into the driveway in front of her home, careful to avoid the pothole that had bounced her unpleasantly on her first trip. She liked knowing that she had a tab at the local shop and what she hoped was the beginning of a friendship with the local shopkeeper. The lines and colors of McNamara were already beginning to etch into her mind, like she was meant to be here. Still, it had been disconcerting to learn about the bleak history of her house.

The sun was low enough now in the west to turn the front window into a sheet of mirrored glass. When she got out of her car, the blur of her thin frame moving fluidly across the windowpane made her red shirt dance like a flame. The tall trees loomed across the darkened glass in a beautiful, eerie version of reality. She paused and stared at the distorted image. Kylie had said the hunters had been in the woods by the lake. Had they been hidden in the same trees reflected in the glass before her? She imagined a bullet piercing the window, moving quickly enough to stop a man's heart, as effortlessly as her nurse's needle used to puncture layers of skin.

She shook her head to stop herself from turning her dream into something ugly. She had come here to let go of the past. It didn't matter what had happened in this home before she arrived, just like it didn't matter what had happened when she was married to Graham. She was here to start over.

But Mallory had never been good at letting things go. The thought of Graham lingered as she went to the kitchen and began to unpack her groceries, growing as sharp as the cry of a gull outside as she realized that she had inadvertently slid a bar of Graham's favorite soap into her grocery cart. The spicy sweetness of the scent that used to linger on his skin long after he showered filled the small kitchen. Once again, Mallory's tears began to fall. This time, she didn't have anyone to comfort her as she wept.

~

Ten years ago, a few months after their small wedding, attended by a handful of their closest friends and family, Mallory had proposed a trip. The hospital board was offering employees a free ticket to Guatemala if they committed to volunteering at a mission. Despite Mallory's argument that it was a once-in-a-lifetime opportunity, Graham had been reluctant. Both she and Graham were atheists, and the overly enthusiastic declarations of faith during Mallory's holiday work parties often made Graham feel uncomfortable. He worried that their role in Guatemala would be to spread a belief system he knew little about. For months, Mallory urged him to consider it. *It's a free trip,* she'd said. *We can do something good, then take time for ourselves after the work is done.* Graham finally agreed, and the vacation turned out better than he had expected. Until they returned home.

Weeks after their arrival, Graham had complained of a rash spreading across his stomach. Mallory had examined it and told him that it was likely contact dermatitis. She brought home a light over-the-counter steroid cream and his patchy skin had cleared up almost immediately. But then a fever set in, along with aches and a headache that he could dull only with hourly doses of aspirin. When the symptoms continued for more than a week, Graham visited his general practitioner at Mallory's insistence. *This has been going around,* the doctor had said, shrugging, after a full-body physical. *Nasty flu this year.* Following the lack of diagnosis, Graham allowed Mallory to start him on a wellness plan: lots of water, a daily walk, and enormous helpings of vegetables at every meal. Though it had taken nearly two months to recover from the headaches, which continued to flare up when he was fatigued or stressed, Graham had been grateful to her when he finally felt like himself again.

Definitely getting a flu shot next year, he had joked. Mallory had laughed with him, though secretly, Graham's ailment had made her hyperaware of the age difference between them. When she had met him through a friend the year she turned twenty-eight, he had still been three years shy of forty, and his clear skin and athletic frame made him seem younger than that. But the long illness had aged him considerably, painting shadows under his eyes that he never managed to fully erase. The weight loss it caused made his frame seem frailer even after he became strong enough to return to his beloved long-distance running. Mallory had been shaken by the reminder of his mortality, but her unease had faded in the same way as the faint marks on his skin where his rash had been.

For nearly a decade, his bad flu remained nothing more than a reminder for them both to wash their hands diligently during the winter months. She had nearly forgotten about it completely until she received the call from her husband's secretary fourteen months ago. *He collapsed at his desk,* she said frantically. *He's in the ambulance now.* Mallory had met them at the hospital, grateful for her staff parking spot as she raced into the emergency room. Heart attack, her friend and the attending physician told her. *Does he have any history of heart disease in his family?*

Graham did not. His entire family was long-lived, prone to dying peacefully in their beds, not on operating tables. His age was a slight risk factor, but though he was about to turn fifty, he had noticed none of the standard markers for poor heart health until that very moment. Like her, he was a runner who had never experienced chest pains or shortness of breath during his many races. Largely due to her influence, he ate well, nearly vegetarian, rarely drank, and had never smoked. It took two blood tests, the second an unusually thorough analysis done only because Mallory knew which strings to pull at the laboratory, to get a diagnosis. She was stunned to find the answer provided less hope than the mystery.

Chagas disease, she repeated after the doctor had relayed the information to them. She had been dumbfounded. The name sounded vaguely insectile and tropical, something that didn't belong in the middle-class suburb where she and her husband lived. In the weeks that followed, the more she learned, the less it seemed like she knew, despite hours spent interviewing her colleagues and poring through medical journals. Her research yielded one disturbing fact after another, which she dutifully relayed to Graham every evening despite the way the process left them both withdrawn and miserable as they struggled to absorb the death sentence he'd been given.

Tell me everything, he had said. *Don't sugarcoat it.*

As a nurse and a systems analyst, she and Graham had both spent their lives developing plans and programs based on the best available data. They approached his death in the same way.

Chagas was passed on by a tiny biting insect, rare in North America but common in Central America. For most people, the first symptoms looked a lot like Graham's: a rash, headaches, chronic fatigue. Sometimes, that was as bad as it got, passing through the body quickly and leaving little trace of its presence behind. But for people like Graham, the infection left behind by the small bugs silently eroded the heart's function, often going undetected until it was too late. Graham's two-month-long flu had been the only sign of the struggle his body was undergoing, like a white hand of a drowning victim briefly raised above waters unprotected by a lifeguard. No one had noticed until the damage in his heart was so extensive that it couldn't be reversed.

Graham needed a transplant. His doctors put his name on the list, but with each passing month, their hope dimmed. When he began wheezing so hard with each step that Mallory's own chest tightened in sympathetic panic, she took a leave of absence to be his home nurse. Their insurance also covered a day nurse to come in once a week to give Mallory an eight-hour break so she could sleep during the night. *Relax and rest,* the nurse had told her. *Let me do my job.* But Mallory rarely took her up on the offer. She found herself tense and alert while the woman was present, constantly prepared for the sound of Graham calling.

Their friends offered to help as well. The couple next door, who they used to meet with once a week for a game night, tried to take shifts with Graham in the evenings to give her a break. As Graham's health grew worse, however, she had told the couple that she couldn't bear to be away from him. The moment the door clicked shut behind her, panic that Graham would die as she giggled stupidly in a dark movie theater or gritted her teeth during dinner with her mother made her desperate to return home immediately. But it didn't matter how hard she tried to keep him alive. Her fear hadn't changed anything at all.

∼

Mallory had just placed the last of an astonishing number and variety of canned and dried beans on the shelf when she heard the knock on the front door. Her jaw clenched as the sound of pounding echoed around the empty rooms. Had Sergeant Benson discovered something else? She approached the door warily, realizing from a few feet away that it was not equipped with a spy hole as her door in Vancouver had been. She wondered if anyone in McNamara owned a door that allowed them to know what was on the other side before giving it the chance to get in. Just then, the sun sank behind the tree line, draining the house of the last of the day's dim light. Prickles nipped at the back of her neck as Mallory sensed the presence of the uncurtained back window behind her like a person staring menacingly.

She ran her hand along the wall in search of a light switch but failed to find one. The shadows in the foyer swarmed as she braced herself and swung open the door.

In front of her stood a beaming Kylie. "Special delivery!" she cried.

Mallory attempted equal enthusiasm, but her confusion and lingering fear suffocated her smile. "Delivery of what?"

Kylie turned and pointed behind her. "I brought you a bed!"

"What? Why?"

Mallory squinted out into the swimming darkness, but all she could make out was a vague outline of a truck.

"Joel mentioned you didn't have any furniture and I thought, *That's no way for her to spend her first night in McNamara.* We have loads of extra furniture. My dad always says that there's always someone in need of things that don't matter to you anymore. So come around here. Let's get this into your place."

Despite her discomfiture at the unexpected gift, Mallory obeyed and soon found herself struggling with the corner of an oak frame. The two women wedged the bed through the front door and past the tower of boxes in the foyer before shuffling into the hallway. Despite the weight, Kylie kept up a stream of conversation, and her words were a comforting backdrop to Mallory's first foray into the west side of the house, where the bedrooms were located. Kylie walked quickly down the hall, though she was moving backward with an awkward bed frame cupped in her small hands. At the end, she ignored the open door on the left as she jostled to angle the bed to the right into the other room. As Mallory followed her, carefully sliding the bed frame through the door, she saw a small bathroom where the hallway ended, dividing the two rooms, as Betty had described. She half lifted and half pushed her side of the bed into the room Kylie had selected for her, tilting it into position with Kylie's direction.

"This is the best room," Kylie said. "You can't beat that view of the lake."

Her certainty was disarming. Mallory was both disconcerted and mesmerized by the dark water outside the large window, lit only by one long streak of moonlight illuminating the strands of mist floating above the gently rolling surface. Like the two windows in the dining room, it too had no curtains. The view filled her with a sense of peace that kept her going as she followed Kylie once more out to the truck to get the mattress.

"I wasn't sure if you'd need these," Kylie said as she grabbed a tall stack of sheets from her front seat.

"I do."

Her admission that she had somehow reverted back to a person who didn't own a single set of sheets, like a college freshman or a homeless person, made her shy.

"Then I'm glad I tucked them in," Kylie said without discernible judgment.

They returned to the bedroom, and Kylie flicked her wrists to let the top sheet rise and fall gently onto the bed. Mallory smoothed the opposite corners across the mattress, tucking them in tightly as she had been trained to do.

"I don't know how to thank you," Mallory said as they laid a heavy quilt on top of the sheets. The smooth, soft curves of the bed looked much more inviting than the foam mattress and sleeping bag she had been planning to sleep on that night.

"Well, there's only one way you can," Kylie said with the now familiar sparkle returning to her eye.

Mallory wondered if the woman was going to ask for money, but she immediately scolded herself for thinking the worst as Kylie giggled.

"Buy me a drink at Logan's!" Kylie said.

Her joy was infectious.

"Absolutely," Mallory replied. "What's Logan's?"

"The only bar in town. If we leave now, we should be able to catch happy hour."

Mallory was taken aback by the unexpectedly sudden nature of the invitation. She had assumed that her offer would be claimed by Kylie at another time in the future, not immediately. But she didn't have anything else to do, and the thought of spending more time with the young woman was appealing.

As they neared the door, the tinny music of her cell phone began to play from its place inside her purse. The sound was muffled but unmistakable.

"Do you need to get that?" Kylie asked. "Probably someone checking to see if you arrived okay."

Mallory silenced the phone with one hand as she slung her purse over her shoulder. There was no one she wanted to speak to besides the cheerful woman in front of her.

"I'll listen to my voice mail later," she said. This time, she didn't have to work hard to coax a smile onto her face.

CHAPTER FIVE

Kylie pulled her four-by-four truck into the dirt parking lot of the small pub. It spluttered as she turned it off. Mallory could hear the twang of old country music coming from inside the knotted planks of the wooden building she had noticed earlier. Her stomach rolled as she and Kylie walked up the six front steps and through the pub's front door. She couldn't tell if she was scared or nervous to see another part of McNamara—or both.

The interior of Logan's Pub was somehow exactly what she had expected and also completely different than she would have guessed. It was decorated in the style of an old man's den, with televisions mounted high in two corners of the room, each offering a different channel to compete with the music thrumming from the speakers. The wood-paneled walls were similar to those in Mallory's new home, but these were so full of decoration that Mallory felt claustrophobic. Several posters featured women from the early '80s clad in high-cut one-piece swimsuits that clung to their bodies as they posed while seductively holding a beer. But it was the three sets of shelves running the length of the wall immediately facing the entrance that were the most jarring. The narrow spaces were so crammed that Mallory could see the dip at the center of each where the jumbled collection had weighed them down over time.

The first things Mallory was able to pick out of the crowded pile on the shelf at eye level were half a dozen snow globes that looked identical to the ones Kylie had in her store. The same sluglike creatures undulated in the glass balls as Mallory had seen in the ones beside Kylie's Buddha. At Logan's, however, the snow globes were only part of a collection of monster-themed memorabilia. Mallory stepped closer to the stacked shelves to examine the offerings. Nestled beside the round figurines were four stuffed versions of a sea monster covered in light-green faux fur and adorned with goofy grins. At both ends of the shelf were huge jars jammed full of bright-green pinwheels featuring a different version of a serpent. In between were pennants, baseball hats, and brightly colored scarves, each with another rendering of the monster's form. The lack of uniformity suggested the Loss Lake monster had yet to find a clear brand. Each item was pasted with a bright-pink price tag. Above them all was a laminated sign.

HERE WE FEATURE OUR LOCAL CREATURE.
BRING IT HOME SO IT CAN MEETCHA.

The lettering was in a jaunty font favored by baby boomers for their email signatures and small children for their birthday invitations. Mallory bit her lip to stifle a condescending smile.

"See anything you like?" Kylie asked.

"They're definitely interesting."

Kylie began to move and Mallory followed. She wanted to quiz her companion about who had created the display, but there were too many curious eyes on them for her to ask the question undetected. Mallory returned a few smiles from people as they tipped their drinks toward her and Kylie walking through the room. It seemed she was the only unfamiliar face in the place that night. The interested glances made her feel intriguing rather than self-conscious. Mallory had never been so notable before. She had lived in the same place all her life. Now, at forty years old, she finally knew how it felt to be the new kid. It was strangely exhilarating to realize that no one in the entire bar knew her. Whatever she told them would become her story.

"It's so busy," she said in a low voice as they passed two pool tables lined up along the side wall of the room.

Kylie shrugged. "Saturday night. A lot of people need to blow off steam."

Mallory hadn't realized she had arrived in McNamara on a weekend. Since Graham's illness, she had ceased to notice the days of the week, focusing instead on the tasks at hand. But given the way the conversation rose and fell at several decibels above necessary as she and Kylie made their way to a small booth in the back, she was clearly the only one in the place who had come unprepared to celebrate.

They settled into the booth at the back of the bar, which was mercifully positioned away from the speakers. Mallory slid into the side that faced the busy room. To her left was an open space where there were two dartboards on the wall beside a jukebox and a dance floor. The combination seemed dangerous. A lone woman nursed a drink at a table tucked in the corner.

"We're lucky to get a seat," Kylie said with a grin.

At the other end of the room, past the entryway and the shelves of merchandise, Mallory noticed a wizened man pulling pints behind a large bar.

"Will someone come around to serve us drinks?"

Kylie shook her head. "Not in this place. It's bar service. Logan Carruthers works alone. He's been the only bartender for over forty years."

"Wow," Mallory said, quickly doing the math. Logan must be in his sixties or seventies. Graham had started at his IT firm at the age of twenty-two. He had worked at the same company until he was forced to leave due to his ill health. He hadn't liked change, so it was possible that he might have claimed five decades in the position had he lived. But being close to retirement age in a desk job was a lot more common than for a bartender. She blinked and focused on Kylie. "That's hard work for someone his age."

"It's a bit weird, but he's in good shape. No one's in a real rush around here. People let him move at his own pace. Besides, it keeps him from trying to get everyone to turn this into the Canadian Loch Ness. All that stuff he's trying to sell is his retirement plan, but it doesn't look like he'll be able to close his doors anytime soon. At his insistence, I stocked a few of his things last year, and they've been on the shelf collecting dust ever since."

Mallory laughed. That explained the less-than-prominent placement of the items in Kylie's store. "All right, I owe you a drink. What will it be?"

"White wine, please," Kylie said.

"Coming right up."

Mallory slipped out of the booth and walked toward the bar. This time, only a few people met her eyes as she passed, but the feeling in the room remained congenial.

When she reached the bar, Logan Carruthers was pouring for a customer who was wearing a hat emblazoned with another version of the Loss Lake monster. Logan called out to her. "Hello. What would you like?"

Mallory paused for a moment before answering. She rarely drank. Since her first sip of wine at a cousin's wedding when she was thirteen, she had found alcohol to be both foul tasting and prone to leave her with a light but hard-to-shake headache. During Graham's last months, she had not touched a drop. It was important for her to be clearheaded, as he often called to her in the middle of the night if he was having trouble finding his pills. But tonight was special. It seemed right to celebrate it with a proper drink. The older man looked at her questioningly, clearly not used to waiting so long for an answer.

"Two glasses of white wine, please."

The bartender turned to the fridge. He was thin. Through his well-worn plaid shirt, Mallory could see the distinct outlines of his shoulder bones, but his movements were fluid and certain. Operating behind the bar appeared to be second nature for him, which made sense after decades of practice. Mallory let her eyes travel around the room. The place smelled of long-ago cigarettes, though no one was currently smoking. It seemed that the faux wood paneling and the extraordinary number of knickknacks, collectibles, and peeling posters had absorbed too many pollutants over the years to remain scent-free. The clientele was a mix of men in quilted plaid jackets and women with hairstyles that defied both gravity and current fashion trends. The whole place was roughly one thousand square feet. The booth where Kylie was sitting was one of six lining the wall farthest away from the double entrance doors.

As she turned back to the man pouring drinks, she noticed that behind the bar, the top shelf above a row of liquor bottles was also piled with small collectibles and trinkets. She narrowed her eyes to make out the individual items contained within. Unlike the collection of monster merchandise, this shelf contained mostly unmatched ephemera. A silver metal snowmobile the size of an egg poised precariously in a heap that also contained two balls made of rubber bands, several boxes of matches, and the caboose from a model train set. All of it rested on a stack of books that was draped in tinsel and glittering lights crowned by a bright book whose spine read *Lake of Loss* by Frederich Menzel. The color of the spine was luridly blue, and she couldn't take her eyes off it. Logan slid the drinks toward her and followed her gaze.

"You're new in town. Mallory Dent, right?" he said with a nod as he extended his hand across the bar. She smiled back. Already, she was getting used to others knowing her name before she introduced herself. "I'm Logan Carruthers. President of the Business Owners Association."

He huffed a little as he announced his title. She shook his hand. Up close, deep and fine lines creased his face like that of the apple doll her mother had refused to part with during Mallory's childhood. She placed him as well into his seventies. Sadly, any sense of aged wisdom within the man was undermined by his pompous demeanor. Logan seemed like a man who liked to feel important but never really did. She supposed working in the service industry for years would erode anyone's confidence.

"Nice to meet you," Mallory said as she offered her credit card in payment.

Logan spoke with a wry grin. "No cards accepted, ma'am. I'll start you a tab. We trust each other around here."

Mallory smiled at the simplicity of businesses in McNamara.

"Listen, I saw your curiosity was piqued by the monster of Loss Lake." He gestured toward the toppling pile of trinkets on the shelf above their heads. "Why not learn a little more about the area? I'm going to add a copy of Freddie's book to your tab. He published it himself a few years ago. Only ten bucks, and it will help you to understand the truth."

Before she could answer, Logan stretched his arm up and deftly dislodged the blue book from the stack. Mallory accepted it, then made her way back to Kylie. When Mallory sat back down at the booth, Kylie laughed as she realized what Mallory had tucked under her arm.

"So Logan managed to sell you this. Maybe his retirement plans aren't so crazy," Kylie said with a wink.

"I didn't feel like I could say no." Mallory was sheepish.

"Cheers. To Logan's rich old age," Kylie said happily, clinking her glass against the side of Mallory's.

The two women sipped their drinks. The vinegary tang of the white wine immediately made her mouth feel dry, and she wished she had asked for a glass of water as well. She looked back at the bar to see if there was a line and was startled to notice a large rifle mounted on two hooks above the counter where she had placed her order, similar to the ones she had seen in the window of the hardware store. Its black barrel shone menacingly in the half-light. Why did Logan keep a weapon like that in a quiet town? It seemed so at odds with his eager demeanor. She turned back to Kylie to ask, but the woman was busy flipping through the blue book. Mallory thought she might as well learn more about her recent purchase.

"Is Frederich Menzel a well-known local author?"

"More like a well-known kook. Harmless, but kind of . . . fixated?" Kylie's cheeks were beginning to pink up as alcohol crept through her body. "He's German, I think, and moved here the year before the valley flooded. My dad knows him better than I do, but he's a big part of the community theater."

She looked at Mallory to verify her interest, so Mallory nodded.

"Anyway, before she died, my mom told me that he got pretty obsessed with the idea of the monster. Obviously, right? He literally wrote a book on it."

Mallory wanted to learn more about Kylie's mother, but before she could ask, a young man with a face so cleanly shaved it made his ruddy cheeks look as dimpled as an orange unexpectedly slid into the booth beside her. His light-brown hair was heavy with gel, and a waft of cologne made Mallory's nostrils sting. She noticed that his eyes were the color of new grass, and they sparkled just like Kylie's as he leaned toward her.

"The boss let you out today?" he said as he tipped his nearly empty beer bottle in the direction of Kylie's wineglass.

"Yeah, despite being only two years old, she's a real hard-ass, but I managed to sneak away," Kylie replied, and the man chuckled. "Mallory, this is my youngest brother, Henry."

He extended his hand. "Officer Shine at your service."

"Nice to meet you," she said, taking a drink to hide her confusion. If Henry's last name was Shine, that meant Kylie hadn't married into it after all. Heat rose to her own face, as the kindness of her new community members mingled with her curiosity and the wine. She suppressed a laugh at the memory of Kylie's story about her monstrous guinea pig before registering the title Henry had used. Both of Kylie's brothers were police officers? Henry must be the deputy that Sergeant Benson had mentioned earlier. She wondered if he was involved in the drowning investigation as well, but the young man didn't seem anything but friendly as he grinned.

"It's very nice to meet you as well, particularly since you have somehow performed the magical feat of getting my sister away from her daughter and into the bar!"

"I didn't realize you had children," Mallory said, grateful for a subject that didn't trigger her concern about the ongoing investigation. She hadn't thought about Kylie being a mother, but it made sense, given her thoughtful gift of the bed and sheets.

Kylie's blush deepened. "Yes. I have a little girl at home. Aura. She's asleep now, and fingers crossed she stays that way, but I'm sure Dad will call me if there's any change."

"Her grandfather is looking after her?"

"Yes. He's a wonderful help."

Mallory tamped down the urge to ask where the girl's father was. It was none of her business, though she found it strange that her friend hadn't thought to mention him.

Kylie smiled as she continued speaking. "There's not a lot of parents in McNamara these days. Mostly old folks. What about you? Do you have children?"

The young woman looked at her eagerly, and Mallory felt uncomfortable for the first time that evening.

"No, not me. It was never in the cards."

Both Kylie and Henry looked at her in concern. She rushed to clarify. "Not because there's anything, you know, wrong with me. It wasn't a physical problem. Just . . . my husband and I decided it wasn't right for us."

Her babbling deepened the identical furrows in Henry's and Kylie's foreheads. It had been so long since she'd met people who were totally new to her that it was difficult to explain how Graham had always told her having children provided life with false purpose. That it was too easy to devote yourself to raising other humans at the cost of pursuing something that would truly fulfill you. *It's a cliché to think children will make you happy,* he had said. *There's so much more to life than wiping butts and noses.*

She had agreed to not have children, though not for entirely the same reasons. For many years, she had been so devoted to her studies and then her work that the few men she had dated had failed to capture her interest enough to pursue a serious relationship. She hadn't considered or desired marriage until Graham came along. His approach to life had made sense to her—she loved the way his commitment to his work and running complemented her devotion to medicine and health.

But nursing Graham had dampened her love of her job to the point where she wasn't sure she would ever do it again. Since his death, she had wondered if it would be easier if she had children with her, to tether her to something besides her own sadness. There had been so many days in the last two months when she had not spoken to a single other person. A familiar catch in her throat warned her that she needed a moment alone. She smiled at the two people across the table, who were looking at her in respectful silence.

"Excuse me. I need to freshen up. Kylie, where's the bathroom?"

The young woman smiled back like she was just as grateful to end the awkward conversation and pointed to a small door beside the jukebox. Mallory passed the solitary hard-faced woman nursing a beer in the corner by the dartboards. Her hair was dyed the color of summer wheat, which had unfortunately rendered its texture to something similar. As Mallory brushed by, the woman looked up, and her expression was raw enough to make Mallory wonder what she had been thinking. She smiled quickly, then let her eyes pass over the woman's dark expression.

Mallory entered the single bathroom and closed the door. As she washed her hands, she caught sight of herself in the mirror. Though it was fogged in the corner and the light in the small room was dim enough to be kind, she could still see the lines the last year had carved in her face. Lately, she had been avoiding mirrors. It was hard to acknowledge the marks Graham's illness had left on her. During her adolescence and early adulthood, she had given little thought to her appearance but had enjoyed applying lipstick and mascara for a special night to brighten up her pretty, if unspectacular, features. Now she knew that no amount of makeup could change the way the contours under her eyes had darkened and the creases around her mouth had deepened. Graham's death had aged her irrevocably.

She smoothed her wavy brown hair flat against her head and focused on her eyes, happy to see a spark of hope within them for the first time in a year. McNamara was a place where she could finally breathe, and she needed to believe it. She was finally exactly where she was supposed to be. "You can do this," she said to herself softly. The older woman in the mirror smiled gently back. She walked back to the table, where Kylie and Henry beamed at her, both laughing at a joke she had missed.

Henry spoke as soon as she sat down. "So what brings you to McNamara, Mallory? Are you a monster hunter?" He pointed to the book on the table, and Mallory laughed too.

"Not exactly."

"Then you haven't heard the right stories yet," Henry said as he wove his fingers together, then stretched them out to crack the knuckles.

Kylie rolled her eyes dramatically toward Mallory. A thrum of shared affection passed between them.

"Oh, that's right. Kylie said you have some theories about the lake monster."

Immediately, Henry's pink cheeks brightened further.

"I'm giving you ten minutes," Kylie said to her brother as she shoved him over so she could slide out of the booth. "But if we are going to talk about the monster, I'm going to need more wine."

She grabbed Mallory's glass as well, which Mallory was surprised to see was nearly empty. Mallory knew she shouldn't let herself be carried away by her lovely companions, the rising music, and the noisy conversation around them. But there was an energy to the night that made her feel more alive than she had since Graham had first been diagnosed. Still, she had to be careful. No one knew her here. One wrong step could create the wrong impression—especially with the local law enforcement.

Henry took a big swig from his beer and an even deeper breath, then began to speak.

"Okay, so let's start with a little background. When the valley flooded in 1974, Loss Lake was created, right?"

Mallory murmured agreement.

"The water came in hard and fast and merged with the other waterways in the valley. Loss Lake was immediately connected to the Turner River, a huge channel that leads straight to the ocean. So that's important to know. It's deep out there, three thousand feet or so. Some people think it's deep enough to have allowed something to swim up the Turner River. You know, explore the new territory."

"Something like what?"

Henry grinned, then held up one finger as Kylie returned with their drinks. She plunked down Mallory's wine and another beer for her brother.

Henry thanked her and then continued. "Something prehistoric maybe? The fishermen off the coast have caught massive sturgeons— like twelve, fifteen feet long. These fish are big, Mallory. I heard once about a fish that was reeled in with an eagle skeleton dug into its back. Its talons had clipped onto the fish's spine, and the bird couldn't retract them as the fish dove deep and drowned it. It decomposed and became part of the fish's body."

"So you think the Loss Lake monster is a sturgeon?" Mallory was struggling to follow his argument.

"No, ma'am." Henry grinned wickedly. "I'm saying if there's fish out there that are that big, it makes me wonder if there's something out there that's feeding on them. You know, something that's been at the top of the food chain for a lot longer than us."

"A dinosaur?"

"Who knows? Those underwater channels are real deep." Henry took another gulp of beer, confident he had proven his point.

"Sorry, I'm still confused," Mallory said.

"Join the club," Kylie snorted. Her brother elbowed her good-naturedly.

"Okay, here's the deal," Henry said as he arranged two bar napkins flat on the table, placing a miniature pencil from the keno tray in between them. "This one is the ocean, right? The pencil is the Turner River. And the other one is Loss Lake."

He wiggled his fingers menacingly as he mimed them moving from one napkin to the other, using the pencil as a pathway.

"I think the monster was living off the coast, feeding on those big fish. Then, when the flood happened, it decided to explore."

"But what does it eat in Loss Lake? Surely there aren't any big fish here like those saltwater sturgeons."

Henry raised his eyebrows. "It might have been eating fish to get by, but I think it's always preferred a much different kind of prey."

"What do you mean?"

Kylie sighed again, but this time Mallory didn't meet her eyes. Henry's words had chilled her.

"Our dad was a logger when he was young. Pretty much everyone was in those days. Back before the flood, right? Loss Lake didn't exist yet. He worked in the mill yards right on the ocean, on the coast. It was where they kept all the timber they pulled out of these forests before shipping it down to Vancouver. He told me that there was a foreman back then that everyone hated. Apparently, the guy was a real dirtbag. Beat the hell out of his wife in a trailer on-site where everyone could hear her screams, then came out with his knuckles bruised and a smile on his face.

"So one day, the foreman was trying to show off. Even though it was freezing—middle of October—he dove into the ocean and swam out far. My dad said he was kind of yelling and taunting them all for staying close to the shore. Then"—Henry snapped his fingers for effect—"he was gone. According to my dad, it looked like a whirlpool formed around him, big and wide and then smaller and tighter until it sucked him right down."

The beat of the music seemed foreboding as Henry paused to let her take in his words. Kylie refrained from teasing him. Mallory felt compelled to ask.

"What did your dad think it was?"

"A monster, for sure."

Kylie cleared her throat and looked at her brother with a mix of tolerance and exasperation.

"I don't know if Dad is so convinced it was a monster, Henry. He's talked a lot about jammed logs off the coast where the mill was. How they can change water patterns in a weird way and cause unexpected currents. Also, it was freezing. The man could have drowned because of the temperature."

"Both of those things do seem more plausible than a monster," Mallory said. Kylie gave her a quick smile to thank her for reining her brother in.

Henry seemed to sense his spell had been broken. He shrugged.

"Listen, I'm a practical guy. I'm a cop, for Pete's sake. If I believe something is unexplainable, it probably is. Besides, Logan is convinced the tourists are soon to come a-knocking, and anything that stimulates the local economy is a good thing, in my opinion. But what you believe is up to you." He winked to indicate that he was a good sport.

Mallory took a sip of wine, wondering if this was the right moment to bring up the drowning earlier that day when the music stopped abruptly. A few seconds later, it returned at nearly twice the volume, loud enough to make her ears vibrate painfully. Henry and Kylie looked to the small dance floor, and Mallory followed suit. The woman she had seen by the dartboard was now swaying in time with the raucous vocals of Nickelback.

"Here we go," Henry said loudly to Kylie.

When the chorus began, the woman sang along at a volume loud enough to be audible over the lead singer's emotional belting. Her voice was even less pleasant. As she spun around in a slow circle, Mallory found it hard to tell whether she was in her thirties or forties. It was clear that life had treated her badly. Hard lines were drawn around her mouth and across her forehead. Between that and her tightly closed eyes, she looked both extremely sad and very drunk.

"Suzanne! Can you turn it down a little?" Henry hollered.

"Who is that?" Mallory asked Kylie. The volume of the music meant she couldn't hear her own voice, but Kylie was either good at lipreading or prepared for the question.

She leaned across the table and Mallory did the same. "That's Suzanne Young," Kylie replied with her mouth close to Mallory's ear. "She lives in the trailer at the corner of the turnoff to your place."

Mallory tried not to let it show how unusual she found it to run into her neighbors. It made sense that the woman was just as disheveled and unruly as the exterior of her home had suggested she would be. Suzanne turned toward them in response to Henry's call. The hostility on her face was palpable.

"Screw off," she called in their direction.

"That's no way for a lady to talk," Henry said. His words were teasing, but his tone had an edge.

"Who are you to tell me what to do?"

Suzanne's tongue was thickened by enough alcohol to make her words run together. Mallory cringed at the woman's visible drunkenness. It reminded her of her father.

"Come on, Suzanne. We're here to have fun," Kylie said. "Can you calm down a little?"

"You can shut up too, Kylie. You're just as bad as him, and you all know it."

The people at the tables close to them stared down at their drinks. Henry had half risen, as if about to confront her, when Kylie put her hand on his arm.

"Leave it. You're off duty. She's drunk. Let's go."

Suzanne tossed her head like Henry or Kylie had responded to her. "Who are you to tell me not to play this song? It was our song, Henry. The least you can do is let me play it."

Mallory tried to make sense of the animosity between her new friends and her neighbor, but she found herself at a loss for words. Suddenly, the miles she had traveled and the tension in the bar caught up with her. She was exhausted.

"It's probably best for me to call it a night anyway," Mallory said.

Kylie looked at her with worry in her eyes. "Don't mind Suzanne, Mallory. Every town's got a bitter drunk or two. It's nothing personal."

Mallory smiled back at her friend to show her that she wasn't taking Suzanne's insults seriously. "I may be new to this town, but I'm familiar with the type."

She, Henry, and Kylie downed the last of their drinks and wove their way through the bar, which had become more crowded since they had arrived. Mallory caught a glimpse of Logan giving them a quick wave behind a lineup of people at the bar. The women said goodbye to Henry in the parking lot. As Kylie's truck rumbled over the bumps in the road, Mallory became as drowsy as a child on a long car trip. She spoke little as Kylie filled her in on who to hire to plow her driveway after the first snowfall and where to go to buy a proper pair of winter boots.

"I know it feels like fall has just begun, but winter can sneak up on you this far north," Kylie said.

Mallory made a sound that she hoped was agreeable. She knew she wasn't going to remember the specifics of what Kylie had told her, but the young woman didn't seem like the type of person who would be offended if Mallory asked her again.

"Here we are," Kylie said cheerfully as she pulled up in front of Mallory's new home. The ranch house was lit up in welcome, thanks to her having left the kitchen light on. She thanked Kylie before making her way through the darkness and into her first night in her new home.

Once inside, the silence of the house, so quiet compared to the crowded bar and the chatty ride home, had a nearly hypnotic effect. She turned the kitchen light off and walked down the carpeted hall. As she slipped under the flannel covers worn thin with washing, she was grateful to Kylie for her kindness. The sheets smelled vaguely but not unpleasantly of someone else: slightly smoky and rich. As she drifted off to sleep, she found herself wondering what Joel Benson smelled like. The thought made her nestle into the soft fabric with a small smile on her lips.

CHAPTER SIX

Mallory blinked awake. The room was so bright her eyelashes seemed to brush against the sunlight. She was confused to see a room with unfamiliar dimensions. Her bedroom was dark, located at the back of the house and shaded by trees. She was bewildered yet hopeful, as if she had stayed the night in a luxury hotel. She lifted her head to identify the source of the lemon-yellow light flooding the room and found herself looking at the lake. Its calm surface rolled and dipped, catching bowls of sunshine in its hollows. The sight of it made her remember where she was and what she had chosen.

She snuggled into the heavy quilt, watching the water and light dance together for a few moments as she recalled the conversation from the night before. It was hard to imagine a monster beneath the surface, and the thought of Henry's youthful beliefs made her smile, stretch, and pull herself out of bed. She was halfway down the hall when she realized that, for the first time in decades, her morning wouldn't begin with a cup of coffee. She hoped Kylie was more trustworthy about the uplifting effects of chicory, which she had sworn by while filling Mallory's cart, than she was about the addictive effect of the other concoction she had brewed.

New home, new town, new drink, she thought as she ran her hand lightly down the wood paneling in the hall. Every inch of the place was new and exciting. She had forgotten the way an unfamiliar place generated hope and wonder, which wasn't surprising given the fact that she had experienced the feeling only three times before. Once, when she had moved into her college dorm at UBC, but back then the newness had been so overwhelming it was almost frightening. The second and third times had been less jarring but also less exciting. Moving in with nursing school friends and then a fiancé was inevitable and predictable. This felt like her first real new home. She savored the moment as the hallway opened up to the kitchen. The sun was shining as much through the kitchen windows as it had been in the bedroom, and the rooms seemed to glow with pride, showing off for her.

As she put her brand-new kettle on to boil, countless reflections from the sunshine on the water spotted the walls and floor around her, flitting like fireflies. Her early-morning buoyancy allowed her to overcome a snag of hesitation at getting close to the plate-glass window in the living room that she now knew had once been shattered by a bullet. She turned her back to the window that faced the forest and stared directly at the lake, feeling like she was standing directly at the water's edge. Rays of sun slid up and over the gentle waves. Gold and azure shimmered to her in welcome, dissolving the troubling news of the day before. Finally, she was home.

The feeble sputter of the kettle beginning to boil startled her out of her reverie. Though she longed to go outside and explore the small trail that led to the beach, she hadn't yet earned her opportunity to sink her feet into the sand. Mallory had been taught by her parents, then trained by her profession, to make sure everything was in order before she allowed herself a break. When she dipped her toes into the water, she wanted to be prepared. As she made her chicory, hoping it was a more palatable mix than the crumbling bark in her cup suggested, Mallory resolved to find out more about the lake. But first, she needed to unpack.

She took a moment to sip the earthy liquid and found it not entirely unpleasant, though it didn't have the familiar punch of her beloved coffee. She extracted her phone from her purse and called her mother, ignoring the notification of a missed call from the night before. She was relieved to hear it go straight to voice mail. Neither of her parents were early risers. She left an enthusiastic message stating that she had arrived safely and assuring them she would call again soon. Then she turned to the boxes and suitcases she had brought from her old home, which were still piled in the foyer. After pulling the largest one into the back bedroom, she opened the zippered compartment and caught a faint scent of her former home: the sweet smell of the cedar trees that had bordered their property mixed with the chemical smell of disinfectant she used to keep the house free of potential infections. Underlying it all was the staleness that had emanated from Graham's body. She opened a window, but the smell seemed to grow stronger.

Despite her training as a nurse, she had agreed wholeheartedly with Graham's decision to avoid a hospital for as long as possible. She had watched too many family members huddle around a dying person's bed for endless hours lit by fluorescent lights bleeding into darkened nights. She could see the boredom they were fighting to ignore and the guilt that came with it. It was unfair for the living to notice the tedium of death, let alone be troubled by the fact that the rhythm of electronic beeps and pulses was the only way to mark the passing of time. She knew it was excruciating for the family members to hint at their desire to know when it would all end, to ask the doctors if they had any sense of the moment when death would finally occur. So they waited, sitting on the uncomfortable chairs upholstered with stainproof fabric, wishing that they could leave while punishing themselves with the knowledge of what it was they were hoping for.

She hadn't wanted that ending for Graham, and he hadn't wanted it for himself either. His parents had chosen to have him late in life and had passed away when he was in his early thirties. He was born an only child, so no siblings were present to offer a counteropinion for his care. She had worked around the clock for him, barring the few hours in which they had help, without a single complaint. Only after he died did she realize that hospitals had not been created exclusively for the sole purpose of extending life, as she had been taught. The hustle of activity, the wires and cords that tracked every vital function, and especially the half circle of hard, hovering chairs around the deathbed existed so that no one would die alone. The final moment would always be accompanied and acknowledged. A hospital was a place where death was noticed and the proper attention was paid.

The more clothing she removed from the suitcase, the stronger the scent of her past became, until it was unbearable. She shoved everything back in, zipping the suitcase up and wheeling it straight into the bathroom, which housed the washer and dryer. She pulled a pair of simple black pants and a striped long-sleeved T-shirt out of the case before loading the rest, along with the lemon-and-lavender powder that Kylie had selected for her, into the washing machine.

She placed the laundry detergent on the small shelf above the washing machine, which seemed to have been installed exactly for that purpose, but the smooth slide of the box was hindered by something caught underneath it. She stood on her tiptoes to see what was causing the problem. It was a small piece of paper, crumpled in the way of something pulled hurriedly from a pair of pants before washing them. She smoothed it out and realized it was an old shopping list. The printing was in all capitals, blocky and uniform, like that of a student who had perfected the strokes of each letter but hadn't yet learned to give them a signature shape. The contents of the list were meticulous, each item categorized not only by its product type but also by the manufacturer with further specifications included.

RISING STAR OATMEAL (STEEL-CUT)

FOUR NAVEL ORANGES (MEDIUM)

ONE PINT OF SUNNY DAYS ORANGE JUICE (LOW-PULP)

Mallory was unnerved as she scanned the forgotten list, as if she were eavesdropping on a private conversation. After discarding the note, she became more eager to be finished with her tasks and hurriedly unpacked several more boxes in the kitchen, bathroom, and small utility closet off the kitchen. As she worked, she wondered if she had left anything, like the grocery list, behind in her old home. She hoped not. The idea of someone handling an inconsequential object that provided such a deep intimacy made her feel uncomfortable. Her greatest hope in leaving her old life was to disappear without a trace.

She gulped the last of the chicory and realized that, though it had become measurably more tolerable, it was not enough to dissuade her from trying to find a source of real coffee. It was time for another trip to town.

As she walked out the door, the air that met her exposed face and hands was surprisingly cold, more so than the breeze that had blown through the window. It smelled of autumn, change, and vegetal decay. A light jacket would have been enough to ward off the morning chill, but she didn't bother to go back into the house for a warmer layer. Though she had no reason to rush, urgency bubbled through her body like an underground spring. She gripped the cold steering wheel in her hands and flicked the heat to high, deciding that the library would be her first stop. She could meet her closest neighbor and learn more about her new home.

Mallory had always been a meticulous researcher. She had sailed through nursing school due to her genuine fascination with the information in her textbooks. Her classmates used to laugh at her enthusiastic description of the mechanical beauty of the human hand, teasing her for being a nerd shortly before pleading to borrow her notes. Knowledge was what had always helped Mallory situate herself in the world. She wanted to take out a few more books on McNamara to supplement the work of Frederich Menzel she had purchased last night.

Her heater finally began to blow warm once she was through the forest. Kylie's story of the errant hunter made sense of the chain-link fence's purpose, but the understanding gave Mallory no satisfaction.

Instead, she found the dull metal barrier more unnerving. As she passed Carlotta's cottage, she checked her rearview mirror, and, seeing no cars on the road behind her, she slowed to a crawl so she could look more closely at the finely maintained two-story house. She hadn't noticed yesterday that the white walls and yellow door were offset by bright-red trim, which gave it the feeling of a gingerbread house perched on the top of a small rolling hill. The two large raised beds at the front of the house were bursting with the last produce of the season: bright-orange pumpkins shone under leaves the size of shoeboxes, and golden squash lay on the ground like plump ambassadors of autumn. The property told of a tenderhearted and friendly person who took care of it.

No such feeling of kinship arose as she passed the run-down trailer she now knew belonged to Suzanne, the blowsy woman from the pub last night. Its formerly white exterior had been dulled by years of weather and road dust, and the property was in similar disrepair. Mallory spotted an ATV on its side about ten feet from the door, a bicycle wheel propped up on a tattered canvas chair, and a firepit that looked like it was fueled with more garbage than wood, judging by the half-blackened cans and shriveled plastic milk jugs. She wondered about the bitterness in the woman she had seen last night, dancing by herself to a melancholy song, and tried not to condemn her for her sullen exterior. There was a sadness that seemed to inform her anger, which Mallory understood all too well.

A few minutes later, she pulled her car into the empty parking lot beside the library, marveling at the luxury of space that McNamara provided. She had never noticed the tense awareness that the crowding of the city had required of her—a part of her always aware of the path of other people. It was nice to move around without worrying about whether she was in someone else's way. The library was a squat clay-brick building with a freshly mowed lawn on either side of the stone path that led to its glass door. The flower beds were tidily mulched in preparation for winter, lovingly tended in the same way as the woman's home and garden. The windows were dark, however, and Mallory realized that a small-town library might not keep the same hours as its urban counterparts. It was Sunday after all. Maybe no businesses were open. As she stared at the building and wondered what to do, it brightened before her eyes. Given the warm reception she had received from Kylie and Henry and the welcoming exterior of the two buildings associated with Carlotta, Mallory left her car, walked to the entrance, and pulled open the door with a happy expectation of who she would find inside.

Sure enough, the library was painted a pleasant shade of buttery yellow that made the light wooden shelves immediately to the left and right of the entrance shine. About ten feet in front of the door, past several freestanding shelves, stood a large circulation desk with an ancient-looking computer on one side and a stack of books on the other. Behind the desk stood a woman in her early sixties with wiry gray hair pulled into a loose bun, who looked up as she came in the door. A light-blue hand-knit cardigan, pulled baggy at the elbows with age and wear, hung from her thin shoulders. Mallory greeted her brightly. Though the woman continued staring straight at her, there was no trace of a smile on her face.

"You must be my new neighbor," the woman said.

Mallory walked to the front of the desk. "Yes, I'm Mallory Dent."

"Carlotta Gray."

"This is a lovely library. I was happy to find it open."

"Every Sunday at ten a.m. Some people worship in churches, but words will always be what I turn to for faith."

"I couldn't agree more," Mallory said. "In fact, I'm hoping to take out some books today about McNamara. It would be nice to know the history of the place."

Carlotta's eyes hardened unexpectedly at her words. "History is important. I hope you aren't one of those people who move here and want to change everything. Betty Barber mentioned you wanted to thin some trees. I don't agree with forest management, and I think you should leave those woods alone. I don't want anything cut down on my side of the property line. The deed is available to you in the map drawers at the back if you've misplaced the one that was issued to you."

The woman's curt words were punctuated with a sniff of disdain. She spoke like she was well aware of Mallory's confusion about her land the day before. Mallory was so stunned at the undeserved reproof that she took a step back from the desk. She vaguely remembered making an offhand comment about reducing the risk of a tree falling on the house, but she couldn't recall saying anything definite to Betty. Certainly nothing that would warrant this level of suspicion.

"No, not at all. In fact, I plan to keep the property exactly as it is."

"Good." The coldness in the woman's eyes thawed by a fraction. Her stern words seemed to have been issued more to establish her superiority than to discuss land management. Mallory was reminded of the older nurses who had bullied her when she was younger.

"For now, anyway," Mallory couldn't stop herself from adding.

Though she had expected the woman to recoil, she saw the side of Carlotta's mouth curl up in amusement. Her tone was noticeably less sharp when she spoke again.

"Well, what can I do for you?"

"I came to get a library card."

The tension in the other woman's face eased again, though her expression remained closer to a scowl than a smile. "Did you bring proof of residence?"

Again, Mallory was caught off guard, but she tried not to show it. She hadn't changed her identification yet. It seemed odd that the town was small enough for Carlotta to recognize her on sight yet not small enough apparently to issue a library card without going through the formal process. Luckily, she had slipped her first electric bill into her purse before leaving the house, hoping that the utilities company could help her determine who would set up internet and a landline for her home.

"Of course," Mallory said, handing the woman the paper.

The librarian frowned as she smoothed it out unnecessarily on the surface of her desk. She turned and began typing the information into her computer. Mallory stood awkwardly, wondering if the librarian would think her rude if she started browsing before she had official permission to do so. She decided the answer was yes, so she stayed in her spot, keeping a respectful silence until the librarian's printer shuddered to a start and whined its way through the card's production. Carlotta passed the nonlaminated square across the counter to Mallory without a word.

"Thank you," Mallory said. "Could you direct me to the local history section?"

Carlotta pointed to a shelf on her right. "The section is small, but it's located over there beside wilderness survival skills, which is the section you should be consulting. You're from the city. There are things here that you should learn. Especially before the snow falls."

Mallory tried to react with grace to the unsolicited advice. "Thank you."

As she turned, Carlotta called out to her back, "But if you're looking for more information on the Loss Lake deaths, the archives at the Turner library have a lot more than we do."

Mallory was startled. "Why would I be looking for information about the deaths?"

"I thought you might be curious. Suzanne mentioned you were discussing it last night with the Shine children," Carlotta said before turning back to the stack of books beside her.

Mallory frowned. Once again, news about her seemed to be traveling faster than she was. It was going to take her some time to get used to the size of McNamara and the information sharing that occurred here. What would have been an unsettling coincidence in her former life was now a daily occurrence. She took a breath to clear her head as she walked to the shelves.

Once at the section to which Carlotta had directed her, Mallory let her fingers trail along the spines of the dozen or so books. Most were focused on the history of logging, sawmills, and timber yards in the northwestern part of the province as a whole. Then she saw the vivid blue cover of Frederich Menzel's work. Beside it, a thin book titled *McNamara: For the Love of the Logs* by Nathaniel Shine caught her eye. The author must be related to her two new friends, which suggested a distinctly local focus. She took it in hand and sat down at a small table tucked in the back of the library.

The history book began at the turn of the century, when McNamara had been nothing more than a small logging camp designed to house timber workers while they cut swathes through the forest around them. Like Frederich's work, the book was clearly self-published. The language was melodramatic, and the book was littered with both grammatical and spelling errors.

Mallory skimmed the early chapters, which dealt with road building to the coast and log rolling down the ocean to the larger markets in southern cities. It wasn't until she got to the last chapter in the book that she found what she was looking for:

> In October of the year of nineteen seventy-four, an accident befell the town that would change it forever. For years, the Turner Dam had stood as both a guardian against the river's frequent floods and surges due to storms and snow melt as well as the only source of its electricity from hydropower. The concrete walls of the dam could only withstand so much. During a particularly violent autumn, when the rains poured down from the heavens as if unleashed by God himself, nothing could stand the force. Cracks began forming, but despite the engineers best efforts, before they could come up with a solution, all hell broke loose at midnight.

The dam was pulverized by a logjam that served as a battering ram. Enough water to flood the entire valley flowed freely, leaving a lake where there had formerly been a field and death where there had formerly been life.

Thanks be to heaven that only one home was located in the path of the water's destruction, but, unluckily, the home was occupied at the time of the water's rise. The widow Alice Halloway was drowned in her bed that night, survived by her only son. Her body was recovered days later by a courageous timber worker. The man embodied the courage and fortitude so often seen in the making of our beloved McNamara.

Upon the heels of the tragedy, the *Vancouver Tribune* covered the story, stating that the company who owned the dam would have no choice but to take a loss on the damage which had been inflicted by the formation of the large lake. Locals coined the term immediately to name the incredible expanse of water which now existed in the valley, and Loss Lake was born.

Mallory was disappointed that the book ended there without an author's note or acknowledgments. She checked the date of publication. Nineteen seventy-six, just two years after the lake had been created. She returned to the shelf, looking for anything else that might be helpful, but she came up empty.

Carlotta looked up as she approached the desk with Nathaniel Shine's book. She sniffed as she picked up the book.

"There is another text on McNamara that is more fanciful than this but still worth reading," the librarian said. "It's written by Frederich Menzel."

"I have a copy of that," Mallory said. "I picked it up from Logan Carruthers last night."

Carlotta breathed out through her nose, and Mallory sensed her disapproval at the mention of the bar.

"I see."

"I'm interested in the last fifty years of the town's history. Is there anything else you can suggest?"

Carlotta sighed. "That is a problem unless you're willing to drive to Turner as I mentioned. They carry newspaper archives which might be helpful, but there's little that's been published beyond that. Word of mouth is how most of the local stories get passed around now. Betty Barber has a long memory and likely wouldn't mind sharing some local history. But if you really want to know more about McNamara, the best place to go is Tuck's around this time of day. It's where a lot of the older men tend to take their midday meal, and heaven knows they enjoy telling their stories."

"Tuck's?"

Carlotta raised her eyebrows. "You really are new here. The gas station across the street."

Mallory tried not to give away her shock that the run-down service station was permitted to serve food.

"Thanks, I'll give it a try."

"Jonathan Shine is often there for lunch. He's the right person to ask."

Despite the fact that, for the first time since Mallory had entered the library, Carlotta was offering something like friendly advice, the woman's mouth pursed like a lemon when she said his name. It made Mallory feel better about the woman's clear disdain for her. Carlotta didn't seem to have much time for anyone.

Mallory realized the man must be related to Kylie and Henry, and Joel, though she still hadn't worked out the intricacies of why Joel used the surname Benson rather than Shine.

"Is Mr. Shine a historian?"

Carlotta shook her head. "Not of any note. But his father was the one who wrote that book in your hand, and Jonathan was mentioned in it. You might have noticed the family bias."

Mallory's eyebrows knit together. "Was he one of the engineers who worked to fix the dam?"

Carlotta's face darkened. "Hardly. He was the logger who found Alice Halloway's body."

CHAPTER SEVEN

Mallory crossed the street toward the gas station with quick steps to try to walk off the chill that still hung in the air. As she stepped onto the opposite sidewalk, the door to the realty office opened and out walked Betty Barber.

"Mallory Dent! Is that you?" the unexpectedly tanned woman cried.

"Yes, hello. Nice to meet you in person."

Mallory had seen Betty only in photos, and the flash of the camera had tempered her overreliance on self-tanner. In contrast to her bright-blonde bob, her bronzed skin made her wrinkles as pronounced as lines carved into a copper statue. Betty was about sixty years old, though she seemed to be working hard to appear younger.

"You made it!"

"I arrived yesterday," Mallory said, allowing herself to be embraced. Betty was a tiny woman, and Mallory's chin brushed the top of her fragrant hair. It was like hugging a hummingbird that had been rescued from a perfume counter as Betty darted in and out of her arms.

As she stepped back, Betty beamed with teeth so white that Mallory was momentarily distracted by the thought that they must be dentures.

"How's the new place? Do you need anything?"

As Betty spoke, her head wove back and forth to allow her to examine Mallory's face. Mallory hesitated and Betty noticed.

"What's wrong, sweetie? Is something the matter?"

Mallory couldn't hide her dissatisfaction with the way the woman had handled the sale of her home.

"It's just . . . I was a little taken aback when I discovered that there had been a death in my house. Isn't that something that needs to be disclosed to a buyer?"

Betty stepped closer to Mallory, then moved back again. The woman's constant motion made it difficult for Mallory to focus. A series of expressions flitted across Betty's face: confusion, remorse, then certainty as she came to a decision.

"Oh no. I knew I should have written it down for you."

"What do you mean?"

"Sweetie, I did disclose it. During the last talk we had before we finalized. We had a long conversation about the house's history, but you were so distraught." Betty's eyes grew glassy as she patted Mallory's arm with a velvety-soft palm that she pulled away almost immediately. "I lost my husband a few years ago. I should have known that what I was saying to you wasn't going to stick."

"You . . . told me?" Mallory reddened with embarrassment. The blanks in her memory were becoming increasingly concerning, especially in light of Carlotta's reproachful mention of Mallory's desire to clear the land. How much of her life was happening without her recording it? The idea that she could no longer trust herself was as terrifying as it was unfamiliar, particularly given the ongoing investigation of negligence on her property. Mallory was not a forgetful person. Her colleagues used to double-check charts with her when information was poorly recorded. Graham used to rely on her for the location of nearly everything in the house. The dissolution of her memory was eroding the core of who she had always considered herself to be.

"Sure did. It was right before I sent you the papers. I wanted you to be prepared." Betty touched Mallory's arm again. Her fingertips tapped like the turn indicator on a car as she motioned for Mallory to follow her back into the office. "I was about to stage a house down the road from you, but there's no rush. Why don't you come in? I'm happy to answer any questions you have."

She was amazed at Betty's kindness in the face of her failing. It was so different from the reaction she would have expected from her husband or her colleagues had she been less capable than they needed her to be. Besides, as Carlotta had mentioned, Betty might prove to be a far greater source of information in McNamara than the library.

She followed the woman up the small path made with paving stones surrounded by a bed of pristine white gravel. The face of the building was painted an immaculate pale pink, which contrasted with the oil-stained pavement and tacky signs of the gas station to one side and the cracked sidewalk and cluttered windows of the hardware store to the other. Mallory respected Betty's dedication to her aesthetic. It reminded her of her mother's unfashionable but much-beloved doll collection that she housed in a cupboard in a hulking china cabinet in her kitchen, along with the ugly apple doll that Logan had brought to her mind. As a child, Mallory had hated the way her mother had put her most beloved possessions on display but out of reach, suggesting that the best things in life should be kept at a distance.

Unsurprisingly, the inside of Betty's office was also immaculate and decidedly fussy. Mallory scanned a row of porcelain dolls staring emptily from a high shelf and was relieved to find no wrinkled apple faces among them. She settled into a wicker chair plumped by an overstuffed, dusty-rose seat cushion and accepted Betty's offer of a cup of tea. While the woman bustled about in the small kitchen in the corner, Mallory took the opportunity to look around more. Unlike the realty office Mallory had used in the city to sell her previous house, Betty had no listings of new properties plastered on a window or tacked to a bulletin board. Instead, the white walls were covered in oversize photos of small, cute animals. Like Logan's bar, there was also a display shelf of monster-themed memorabilia, including several of the ubiquitous snow globes. Mallory's eye was caught by a hoop of embroidery hanging on the wall.

A cartoon puppy cuddling the cutest version of the sea monster Mallory had seen yet was threaded across the cloth with the caption "Have You Hugged Your Monster Today?" emblazoned along the top. Betty returned with two china cups balanced on matching saucers.

"There you go, sweetie."

Mallory pointed toward the wall where the stitching hung.

"That piece is so beautiful. Is it your work?"

Betty blushed. "Well, Logan Carruthers and I go way back. We went to school together, you know. Back when all we had was a one-room schoolhouse, before they started busing kids to Turner for high school."

Logan had looked to be in his midseventies. If Betty had gone to school with him, Mallory would need to seriously reconsider the woman's bronzer routine, as it had clearly made her appear younger than she was. Betty took two quick sips of her tea, then set the cup and saucer on the table.

"Now, where do you want me to start, dear?"

"Start?"

"Tell me what you want to know about Sean. I'll fill you in on everything. I don't want you to be taken off guard again if anyone in town mentions something."

Mallory's mind started racing at the sound of the man's name. She wasn't sure if it was because of the opportunity Betty was offering or the way hearing it made him a real person who had lived and died in the house she now owned.

Betty read her pause as confusion. "Maybe I should write it down?"

"No, no, I'll remember," Mallory said hurriedly.

Betty smiled back. "Take your time, dear. I'll be here whenever you need me to go over it again. It was a bad business and hard to hear. You're grieving right now. It's a difficult state to be in, but it protects you from absorbing too much."

"You think grief protects a person?"

Mallory was incredulous at the idea. She thought of her grief as more of a suffocating blanket than a comforting cloak. Betty took a deep breath before she answered. Her eyes shone as she spoke.

"It doesn't feel like it at first, I suppose. At first, it's a weight that drags you down. Some mornings after my Bill passed away, I woke up and felt like a force was pressing me back into my bed, no matter how hard I tried to get back to my regular routine. I slept so much in those days. Everything was harder than it used to be. Heavy, like an anchor."

Mallory's own eyes began filling with tears. Betty reached for a box of tissues housed in a box made of pink quilting. She let her hand flutter on Mallory's arm again before pulling away.

"I'm guessing that's where you're at now. How long has it been?"

"Eight weeks," Mallory said softly, then corrected herself. "No, nine."

"Oh dear. It's all still so fresh for you. I promise this isn't how it's going to be forever. It took close to a year before I realized that the thing crushing me wasn't there to hurt me. It was a dampening, a way for my mind to slowly come back to a life without him in it. A life that I had never wanted to live. It's been two years for me now. I've got a different perspective, I suppose. I think of that grief, that heaviness, as something different now. I think of it as being more like a cocoon. Something that sheltered me until I was ready to change into the person that my husband's death forced me to become."

Mallory took a drink of tea to swallow the sob that was thickening her throat. It was warm and sweet, like Betty herself. She hoped the woman was right. The chance to become whole again, without Graham, was exactly the transformation she had wished for herself in McNamara. Once she had gained control of herself, she spoke.

"That's very beautiful, Betty. Thank you."

"You're welcome, my dear. So tell me. How is the house?"

Mallory thought of the sunshine on the lake that morning.

"It's wonderful."

Betty's face relaxed in relief, and she patted the side of her bob to congratulate herself. "Well, thank goodness for that. You seemed so harried when I first saw you. I was worried that the old story had you spooked."

Mallory was taken aback by the woman's description of her. She had felt more confident that morning than she had since Graham's death. It concerned her to learn that her outward appearance still showed a woman in chaos. Was that how Carlotta, Kylie, and Henry had seen her? Or worse, Sergeant Benson? She realized that Betty was looking at her expectantly and she hurried to answer, lest she come off as more unhinged.

"I suppose the idea of a death in the house did make me nervous. Maybe you can start at the beginning. How did it happen?"

Betty took a sip of tea with her bright eyes fixed on Mallory and leaned in. Mallory was relieved to see that the woman seemed keen to speak. Mallory suspected that there were not too many stories that Betty didn't relish imparting to newcomers. It was a strange thing, she thought, as Betty plucked at the string of pearls around her neck, to have a town so full of history with so few people who didn't know the tales by heart. No wonder everyone wanted to confide in her. It was possible that she was the only new person they'd had to speak with in years.

"It happened ten years ago. Almost to the week, in fact. Poor Sean," Betty murmured. "He had been through so much, and we were all rooting for him to make it, and then he gets killed in that way. It was a crying shame."

"So you knew him as a child?"

"Oh, he didn't have an easy upbringing, neither him nor his older brother. Their mother, bless her soul, was a sweet girl, but she had the most appalling taste in men. The man she shacked up with—Carl Benson—was a drunk and a mean one at that."

Mallory's attention was caught by the familiar last name, but she didn't dare interrupt Betty, who had become agitated as she described Carl.

"All he really gave her was a last name for her children and a black eye every Saturday night. At the time, there wasn't the help and services for someone like her in that kind of situation." She dropped her voice to a near whisper. "Sean's older brother probably saw a lot of violence, before he was old enough to know it was wrong. Things like that get imprinted on a child, you know. Bill and I used to worry about her and her babies, all alone in that house with her husband running around drinking and coming home and doing God knows what. I'd drop care packages at her doorstep every week, and I know I wasn't alone. Dee Shine used to do the same."

Mallory struggled to keep up. "Dee Shine? Kylie Shine's mother?"

"Yes, indeed. She passed away about five years ago. Emphysema. What a tragedy. She was ten years younger than Jonathan, yet she went so much earlier than him. I hope you don't smoke, dear. Nothing good comes of that habit."

Mallory shook her head to indicate she didn't. She tried to redirect Betty to the point of the story. "So Sean and his brother grew up in my house?"

"No, no. That came later. When they were young, they lived in a trailer closer to Main Street. Their father was killed in an accident two weeks after Sean was born. Not that he was around much when he was alive. And like that"—Betty snapped her fingers, and Mallory noticed her nail polish was an exact match for the slipcovers—"their mother packed up and left town without a thank-you or a forwarding address. Up and ran off with two boys under the age of four years old. Nobody knew the whole story, but there was talk of another man sweeping her off her feet." Betty clicked her tongue in disapproval. "This was still a logging town in those days, you know. Plenty of men with plenty of promises for a pretty young girl."

Mallory was skeptical that a young mother would find another suitor so quickly, but it was beside the point.

"So Sean and his brother didn't actually grow up here?" she asked. Maybe she had misread Kylie's sentiment the day before. It seemed that she had known him well, and Mallory had assumed they had a childhood connection.

Betty inhaled like she'd been waiting for Mallory to ask precisely that question.

"Well, that's just it, dear. The year after they left town, their mother was killed in a car accident. Of course, her mysterious new man was nowhere to be seen. The boys were orphaned. Sean was three years old and Joel was only five."

Mallory blinked as she realized what Betty was saying.

"Joel Benson, the sergeant?"

"Yes indeed. If it wasn't for Jonathan and Dee, who knows where they might have ended up? Oh, those two were a lovely couple. God rest her soul."

Mallory was struggling to keep track of the births and deaths.

"So they adopted Joel and Sean and brought them back here?"

That explained Joel's relationship with Kylie and Henry, though Mallory still found it curious that he chose not to use his adopted surname.

"Yes," Betty said with a nod. "Which was what made Sean's death all the more tragic. They had a lot of good years together. Dee and Jonathan raised those boys like their own." She lowered her voice again. "Dee had a hard time having babies, you know. The boys were a godsend to her. Then, wouldn't you know it, Kylie came along the year Joel turned nine. Everyone thought that was it for them until Henry astonished us all ten years after that. Change-of-life babies. It's important for a lady to be careful in that period."

She paused and met Mallory's eyes knowingly, which made Mallory feel an uncomfortable urge to reassure the older woman that there was no need to worry on her behalf. Fortunately, Betty continued.

"Anyway, as far as we were concerned, there was no difference in their or anyone else's mind between their natural children and their adopted ones. Even now, you can watch the way the three kids treat each other. Closer than most blood families. They all still live on the same property, you know. Imagine that."

"It's a shame that Sean isn't around to be a part of it too."

"It was so sad. Senseless too, Sean's death. Only thirty-three years old. He was standing looking out the window facing the lake when the bullet came at him from behind. So many bright years ahead of him. His law practice had only been open for seven years."

"How awful."

At least with Graham, she had known what to expect. Of course, if she was honest with herself, the long period of his suffering hadn't been easy on either of them. It made her feel terrible to remember the moments when she had wished it would end. During her nursing career, she had been taught that death was simple. Once a heart stopped, a body ceased to live. But she'd had no idea that grief was so complicated.

"Kylie mentioned it was a hunting accident."

Betty dipped her head once to confirm. "One stray bullet from a hunting rifle back in the woods between your house and Carlotta's. The hunter was never found, and it's pretty much assumed it was an outsider who was being careless. That forest is thick in parts. Maybe they didn't realize how close they were to a residential area. All I know is that no one from around here is foolish enough to hunt in an area so close to houses."

Mallory swallowed hard, and Betty sensed her anxiety.

"That's why it's fenced off, of course. No one can get into that part of your property now without a key or permission from you."

"Of course," Mallory said, remembering the map the sergeant had drawn for her.

Both women sat in silence for a moment before Betty cleared her throat and tried for a brighter tone.

"Anyway, that's the story. It's an awful one, but it has a happy ending. I know we're all thrilled to have someone like you in the house now. Everyone here wants a fresh start for the property just like you wanted a new beginning for yourself. When I heard about your situation, I knew it was the perfect place for you to buy."

Mallory drew in a breath. She was discomfited by the woman's rapid switch to a happy voice. Once again, Betty seemed to understand Mallory's hesitation. She dropped the cheery act as she spoke again.

"Houses are like people, Mallory. They all have histories. Some are sad, but they can change. A death is just another chapter as the story keeps getting written." Betty stood up and dusted off her pale-lilac trousers. "Now, I'll be here whenever you need me. But I really must get going."

Mallory rose as well, thanking Betty for her time. As the older woman leaned in to embrace her, Mallory's stomach grumbled.

Betty laughed. "Well, that tells me exactly where you should be heading next. Tuck's, right next door."

"I think I'll grab something at home," Mallory said.

Despite the advice of both Betty and Carlotta and her desire to meet Jonathan Shine, she still thought it strange to eat at a place that looked like it had been built before unleaded gasoline was in common use. Besides, given the number of people she'd met in the last day, it seemed that she'd be running into Jonathan Shine soon enough.

"Don't be silly. Tuck's getting too old to work much these days, but every week his wife comes to the shop and delivers the best darn beef on a bun you've ever tried," Betty said, all but shooing Mallory in the direction of the dilapidated service station. Mallory's stomach growled again, and it prompted her to acquiesce to the woman's urging. She had nothing else planned for the day if the food ended up not sitting well.

When in Rome, she thought as she walked across the buckling asphalt toward Tuck's. If people in McNamara ate at gas stations, she supposed she could choke something down. It was important to fit in. After all, this was her home now.

CHAPTER EIGHT

Mallory nearly bumped into a woman wearing a thick wool cap as she stepped into the crowded entryway of Tuck's Fuel and Food. She murmured an apology, and the woman turned and offered her a smile. From her place at the end of the long line, Mallory could see that the gas station had a checkout counter six feet in front of the door and rows of wire shelves offering packaged goods to the right and left of her. Surprisingly, she didn't see a single monster-related piece of memorabilia placed among the bags of chips and containers of motor oil. She counted seven people queued up in the small space in front of the cash register. The gas station smelled of roasted meat and freshly baked bread. In spite of her earlier misgivings, Mallory's mouth watered as she shuffled forward.

When she was third in line, she noticed several small folding tables and chairs had been set up close to the steamy windows to her left. Several people were enthusiastically unwrapping sandwiches wrapped in shiny foil, while others were happily munching away. Mallory noticed Kylie, who waved at her and gestured for Mallory to join her and the rest of her group, which included Sergeant Benson and an older man Mallory didn't recognize, likely Jonathan Shine. She was nervous about sitting with them, but Kylie's open face was enough to put her at ease. It was funny to see the young woman who had filled her grocery basket with every kind of bean imaginable eating a heaping pile of gas station beef.

"What'll it be?" said the woman behind the counter when Mallory got to the front of the line.

Though her bleached-blonde hair was pulled back in a careless ponytail flattened under a forest-green mesh ball cap with the name of the gas station scrawled on it, Mallory immediately recognized the cashier as Suzanne, the woman who had been belligerent to Henry in Logan's bar. Lingering remnants of her makeup from the night before had collected in the corners of her faded blue eyes to form a blackened crust. Red lines snaking around the pupils hardened them almost as much as Suzanne's disinterested glare.

"I'll have a sandwich, please," Mallory said pleasantly.

"Beef on a bun?"

"Yes, please."

The woman's eyes narrowed, trying and failing to place Mallory. She held her breath and hoped that Suzanne wouldn't connect her with the Shine family and reenact her angry outburst. The woman seemed to grow bored of her attempt to identify Mallory, and she held out a flat hand, palm facing up.

"Five bucks," she said.

Mallory pulled out her credit card and looked for the machine.

"Cash only," the woman said impatiently.

Mallory flushed. She couldn't remember the last time she had carried actual dollar bills, though it was clear she would need to start doing so to get by in McNamara. She and Graham had been diligent about paying with their cards to accrue the points awarded to them, which they used for their annual vacation. A man behind her cleared his throat pointedly, and Mallory craned her neck from side to side, as much to search for a solution as to shake off the mundane memory of her husband. It was the small things about their life together that had the most power to destroy her. She could handle the waves of sorrow much more easily than hearing a snippet of a song Graham used to hum under his breath or an ad for the finale of a long-running television show he had been excited to watch.

Mallory failed to see anything in Tuck's that looked like it dispensed dollar bills, so she sought guidance from the woman whose name she knew but didn't feel comfortable saying.

"Um. Is there a cash machine close by?"

The woman sighed dramatically, then eyed Mallory with a shrewdness that hadn't been present before. "Aren't you the one who moved into the lake house?"

"Yes," Mallory said.

It was the first time she had heard her new home described that way. She liked the feeling of the words, the way the water and the dwelling were made inseparable. It captured the spirit of the property in a way that nothing else did. To Mallory's shock, the blonde woman smiled. The expression was enthusiastic enough to change her entire face. Her teeth were straight, though both of her incisors were beginning to yellow. For a moment, Suzanne looked pretty, until Mallory saw a flicker of something unkind underneath the pleasant expression.

"So how about this? Your sandwich is on the house. Welcome to McNamara."

The man behind her coughed again. She was uncomfortable accepting the gesture but was also low-level panicked at the scene her lack of cash was causing.

"Thank you," Mallory said. "I'll make sure to bring money next time."

"Remember the favor. That's how we do it up here." The woman winked as she turned to a huge tray covered in a red-checked cloth behind her. As she unfolded it, a tendril of sweet-smelling steam wafted up from a pile of freshly baked buns underneath. She pulled one out and placed it on a stack of aluminum foil squares on the counter, then opened the lid of a large slow cooker. Mallory could see the cord of the small appliance had been pulled taut to reach an outlet at the end of the counter nearly three feet away. It looked like a fire hazard, but she wasn't about to risk Suzanne's bad temper by pointing it out. Suzanne used tongs to lay several pieces of tender beef onto the bread, which she then rolled into the thin foil with three efficient moves. Fold, fold, roll.

"Enjoy," she said, smiling again as she handed the sandwich over the counter. The kindness in her words wasn't enough to change the ice in her eyes.

Mallory thanked her. The man behind her moved eagerly into her place as she stepped out of the line. The sandwich was heavy in Mallory's hands, both comforting and curious. True to the word of Carlotta and Betty, Mallory was now looking forward to eating something that came from a gas station as she sidestepped through the tight space over to Kylie's table.

Kylie smiled at her and pointed to the empty chair beside her. "Come sit down."

She slid into the chair and found herself directly across the table from Sergeant Benson. She said hello. He greeted her in return before taking another bite of his sandwich. Though she knew he simply happened to be having lunch in the same place she was, Mallory couldn't shake the feeling of being under observation. She wondered if he had discovered something else about the drowning but was hesitant to ask. Then she wondered if it was stranger not to bring it up. Luckily, Kylie rescued her from her own thoughts.

"Mallory Dent, this is my father, Jonathan Shine," Kylie said, gesturing to the older gentleman.

She had been right about the man's identity. She silently congratulated herself on finally knowing someone in McNamara before they knew her.

"Hello," she said as she angled her body toward the older man. "It's nice to meet you. I've heard a lot about you."

The older man raised one eyebrow as he looked at her without a smile. His gray hair was swept back from his head. It was full and thick despite the deep lines that radiated from his eyes. He looked to be in his seventies, but it was hard to tell if the decade was beginning or ending for him. His face was scored from hard weather and work, but his complexion still looked vital with health. Though age had hollowed out his strong frame some, leaving his cheekbones stacked like shelves under his eyes, he gave off a sense of power. Even if she had not been told about his former profession as a logger, Mallory would have sensed he had been a physical laborer of some kind. As he reached out to shake her hand, Mallory noticed a slight tremor in his.

"I'm surprised anyone finds me interesting enough to talk about, but I suppose I'll take it as a compliment," he said. "It's nice to meet you too. How are you settling in?"

"Very well, thank you," Mallory said, and the man looked at her with approval. "People are very kind here. The woman at the counter gave me this sandwich when I realized I didn't have cash."

"Kind?" Kylie snorted. Her father shook his head at her. Though she didn't let him stop her, she dropped her voice so it wouldn't carry beyond their table. "I guess that's one word for Suzanne, though it's not the one I'd use."

"Kylie," her father warned.

"What, Dad? She hasn't had a single good thing to say about us since Sean died."

"That'll be enough of that for now."

Kylie fell silent. Mallory wondered why she had come to Suzanne's place of employment when there was such tension between them, but she supposed in a town as small as McNamara, it was necessary to mix with everyone. Tension zapped the air between Kylie and her father, which Mallory tried to ignore. She was intrigued by the friction she had witnessed the night before, but she didn't want to discuss it in the presence of the Shine family patriarch, who seemed above petty grievances. She made a note to bring it up with Kylie later as she unwrapped her sandwich and took a bite.

As expected, it was delicious, and she realized as she chewed that she hadn't eaten anything the day before besides the granola bars, apples, and cut vegetables she had packed for her road trip from Vancouver. No wonder the two glasses of wine had hit her so hard the night before. Over the last two months, her appetite had been as absent as her memory, as if Graham's death had eliminated her life functions as well. In a strange way, the sandwich made her feel like she was becoming a different version of herself who was integrated with a new community and its customs. As she savored the bite, Sergeant Benson stood abruptly.

The sudden difference in their height drew her attention to his body. He was well over six feet tall, lean and muscled. The synthetic material clung briefly to his thighs before he smoothed them with flat, strong hands. He wasn't wearing a ring. She looked back down at her sandwich, feeling embarrassed at the effect he was having on her. She realized that her nervousness around him was not solely the result of his investigation of the drowning on her property. She was attracted to him. The idea was the most unexpected thing she had experienced since arriving in town, surpassing talk of monsters and unexpected deaths. She took another bite to try to distract herself from the rush of thoughts in her mind as he made his departure.

"I've got to get back to the station."

Kylie said a quick goodbye before the sergeant turned to Mallory. A blush crept up her cheeks.

"Mrs. Dent, I have a few more things to discuss with you. I'll be following up shortly."

She agreed, hoping her face didn't betray her as he held her eye a moment longer than expected, then nodded curtly at the others. Jonathan Shine rose as well, crumpling his sandwich wrapper in one fist.

"I'll join you, Joel. Mallory, I hope you enjoy your lunch. It's nice to have a new face in McNamara."

Mallory smiled in thanks, though her neck was coiling up like a bedspring at the idea of another meeting with Sergeant Benson. The moment the two men walked out the door, Kylie immediately picked up the conversation that her father had admonished her to end.

"Watch out for Suzanne is all I'm saying. She's not as nice as she might seem."

Mallory's mouth was full, but she raised her eyebrows questioningly. Kylie took it as encouragement.

"She was Sean's girlfriend, you know."

"Oh, no. I didn't realize that. How awful for her."

"Well, I guess. But at the funeral, she got drunk and said some horrible things about Henry."

"What kind of things?" Mallory tried to do the math. If Sean had died ten years ago, Kylie would have been in her midtwenties when it happened. Henry would have been a teenager.

"She told my father that she had seen him on the property as she was pulling away from Sean's house the day he died. It was ridiculous. He was sixteen years old and had been dirt biking along the lake. Just because he was close to the house, she assumed he knew something. Or worse, had something to do with it. It was stupid and awful. Like I said, she was drunk. As usual. Ever since then, she's had it out for him. Remember her snapping his head off last night? That's kind of the least of it."

Mallory was honored and a little confused to be brought into Kylie's confidence. It was hard to imagine the fresh-faced, exuberant man she had met the night before doing anything nefarious.

"What was she trying to say? Did she think Henry was responsible for the hunting accident?"

Kylie shrugged, but her face was twisted with anger. "She's never said it directly, but the hints are enough. It's insane. Before he became a police officer, Henry had shot a gun maybe twice. He was more into his bike than my dad's rifles."

"But surely the police investigated it."

"Yes, of course. The Turner police spent days out here at the time. We all had to speak to them. It was awful. We loved Sean so much. When I heard what Suzanne was saying about Henry, I wanted to tell her exactly what I thought of her. But my dad talked me out of it, and I'm grateful for that. He understood how crazy losing someone can make a person. I can see that a lot of my anger was actually grief. Now, I try to avoid her as much as I can. If you want my opinion, you should too."

Mallory wasn't quite ready to drop the subject of Sean. The mystery of what had happened to him was the only part of McNamara that didn't sit right with her.

"But why would Henry do anything to Sean?"

Kylie's green eyes glinted like a cat's. "Exactly. There were plenty of people in town who had a lot more motive to harm Sean than Henry. The Turner detective let it slip that Sean had been working on a case that was starting to get under some people's skin."

"What was the case about?"

"I don't know. My mom would never tell me, and eventually the death was ruled an accident," she said as she gathered the wrapping of her sandwich. "It's all old history now, anyway. It was an irresponsible hunter, plain and simple. Just be careful around her, that's all I'm saying. Listen, I've got to run. It was nice to see you. Stop by the store when you can."

"Will you be there tomorrow?" Mallory asked.

"Oh, I'm always there. See you soon!" Her bright voice made her sound like a different person from the one who was scowling about Suzanne. She left in a drift of patchouli. Quickly, Mallory finished her sandwich, then crossed the street to the library to pick up her car and drive home. When Mallory turned back onto her road, the lake's surface was as smooth as a pane of glass laid over a painting. Only the blurs of deep blue and green in the depths hinted that there might be something unknown below.

CHAPTER NINE

As she shifted her car into park outside her house, Mallory's mood sank once again. The hustle and bustle of the morning and trying to find her bearings in a new town had given way to exhaustion from the trip and the burden of grief that was never far away. She shuddered as she replayed Kylie's description of Suzanne's animosity toward Henry. Though she had known Kylie for only a day, she didn't like the idea of anyone in the community disliking her or her family. It had been so long since she'd made a friend independent of her husband, and the friendships she'd made with Graham hadn't been deep enough to survive his death.

She opened her car door and heard a bird whistling sweetly in the thick forest. It was disarming to think that the lace of leaves and branches had once hidden a person with a gun. Another small song began to play. Through the closed front door, she could make out the tinny music of her cell phone ringing inside. It was probably her mother returning her call. Though she knew she should hurry, her legs became heavy at the idea of rushing in to try to answer it. Instead, she took her time going into the house, moved her wash into the dryer, then opened the small duffel bag that contained her running gear. She slipped on the tights and shoes and went back out the front door, feeling like a warrior who had found her armor. She had given up running during Graham's illness, knowing that each step she took was a reminder to him of the ground he could no longer cover.

Graham had been the real runner of the two of them, competing in a marathon and several shorter races each year. While he tracked his heart rate and calorie intake with the same fervor she had once seen in a patient of hers with an eating disorder, Mallory rarely recorded the length of her runs. She loved to meander freely, letting her route unfold in front of her without a plan. He had teased her for years about her lack of discipline when it came to the pursuit, back before their jokes had an edge of treachery. Once he had compared running with her to training a puppy into a seeing-eye dog. Still, they had gone out together regularly. She knew he would have been devastated to see her go without him. So, she had abandoned it temporarily, feeling guilty each time she saw the duffel bag patiently waiting in her closet until the moment when her husband died. But now here it was.

She walked around the outside of the house and saw an overgrown path leading to the lake through a tangle of low-growing, thorny bushes. The sharp-edged leaves nipped at her ankles as she pushed her way toward the lake one footstep at a time. She felt foolish and brave, like a supplicant approaching an unpredictable god. The water shimmered before her. Once she reached the rocky beach scattered with volcanic stone and wave-polished rocks, Mallory stopped ten feet from the water and stared at the horizon, trying to imagine the dry valley that had once been there. A bird called again from somewhere high, more of a shriek than a song. It sounded like it was in pain.

Mallory thought about the bodies that had never been recovered from Loss Lake, waterlogged and weighted down. She shivered as a cold finger of wind encircled the bare skin around her neck, prompting her to move west, away from Sled Beach and downtown McNamara. The lakeshore was long and curved but not completely empty, as Mallory had assumed. At the farthest point she could see, a house had been built on top of a cliff to face the shore. Mallory estimated it was at least two miles away from where she was standing, but at this distance, the building's tall stature and positioning made it look as solid and trustworthy as a lighthouse. She wondered who lived in it.

Finding purchase on the stones and sand was more challenging than on the paved trails around Vancouver's seawall, but she quickened her pace over the rounded rocks on the beach as her ankles became used to the uneven terrain. Her heart began to beat faster, and she welcomed the throb of blood to her arms and legs. She never felt more alive than when she was running, and though the ground was making her work hard for each step, she welcomed the resistance pulling at her heels. She loved the idea of being in a fight she could win.

The last part of Graham's life had seemed to last so long, as if she had been nursing him for decades rather than months. Though she wasn't religious, she had wondered if the act of dying was so sacred that its proximity changed the passing of time. The spaces between her husband's shuddering breaths had seemed to last forever. Maybe it was the same in the case of a sudden death. The last moment stretched to an impossible length, as the water pulled a person below the surface or a bullet whizzed through the air.

The shoreline curved left in the direction of the tree line, and Mallory saw a figure walking toward her who had previously been obscured. Even from a distance of thirty feet, she recognized the long legs and strong build of the man before she could make out his face.

It was Sergeant Joel Benson.

Mallory fought the urge to turn and race back in the direction she had come. Instead, she closed the distance between them with her heart pounding in her heels. Then it was too late to go back. Sergeant Benson had seen her. He raised his arm, and she waved as she slowed her pace to a walk to calm her ragged breath.

"Hello, ma'am."

She returned his greeting. The patch of beach they were standing on was mainly sand. There was a gentle slope to the slate-colored water, which was almost as gray as the dark clouds piling on top of the horizon. Then, a single ray of sunshine peeked out from behind a cloud. Its liquid-gold light streamed from the sky to the shore to bathe them both. Sergeant Benson looked down at her, and she met his eyes. In the flat light, they were the same color as the cedar box that housed Graham's ashes, which she had placed on the top shelf of her closet.

"Mrs. Dent, I was on my way to knock on your door."

Though Mallory didn't feel prepared to speak with the sergeant in her running clothes, she knew it was better to do it now than to dread it later. A trickle of sweat slid down the back of her neck. Where had the sergeant been coming from? She wondered if the house at the point belonged to him.

"I see. You mentioned you have more questions for me?"

"Yes." He paused, and she willed herself not to drop her gaze, though his eyes continued to unnerve her. "Would you like a cup of coffee?"

Mallory's body responded with a pang of longing as she noticed a thermos in his hand.

"I would, actually. How did you know?"

"Kylie's always trying to dissuade people from caffeine. We stock up in Turner when we can. I thought you might need a pick-me-up."

"That would be fantastic."

"We can talk here for a moment, if you have time."

"Sure," she said.

He removed the cup from the top of the thermos, poured the steaming liquid into it, then passed it over. She sipped it gratefully.

"Thank you."

"You're welcome," he said. "Mind if I begin?"

The heat of the dark liquid spread through her throat and chest. Despite the innocence of his tone, Mallory suddenly realized how effective a good-cop routine could be, especially when it included coffee. She motioned for him to continue.

"Do you have any friends coming up to visit you?"

Mallory's neck stiffened but she kept her voice light. "No, I don't."

"No one who might require your address?"

"Not that I can think of." Mallory finished her coffee and handed the cup back to him. "Has someone been asking about me?"

Sergeant Benson didn't respond to her question. Instead, he cocked his head like they were chatting at a party and she'd said something curious. Then he gave a slight nod, like he had decided something about her.

"I need to follow up on all the information I receive. It's probably nothing. Once we determine the name of the drowning victim, I may come by again, but we're still waiting for records. I appreciate your time."

"Of course. Anything I can do to help."

For the first time over the course of their conversation, he smiled. The expression made him even more attractive, Mallory realized uncomfortably. Almost enough to lessen the unease his questions had stirred up. He rubbed his neck. "It will probably wrap up quickly, but it's important to cross all the t's. Like I said, this lake can be a dangerous place. I want you to take care of yourself."

As she began to say goodbye, the sergeant interrupted her. This time, he didn't meet her eyes but kept his gaze locked on the steely water that had begun to froth with white-capped waves, like frilly gloves beckoning those on shore. The ray of sunlight had disappeared.

"I also wanted to tell you that I'm sorry about your husband. I should have said it yesterday. Losing someone you love is an awful thing."

He sounded far away, caught in his own memories as he honored hers. Mallory guessed he was thinking about Sean.

"Thank you," she said. "I was very sorry to hear about your brother as well."

She took a moment to force her eyes to take back her tears. She was tired of crying and frustrated by the fact that expressing sympathy for someone else was enough to send her back into her own misery. She was here to start again, not to be constantly reminded of what she had lost. She angled her body away from the sergeant and toward the lake. The clouds had thickened and were now winding into long, twisted bands halfway up the sky.

"Looks like rain is coming," she said.

"Or worse. I heard there was a call for snow later in the week. Do you have winter tires on your car?"

Mallory blinked. Graham had taken care of all that. She was ashamed to admit that she wasn't certain. He used to joke that he would be lost without Mallory's cooking, but now here she was, lost without him.

"I'll have to check."

"Bob Miller does the plowing around here, but when a storm comes in hard, he might not be able to get to your road quickly, and the driveway can be a mess if it's not cleared."

Kylie had told her the same thing about snow plowing last night. When she had purchased her new home, the idea of a northern town blanketed by snow had seemed soft and quiet. The reality was more complicated, and panic chilled her like the mist that was beginning to rise up from the water.

"Thanks for the advice," she said.

"Thank you for saving me a trip to your front door," he said. "I'll let you carry on with your run."

She said goodbye and began to jog back the way she had come. A quick glance over her shoulder showed Joel turning in the opposite direction toward the house silhouetted on the far edge of the beach. Despite the welcome buzz of caffeine working its way through her system, the sucking sand made her thighs burn. The conversation had made her feel that though she had traveled more than a thousand miles, it still wasn't far enough to leave the things she wanted to behind.

CHAPTER TEN

When Mallory reached the path leading to her back door, the sky had dulled to the ominous gray of an eclipse. After one last look, Mallory let herself in the back door. She glanced at her watch. Three p.m., but it seemed like the evening was about to arrive. She knew she would have to get used to this northern abbreviation of daylight, but the gathering gloom made it hard to shake the feeling that time was running out. Days in the south stretched longer, and the approach of the shadow season of winter didn't feel so dire. But here, the darkness lurked at the edges of the day in a way she had never experienced before. She distracted herself with the thought that she had been in McNamara for only twenty-four hours. She still had a lot to learn about living in the north, but she would get used to it.

The large room was chilled, and Mallory nudged up the dial on the thermostat she found to the right of the door, then knelt down by the vent on the floor to ensure it was fully open. Warm, dusty air whispered against her cheek. As she rose, her eye was caught by the difference in shade between the linoleum on the floor directly in front of the plate-glass window and that which surrounded the vent. Mallory moved forward in a half crouch to examine it closely. About three feet from the window, she saw the joint where a less-worn version had been knit with another. She realized that the newer patch must have been used to replace the pieces that were too bloodstained to remain. The floor beneath her feet must have been exactly where Sean had been standing when he died.

She stepped back so quickly it was almost a jump, then turned toward the center of the room. The dimming skies cast shadows in the empty corners of the space, making it seem like a place she had never seen before. Her running clothes were damp with sweat, and a chill slithered up her arms as her eyes adjusted. What she saw made her blood needle into her hands and feet.

There was a large, hulking shape in a far corner that should have been vacant. Adrenaline bit at her scalp as she tried to make out who or what had entered her house when she was gone. She hadn't locked the back door when she'd left. Now something or someone was here with her, uninvited. Her accelerated inhales and exhales were so loud that she couldn't tell if there was another person in the room breathing alongside her. In her head, she called for her husband, but she knew there was no point in saying his name out loud. She was alone. She had to deal with this by herself.

She willed her rigid legs into taking a step, scanning the walls for a light switch that would illuminate the bulky shape. It wasn't moving, which Mallory took as a good sign as she lunged toward the panel on the far wall and the room burst into light from the tacky glass chandelier that hung overhead.

As the spots across her eyes faded, she laughed out loud. Instead of a hulking beast, Mallory saw an oversize dark-navy armchair in the corner of her living room. Relief tasted sweet in the back of her throat, like a honey lozenge after a bout of jagged coughing. She had terrified herself over a piece of furniture, and a comfy-looking one at that. Then her blood gathered in her temples in another pulse of concern at the idea of someone coming into her house uninvited. She tried to tamp it down immediately. As everyone kept saying, McNamara was different. People took care of each other up here. As she approached the big chair with the velveteen fabric, a note pinned to the worn arm confirmed that the gift had been made with the best possible intentions.

No home is complete without a cozy place to read. Come by again soon.

Xoxoxoxox Kylie

Mallory smiled and patted the soft arm of the chair. She had been so fixated on getting rid of her possessions that the thought of what she would do for furniture hadn't occurred to her. Though she couldn't quite shake her big-city apprehension about people entering her house without permission, Kylie was the furthest thing from a threat.

She showered quickly to rinse off her sweat and fear and then retrieved her softest flannel pajamas from the dryer. When she circled back to the kitchen, she filled the kettle, staring out the window at the clouds crowding in a thick swarm. Her kitchen was in a state of disarray, and she took her time arranging the scant possessions she had unpacked haphazardly the day before. One chore led to another, and she spent the rest of the afternoon organizing and sorting items for her bedroom, bathroom, and front hall. After everything had been ordered, she prepared a light dinner. Her purse was sitting on the counter where she had left it, and, balancing a plate of cheese, crackers, and cut veggies on top of a mug of tea, she reached into it to pull out the book she had purchased from Logan Carruthers. Her food stack wobbled precariously as she returned to the living room blazing with light, but she made it without incident.

She set her cup of tea on a small side table that Kylie had also thoughtfully brought over and opened Frederich Menzel's book. As she began the first line, she heard the muffled sound of her phone ringing again from inside her bag. She sighed. She was too comfortable to get up, though she knew she owed her mother a phone call. The pestering ringing also reminded her that she had not yet set up internet access and a landline. During the drive, her cell phone service had cut in and out, as the towers around McNamara were few and far between. Though the cell signal seemed strong here for now, she wondered if the winter storms and snowfall everyone was warning her about could play havoc with it later. But all that could wait for another day. When the shrill tones ended, she began to read in peace. The book was written in a pompous style and began by echoing some of what Henry had already told her. After a few sentences, its overly crafted voice grew on her like an overbearing neighbor with a good heart.

Chapter One: A Loss and a Beginning

As the verdant valley began to fill with torrents of icy water, one wonders what it would have been like to stand upon the slope of Sled Hill and bear witness to the end of a grassy meadow and the beginning of a lake. Would one have wondered about the fate of the huge logging machinery soon to be entombed by water to lay at the bottom of the lake forever? Would one have realized that the hill would never again be sung into life by the careless calls of playing children? Did one worry about the small farmhouse which sat directly under the crumbling Turner Dam? Or realize what had been unleashed?

The Turner Dam failing of October 1974 released a flood. It overflowed the Turner River, a waterway that led directly to the deep Pacific Ocean thirty-three miles west of McNamara. Previously, the river had been rendered small and sluggish by the dam upstream. That night, however, it claimed its due and swelled high enough to stretch its fattened fingers all the way to the ocean. The newly created pathway was large enough for a beast to travel into the bloated body of water that would soon be known as Loss Lake.

If something traveled to the lake—and it seems that it most assuredly did—it was a one-way journey. The water in the river corridor fell almost as quickly as it had risen as the lake absorbed the excess flow. Within hours, the river level shrank again, becoming too low for anything of size to pass back to its habitat on the coast. If a migration occurred, whatever came into Loss Lake would never be able to find its way back.

But what could have moved into the newly formed lake? For decades prior to the valley flooding, there had been talk of a creature lurking around the shores of the industrial activities of the sound. Men working on fishing boats and mill sites in the region spoke in low tones of a monster below the surface that killed the immoral, the transgressive, the people who didn't live up to its exacting scrutiny. Reports from a logging company operating on the coast in the early 1970s record three suspicious deaths, all individuals described by their peers as distasteful or just plain bad.

In each case, witnesses swimming close by or watching from shore saw a sucking whirlpool begin around the men, closing in tighter and tighter like the spinning of a top until the men disappeared and the water calmed. One man described the phenomenal death as feeling something like "a reckoning" from the water itself, a judgment and condemnation. As a result of the rumors, few workers dared to swim in the coast channel, lest they too be found unworthy of their own lives.

In the days following the dam failure, no one knew if the creature that had killed on the coastline had made its way into the newly created lake. The community was still struggling to comprehend the new geography of their home and the tragic death of Alice Halloway in the nearly biblical flood. There was no time or reason to ask about what lay beneath the surface. It wasn't until five years later, when her son Dean Halloway was also claimed by the waters in 1979, that questions arose. Had the family been cursed by the monstrous being lurking at the bottom of the lake? Was it possible that they had been targeted for reasons unknowable to human kind?

In the last year of her life, Alice Halloway had been running wild since the tragic logging death of her husband, Tom Halloway, an upstanding member of the community. She drank heavily and ceased to attend church and other community functions. Her farm fell to ruins with crops rotting in the field. Some community members speculate if something nefarious had happened to her husband. Something in which she and her son had been involved in. Something that deserved a reckoning like those that had happened on the coast years before.

How else can one explain the inexplicable accident which befell Dean Halloway during his October canoe trip on Loss Lake? He was, by all accounts, extremely experienced with a boat and a strong swimmer to boot, but he didn't come back. His wife reported him missing when it grew dark without him returning home. A team set out to search to no avail. His body was never recovered but, weeks later, pieces of the canoe washed up on shore. The fiberglass hull had been scoured clean of its paint as if churned through a set of rocky rapids, yet the lake had been placid for weeks. What was it that scraped the man's boat? How did the experienced canoeist tip and drown himself on calm waters?

What really lies below the surface of Loss Lake?

In 1975, three months after the dam's failure, most of the dam staff had already left the north in secret, save for a small few who remained. Though the place was soon forgotten by those who had made it what it was, it will always be remembered for something else. A mystery beneath the depths.

Within this fragile tome, I will seek to answer the question of what lies beneath the depths of Loss Lake, our own West Coast monster that sacrifices men and women for sustenance and even, perhaps, justice. Could it be that the deaths of Loss Lake were not random after all? Could the monster below be serving as the executor of the unjust? Only time and these pages will tell.

As the chapter ended, Mallory closed the book and took the last sip of tea from her mug. Her mind was spinning in the same way as Menzel had described the whirlpool. Though it was good to learn more of the story of the lake, the idea of a place that could either punish or absolve was fascinating and bewildering. She remembered the way the waves had seemed to be calling to her.

She stared in the direction of the water. Night had fallen. The blackness outside turned the glass into a mirror rather than a window, and the sight of herself huddled in the chair made her uneasy. Though it was still early evening, the darkness surrounding her small house suggested it was the dead of night. She was as drained of energy as the world was of light. Slowly, Mallory walked down the hallway and into the bedroom at the end of the hall. As she drifted off to sleep, she saw that the skies had cleared once again. Stars appeared before her, one at a time, before her eyes closed and she fell into a deep sleep.

CHAPTER ELEVEN

The next morning, the knocks on the front door were sharp and insistent, coming in rapid sets of three with intervals of only a few seconds between them. Luckily, Mallory's early night had resulted in an early morning. She was fully dressed, fresh from the shower she had taken to wake herself up in lieu of coffee. She glanced at her watch as she made her way toward the front door. Eight a.m. seemed too early for a social call. She braced herself as she turned the knob, wondering if Sergeant Benson would be on the other side with bad news once again. Instead, she found herself looking at the stern face of Carlotta Gray. The woman's right hand was curled into a fist and raised to eye level inches away from the door as she readied to knock again like the world's most persistent woodpecker.

"Hello," Mallory said. There was more caution in her voice than she had intended, but Carlotta's frowning face suggested she was about to reprimand Mallory for an overdue book.

"I came to bring you these," Carlotta said.

Both women looked down at the brown '70s-era plate Carlotta had balanced on the flat of her left palm. It was piled high with misshapen muffins. Though Mallory had yet to eat breakfast, the sight did not inspire her to do so.

"How nice of you. Please come in."

Mallory stepped back to let Carlotta enter. The woman's current outfit was nearly a polar opposite of the frumpy knitted cardigan and forgettable dress she had been wearing the day before. Now, Carlotta was clothed in a boiled-wool jacket in a dark red-and-black plaid, and her hair was tucked under a thick gray knitted hat. She looked like a cross between a lumberjack and a fisherman fresh off the boat. Carlotta unceremoniously pushed the earthenware plate into Mallory's hands.

"It's a housewarming gift," she said as she kicked the dirt off her boots on the house frame. "I suppose you'll want me to leave this out here."

She gestured to the side of the door. Mallory peered out and was shocked to see a large rifle leaning against her house. She had never been this close to a gun before. Carlotta met her eyes, and Mallory was taken aback by the warmth within them. It seemed at odds with the weapon she was brandishing.

"Deer season just opened. It's an important time of year around here. I wanted to invite you to be a part of it. I liked the look of you yesterday. You seem like a woman who knows how to take care of herself. A good hunting partner."

"Oh, how nice."

Mallory bit the inside of her cheeks to contain her confusion as Carlotta brushed past her, slid off her boots, then followed Mallory toward the kitchen. Carlotta stopped on the opposite side of the counter, in the space that would be a dining area if Mallory had a table. She rested her hand on one of the two folding chairs that Mallory had repositioned from the kitchen, then closed her eyes and took a deep breath. A moment passed. Mallory didn't speak, though questions jostled around inside her head. Carlotta seemed to require silence.

Finally the other woman opened her eyes and spoke in a voice that was almost reverential. It was the opposite of the tone she had taken at the library. "Having you along with Suzanne and me would be good for us all. I've been thinking of you, in this house, all alone."

"Suzanne . . . hunts with you?" Mallory asked.

"She does. I helped her find her strength. I can do the same for you. We all lost our partners. This is a way to heal."

Mallory raised her eyebrows in skepticism, but Carlotta refused to break the gaze between them.

"Hunting will bring back your power."

"I'll definitely consider your invitation, Carlotta," Mallory said. "But I'm in a bit of a rush."

She had been planning to go for a run when the town librarian had arrived. Another storm had brought a cold rain in the early-morning hours, ending shortly after Mallory woke up. She hoped to get out before the clouds opened up again.

Carlotta paused before answering. "Thank you for thinking about it. This isn't a day out in the woods. It's a calling."

"You sound really committed to hunting, Carlotta. But I'm not sure it's for me. I rarely eat meat."

Carlotta spoke firmly. "It's not about the sustenance, though that matters too. It's a chance to find your true self in the forest. I learned how to hunt when I was twenty, right after my husband died. His uncle taught me how important it was to be able to protect myself. To become whole."

Mallory did an internal calculation. Carlotta looked to be in her sixties. It was possible the woman had come before the valley was flooded. After her reading last night, she was intrigued by what it had been like when the dam had failed. She wanted to ask whether Carlotta had witnessed the flood but couldn't get a word in edgewise. Carlotta was still speaking.

"For years, I went by myself, but after Sean died, Suzanne asked me to teach her. When we went out into the forest, I realized that it was important to share my knowledge with other women, especially those who need it the most. Like you. I'm here to invite you to join us. I'm willing to teach you. It's critical for a woman to connect with other women. Especially one who lives alone, Mallory. Especially in this house. It's been standing longer than the lake's been there. There's a history here."

Mallory's eye was drawn to the newer section of the floor, but she kept the glance quick to avoid alerting Carlotta to the macabre mismatching panel.

"Suzanne and I would like to ask you to accompany us in the forest between your home and mine. We need your permission before we go into the gate. Betty Barber must have given you a key."

Mallory's body jerked with dismay. Not only did the older woman want to shoot guns near her, she wanted to do it on Mallory's land. The land that had previously been the site of a hunting accident. Her patience for the incomprehensible request ran out.

"I'm afraid the answer is no. I don't want to kill anything. I don't want you killing anything on my land."

Carlotta's face went blank. "I don't think you fully understand what I'm asking."

Mallory was so insulted by Carlotta's response that she blurted out something she'd never have said after careful consideration.

"I absolutely do. Sean Benson was killed by a bullet because of exactly the type of activity you are proposing. I don't know how you expect me to agree to it. It's dangerous, Carlotta."

Carlotta sighed, suggesting her concern was nearly too foolish to register. "My dear, Sean of all people would have understood how safe it is for us to be in the forest. We'll keep well away from your house. We know what we're doing."

"I'm sorry. I don't feel comfortable with it."

"You shouldn't be alone right now, Mallory."

"I'm fine."

She was surprised to hear a catch in her own voice. Something about the way Carlotta was looking at her made her feel like the woman was aware of things below the surface that Mallory couldn't acknowledge. She changed the subject, motioning to the small, dense-looking mounds on the plate to try to take the edge out of the conversation. "These look good. What are they?"

Carlotta closed her eyes once again, seeming to will herself to drop the subject of the hunt. When she opened them, she attempted a smile. It was thin but detectable.

"Blueberry quinoa loaves. I live a gluten-, sugar-, and dairy-free life. These muffins are absent of all allergens."

Mallory murmured something supportive as she tried not to show how little she wanted to eat one. She picked a clump up and took a large bite, which she instantly regretted. It took a minute for her to chew the fibrous mass into a size she could swallow. Its ragged edges caught in her throat, but she managed to get it down. She set it on the counter and wondered how much longer the woman planned to stay in her home, but she decided she might as well try to be a good host.

"Would you like some tea?"

"Thank you."

"Please sit down."

Carlotta settled on one of the two folding chairs while Mallory busied herself with the kettle, sneaking glances at the older woman as she worked. Carlotta's expression turned sad as she looked around the house. Her gaze stopped short when she spotted the large armchair in the corner.

"Where did that come from?"

"Kylie dropped it off last night," Mallory said as she finished with the kettle and left the tea to steep. She settled on the chair opposite her guest. Carlotta's face was arranged in an expression that seemed a cross between disapproval and sorrow.

"That was kind of her."

Again, an awkward silence fell. Carlotta stood up. Mallory wondered how well Carlotta had known Sean. She half expected Carlotta to make her way to the door, but instead she crossed the room to the blue armchair and touched the arm of it gently, as if stroking a child. The odd moment ended when the woman turned back to Mallory. Her expression was complex but unreadable.

"I do understand your position, Mallory, but I hope you'll reconsider. Things are done differently in McNamara. It's important to help each other. We've all survived so much."

Mallory wondered if she had broken a small-town code and tried to salvage the visit with small talk.

"Was your husband a hunter as well?"

"No. I was only sixteen when I married him. I grew up in Turner, and my father thought it was a good match, but he was interested in . . . other hobbies." She grimaced before continuing. "He passed away four years after our wedding. The truth is, he didn't like guns. He preferred other forms of physical expression."

Mallory felt a growing affinity for the woman. She knew, better than most, that not all marriages were remembered well.

"I'm sorry."

"Thank you. I had a feeling you would understand. Dean Halloway was a complicated man."

Mallory remembered the name from Frederich's book. "Dean Halloway was your husband?"

"Yes," Carlotta said. "In fact, this used to be our house."

Mallory was dazed. No wonder the woman had been acting so oddly. Everyone was connected to everyone else. Except her.

"And you bought the place you live in now after your husband passed away?"

"Well, my husband's uncle gave it to me shortly after. I've been there ever since."

She wanted to ask who Dean's uncle had been, but Carlotta's clouded expression didn't invite questions.

"Oh," Mallory said. The woman spoke like Mallory hadn't.

"He died by drowning, you know. It's why I don't want you to thin those trees. I couldn't bear the sight of the lake that killed him."

Carlotta's words reminded Mallory of the other recent death in the lake. She hurried the conversation along.

"I won't change the forest. But I also don't want you hunting in there."

"And I must respect that for now." Carlotta took two long strides toward Mallory. She was forced to crane her neck to look up at Carlotta when she stopped a foot in front of her chair. "On second thought, I think I will pass on the tea. Thank you for your time. Take care of yourself, Mallory. Remember, I'm down the road if you need me."

Mallory showed the other woman out. When she returned to the living room, she looked out at the slate-gray lake and thought of Sean Benson and Dean Halloway. The muscles in her neck tensed at the thought of not one but two of the past owners dying unexplained deaths while living in the house. Mallory walked to the window and placed a flat palm on the surface. The coldness seemed deeper than the temperature of the glass.

CHAPTER TWELVE

Carlotta's interest in the forest had piqued Mallory's own. She used the small key Betty had provided to unlock the padlock on the chain-link fence, secured it again once she was inside, and then she ran. Her shoes hit the spongy trail like a drum. Up, down. All around her, ferns swayed their leaves in the wind like fan dancers. The air inside her forest was rich in oxygen, and her breathing soon began to match her pace. Carlotta's visit had left her unsettled. As she followed the established line of trail through the woods, her thoughts circled back to the person who had come to her mind during their conversation. Graham.

She understood the reason Carlotta had needed to leave the house she had lived in when her husband died. After Graham's death, Mallory had walked down the stairs each morning with a sense of foreboding so strong it nearly made her choke. Every step in the Vancouver home they had shared had forced her to relive the worst moment of her life. She realized that the memory of discovering Graham's dead body hadn't come to her since she'd arrived in McNamara. Not until Carlotta's revelations had dislodged it once again.

~

The open-concept main floor had seemed so beautiful in their early years of living there and so oppressive in their last, when Graham's hospital bed and medical equipment had replaced half of their sitting area. The beeping and ticking of the machines was a constant hum in the background, like the intermittent whine of a mosquito in a dark room. That morning, the sky had been gray, despite the fact that it was the beginning of August. Mallory had been grateful for the pallor. All summer long, the sunshine had reminded her of the fact that Graham would likely never see another. During Graham's last appointment, the doctor had asked them to be realistic about the slim chance of a heart transplant.

"We're running out of time," she told them.

Mallory tried to meet her husband's eyes, but he looked away.

That morning she had been exhausted, which wasn't unusual. Graham's pharmaceutical schedule required him to receive a dose of medication every four hours, which either she or the home-care nurse— on the one night a week she came—administered. Since Mallory provided all Graham's care during the day, she wasn't able to turn her schedule from day to night to provide the midnight dosage, as she would have during her nursing career. Instead, for six nights a week, she slept on a daybed downstairs beside Graham, setting her alarm for 12:00 a.m. to give Graham what he needed before settling back to sleep. On the seventh night, when their home care was present, she slipped in earplugs and slept in the bed upstairs that she and Graham had shared for a decade. On those mornings, she woke on the right-hand side as if he were still sleeping beside her.

As she rounded the corner of the landing, the first thing Mallory had registered was that the machine attached to Graham's heart wasn't beeping at regular intervals. Instead, there was a solid electronic scream. She ran to his side, nearly rolling her ankle on the bottom step, but as soon as she came close enough to see the blue undertone in his skin, she knew it was too late. Graham had died, alone, in the night. There was no sign of the nurse's presence, nothing to indicate that she'd arrived at all. Her training had kicked in. She checked his pulse and vitals, robotically called emergency services, and waited for them to arrive. Then, she sat by his bed, his cold hand in hers, until they had.

Within an hour, the house became so full of activity that she hadn't seen Graham's cousin, Cynthia Rooney, slip through the crowd. The moment the woman's pale face came into view, Mallory remembered that Cynthia had been scheduled to visit Graham that morning. Mallory had been too dulled by shock to cancel the visit. Graham was an only child, but his mother and aunt had been exceptionally close and united their children on months-long vacations at the family cottage every summer. Cynthia, Graham's ruddy-faced, heavy-drinking, overly hair-sprayed cousin, had never liked her. At times, her attitude approached jealousy. Once, Mallory had walked in on Cynthia asking Graham why he had chosen to be with someone so boring. When Mallory had asked Graham about Cynthia's animosity toward her, Graham had become embarrassed and changed the subject.

Mallory knew that failing to inform Cynthia of Graham's death wasn't going to improve their relationship. Sure enough, Mallory could see anger in her bloodshot brown eyes before Cynthia pulled her into an embrace that was closer to violence than comfort.

"Mallory, how could this happen?"

The volume of her voice made Mallory's ears ring.

"I don't know," Mallory had whispered.

"You were supposed to be taking care of him," the other woman said as she released her hold and took a step backward. "It was your job."

The air between them turned threatening.

"I did the best I could."

Cynthia had shaken her head while pulling out her cell phone. She dialed a number. Mallory walked away without bothering to learn who Cynthia was calling. The woman's accusations had excoriated the protective layer that her shock had provided. Now, the sounds accompanying the end of her husband's life seemed too loud. She wished she could rip Cynthia's bleached-blonde hair from her head and tell her that Graham's death had been inevitable since the bug had bitten him in Guatemala. She wanted to scream at the paramedics, who were lifting him onto the gurney, to get out. She fought the urge to run away from all of them and what they represented. She needed to be alone. But Cynthia wouldn't let her be.

For weeks, Cynthia called her every day, begging and then demanding that Mallory go through the final night of Graham's life over and over. When Mallory began to ignore her calls, the woman recruited her sister, Sadie, to ask Mallory for the same information. The unrelenting requests had worn her down. She cringed at the sound of the telephone and cowered when they knocked on the door. She hadn't felt free until she fled Vancouver. She hoped Carlotta had found the same peace living in a home steps away from the place where her husband had died.

Mallory paused on the trail. Her lungs rattled a little as she breathed deeply enough to taste the slight sweetness of the forest air, full of oxygen and decay. Mallory's legs were loose now, the stiffness of inactivity giving way to the loose buzz of muscles in motion. She looked at her surroundings. She was in a small clearing where the trees were tall enough to filigree the sunlight around her, striping the gentle rolls and slopes of moss at her feet. She had never been so deep into a forest before. She could hear the tiny patter of creatures in the branches above her. A squirrel chittered a warning to whoever was listening about the human in their midst. She had been right to deny hunters entry to this space. She hated the idea of a gunshot silencing the sounds around her.

As her breathing slowed, the squirrel stopped, apparently deciding she wasn't a worthy threat. She walked a few more steps, reveling in the way the forest floor bounced slightly under her feet. The wind picked up, and Mallory could hear the trees brushing against each other like lovers. A single red leaf sauntered down in front of her, floating in the wind like it had all the time in the world to reach the ground.

She had never been able to believe in the saccharine heaven that her mother settled for or the black void that Graham had insisted was the only thing that made sense. The closest thing she had ever come to constructing a vision of death was an extension of Einstein's theory about energy never being created or destroyed. Graham had been composed of energy; he had vibrated with it as he trained for his races and swept her off her feet in the early days of their relationship. He had not been destroyed. His energy still existed somehow and somewhere. Maybe even here. He could be part of the wind. She closed her eyes and tried to feel forgiveness. A bird sang. A breeze skimmed her cheek. For a moment, she came close to believing.

Then she heard the footsteps coming up behind her.

CHAPTER THIRTEEN

Her blood plummeted to her feet in a solid, coagulated lump. Her hands turned ice cold. She couldn't bear to turn to face what was coming, but she didn't dare let it attack her unseen. She clenched her fists and wheeled around, unsure if she was about to see a crazed Carlotta or a stampeding bear. Instead, she found herself looking into the light-brown eyes of Sergeant Joel Benson. Instead of relief, she was angry at being taken aback on her land. He was trespassing.

"What on earth are you doing here?" Her words were loud and sharp enough to send the squirrel back into its vocal spasms. The sergeant's face was impassive but his eyes widened, like he'd been caught cheating at cards.

"Apologies, ma'am. I didn't think anyone would be out here."

"This is my land. It's gated. You have no right." Mallory was too angry to be tactful. She was amazed to see the sergeant's face fall.

"You're right," he said. His voice was quiet and chagrined enough to make Mallory temper her own.

"How did you even get here?"

"There's a sand drift that got blown up on the northeastern side of the fence. It's easy enough to jump over the top now, if you know where to look."

"Do you know this property well?"

The sergeant shrugged. "I suppose I do. I used to come here often to think before the fence went up. There was a trail that went all the way from Sled Beach to my house."

Mallory remembered what Betty had said about Joel and Sean being adopted after the deaths of both their parents. She watched him touch the peeling bark of a paper birch that was leaning gently over the trail. Joel had lost so many people in his life. She softened.

"It is beautiful in here."

"Listen, I'm sorry for scaring you. I like to be around things that humans didn't make once in a while, but this isn't a place I should be."

"It's okay. I understand that feeling."

She and Graham had done most of their long runs in Stanley Park and the North Shore Mountains near Vancouver. The moment she stepped foot on the trails she had felt different from when her feet were on concrete. It had been the same this morning. The forest had helped her sort through the feelings Carlotta had stirred up. Joel continued.

"It's been empty for so long. I got into the habit of coming in here," he said. "But I should have asked your permission, and, for that, I apologize."

"I accept your apology, Sergeant." He smiled and his shoulders relaxed. She felt enough ease to ask him what had been on her mind since he'd mentioned Sled Beach. "How is your investigation going?"

Joel hesitated and his smile faded. Mallory's neck tensed. Then he spoke as if the pause hadn't meant anything at all.

"The coroner hasn't released her report. I can't do much until I get the results of that. And please, call me Joel. Seems as though there's not much need to stand on ceremony at this point."

"I appreciate that. You can call me Mallory."

The man grew silent. At first, Mallory thought he was about to reveal something sensitive, but then she realized that his eye had been caught by something on the ground behind her. He walked toward it quickly, then crouched beside a bed of moss about three feet off the trail. Mallory stared in awe as he tucked his fingers under the edge of the green patch. He pulled it up carefully, and Mallory gasped in unexpected delight. Under the thick layer was a grouping of golden mushrooms. Their scalloped edges looked like the lifted skirts of cancan dancers. When he met her eyes, his were dancing like he'd won a game of hide-and-go-seek.

"Now you've really caught me. This is the real reason I'm out here. It's chanterelle season. Slice these up and fry them in butter and you'll never look at another mushroom the same way again."

She watched as he pulled a knife and a cloth bag from his pocket, then gently cut the mushrooms about an inch from their base, leaving three-quarters of the patch. Mallory found herself transfixed by his long, strong fingers as he transferred them to the bag.

"I try to leave some for the other creatures," he explained. "We're not the only ones in these woods."

Mallory thought of disallowing the hunting in the forest. At least she'd found someone in McNamara who shared her sensibilities. She tried not to dwell on the fact that the person was also the most handsome man she had met in the town, if not in her life. As he placed the last of his find into the bag, he stood up, then offered it to her.

"Take these. Consider it a welcoming gift. And an apology."

Mallory was touched. When he handed the bag over, their hands met. Mallory looked down and noticed the sleeve of his shirt had slid back, revealing a glimpse of color at his wrist. She had no tattoos and neither had Graham. Seeing them on Joel was intriguing. And sexy.

She spoke boldly. "You have a tattoo. Can I see it?"

Joel was unfazed. He undid the button on the cuff and rolled it up, revealing an intricate network of waves and sea life surrounding a deep-orange octopus, whose tentacles swirled around up Joel's forearm.

"Wow," Mallory said. She fought the urge to extend her finger and trace the lines that undulated across his skin. "It's beautiful."

Joel pulled his sleeve down, though his expression was kind. "Thanks. I usually keep it covered."

"Why?"

Joel looked at her closely. "I didn't get it to show the world. My purpose was something different."

She looked at him expectantly, and he laughed as if she had called his bluff.

"I think so many things in life change a person without their consent. The nicks and cuts that scar us and the losses that mark us forever. I've known a lot of moments when everything changed. The ones that make you record your life in before and after. After my mom died, I thought of everything like that: I got that bike before she died. I got this shirt after."

Mallory understood exactly what he was saying. Like him, who had to live in the after of his parents' and his brother's deaths, she was living in the after of Graham's.

"So, that tattoo was a reminder of a moment?"

"Not exactly. My dad died when I was a small child. I don't remember him at all. My mom I do have some memories of, but I was just starting kindergarten when she passed away. Still, those losses took a toll even if I couldn't remember them much."

"So it was to remind yourself of when your brother died?"

Joel was silent. Mallory hoped she hadn't been too forward. Everyone else in town seemed comfortable drawing conclusions about her using information she hadn't given them, but it still felt awkward for her to do so. But Joel's tone wasn't affronted as he continued. Instead, he sounded far away.

"Yes. That changed me most of all," he said, then shook his head like he wanted to empty it of a memory. "When Sean died, I decided that our choices alter us more than our fate. I kept the surname he had used so a part of him would stay with me, and I marked myself to remember the moment everything changed."

Mallory paused as she absorbed the answer to a question that had nagged her.

"But why a sea monster? Is that how you see the creature in the lake?"

Mallory worried that he thought she was making fun of him. Instead, the tall man's eyes lit up, and Mallory was again reminded of cinnamon. He laughed again. "Do you believe in all that?"

Mallory's first instinct was to laugh along with him, but instead she found herself speaking seriously.

"I'm not sure. There's something about the lake that I find . . . unsettling. Not scary necessarily. Certainly not monstrous. But over the last few days, when I look at it, it seems like there's a question I'm supposed to be asking."

A tree creaked gently beside them as he regarded her.

"I know what you mean," Joel said. "I've never put it into words, but I suppose I feel the same way."

She paused. The silence between them became companionable. Though he was hardly more than a stranger, it seemed like she was in the presence of a friend. It was good to be in the company of someone who brought out her thoughts before she knew they were there. Joel spoke first.

"Have you ever heard the story of the wendigo?"

"No, I haven't."

"It's a myth from the northeast, the indigenous Algonquin-speaking bands. The wendigo is a monster who roams the forest, often seen in the winter. It's a monstrous combination of human and evil spirit, sometimes a beast with human characteristics and sometimes a human possessed by something evil. It's huge in size but completely emaciated, thin to the point that its bones are almost protruding from its skin. It feeds on people and other animals, but every time it eats something, it grows in direct proportion to whatever it had consumed."

"So it's always starving," Mallory said. Goose bumps rippled up her arms.

"Exactly. It was a symbol of insatiable greed and the horrible things that happen when we destroy more than we create or take more than we give. The wendigo has no sense of community. Its appetite makes it so ravenous it's willing to unravel the social fabric with its selfishness. Within a culture that relies on everyone sharing what they have and looking out for each other, it embodied the worst characteristics possible. It was a warning and a lesson."

"Is that how you see the monster of Loss Lake?"

"In a way." Joel paused to look in the direction of the lake, though the sight of it was shielded by the thick forest that towered over them. "Loss Lake was an accident. I think the people of McNamara needed to feel that it had a purpose, that there was actually a reason for its presence and for the death of Alice Halloway. That was hard for everyone to understand, how a woman could be killed like that. Then, when her son died, it seemed too coincidental to be natural. So we needed a story to make it understandable. A wendigo, kind of. Something that could explain what was happening. From what I've heard, neither Dean nor Alice or the men who were lost on the coast before the lake was formed were people you'd admire. The Loss Lake monster made their deaths understandable and helped tighten the community."

"So you think the monster is an explanation?"

"I do."

His eyes darkened, and Mallory sensed she'd understood only half of what he was saying.

"And a warning?"

"Something like that. I think it made it easier for everyone to accept the bad things that had happened here if we had a monster who would tell us right from wrong and separate the good people from the bad. It made what happened acceptable."

"But wasn't it also terrifying to know you could die if you swam in the water?"

"Only if you had something to be scared of."

His sudden smile took some of the sting out of his words.

"Besides, there are plenty of people who have survived a swim in Loss Lake. My brothers and sister and I used to go in there all the time when I was a kid. There's a lot more to this place than an imaginary monster, Mallory. Especially one that's trapped in a million cheap snow globes being sold by Logan Carruthers."

Mallory chuckled and dipped her head. Her eyes registered a flash of gold poking up from the moss. She got down on her knees and mimicked his move of pulling up the thick carpet of moss from the edge. Underneath, a cluster of mushrooms stood proud. Joel knelt down as she touched one finger to the supple cap of the largest mushroom. It was smooth and cold.

"You're a natural," he said with a smile.

Mallory was drawn to him so strongly that she imagined leaning forward into a kiss. One second passed, then another. Then the stillness was pierced with an electronic trill. Joel made a face as he reached into his pocket to answer his phone.

"Sergeant Benson here."

He paused as the voice on the other end spoke. Mallory could make out the word "coroner" in the buzz of secondhand conversation.

"I'll be right there," Joel said into the phone. He hung up, then turned to Mallory. "Excuse me, ma—I mean, Mallory. I'm being called back to the scene at Sled Beach."

"Is everything okay?"

"They've managed to retrieve the body. The coroner is about to make an identification."

"That's good news," she said, though she was uncomfortable speaking about the case now that an actual person had been dragged from the lake. It worried her to think of saying the wrong thing at such a fraught moment. Joel wished her goodbye before turning on his heel. She watched him walk back in the direction he had come, his steps hurried but sure on the narrow forest trail. She hoped whatever was going on at Sled Beach wouldn't distract him from what she could feel developing between them.

CHAPTER FOURTEEN

Mallory retraced her steps on the rich loam of the trail. The myriad shades of green swirled around her in a natural kaleidoscope. As she breathed in her last lungfuls of the sweet air, she was as content as she had been in the days before Graham had gripped her hand hard enough to bruise it as the doctor gave his diagnosis. Once she reached the edge of the forest, she made sure to close the gate that girded the wildest section of her land, being careful to slip the padlock through the metal rings attached to the post and the gate itself. She clicked it shut and gave it a tug to ensure it was fully secured. Though she wasn't bothered by the idea of Joel returning to her property through the secret way he had discovered—if anything, the idea of it gave her a quiet thrill—she didn't like the thought of someone else entering her property without her permission. Especially someone like Carlotta, who might come packing a gun. She made a note to herself to walk the entire fence line when she had a chance to see if the second entrance was visible to others and to ensure there were no other ways to sneak onto her property.

She walked up the bumpy section of her driveway from the gate to her front door. Orange, red, and yellow leaves crunched under her feet like cornflakes. Despite the warmth of the sun, her face and hands tingled at the chill in the air. She started when she saw a figure standing outside her door, arms crossed around her chest.

What is Suzanne doing here? Mallory thought. Then she realized that Carlotta must have informed Suzanne right away that Mallory had denied her request. She wondered if the woman was here to plead the case again. Living in a close-knit community like McNamara had its share of drawbacks. Like Carlotta before her, Suzanne was clad in a heavy plaid coat, though this one was the color of spearmint leaves.

Mallory spoke first to hasten the conversation. "Hello, Suzanne," she said, locking her eyes on the woman to avoid rolling them. "I know why you're here."

She closed the distance between them and leaned against her house about a foot away from Suzanne.

"Do you? Okay, then I won't waste my time getting on my knees."

The woman looked healthier than she had the past two times Mallory had seen her. Her eyes were clear. The cold air had put pink in her cheeks, and her overly processed hair was covered with a light-blue knit cap that flattered her coloring. Despite the fact that Mallory suspected her presence was intended to pressure her into changing her mind, the woman's manner was easy. She looked like she was at home.

"It's not that I want to refuse," Mallory began. "I'm not used to guns. The thought of hunting around here makes me nervous."

"What? Who said anything about guns? I'm here to collect my favor," Suzanne said. "I wanted to ask if I could borrow your car."

The words were followed by a laugh, which quickly changed into a chesty cough.

"Right now?"

"Yeah, if that's cool. I stayed the night at Carlotta's, but she went out this morning and I need to get to work. I'll bring it back this afternoon. Okay?"

Mallory stunned herself by being open to the request. There was no harm in showing some good faith in the woman—so long as Suzanne didn't crash the vehicle. She hoped it would soften her earlier dismissal of Carlotta.

"Sure, I suppose. I wasn't planning to go out today. Let me grab my keys."

"Awesome."

Mallory pushed aside her apprehension about the agreement. It was too late to back out now. She opened the door to let Suzanne in, but the woman stayed on the doorstep. Mallory realized that she had inadvertently revealed the fact that she had left her front door unlocked, but Suzanne seemed too distraught to notice. Her face creased with sadness as she peered inside without making a move to enter.

"Being here reminds me of him. Of what happened."

Suzanne's eyes began to shine, and Mallory's throat tightened in response to the admission about her sorrow. Cold air blew into the house from the open door, and Mallory steeled her shoulders to stop a shudder.

"Of course. I'll only be a moment. You can stay out there if you prefer. Or come in for a cup of tea."

Suzanne hesitated.

"It's up to you, of course."

The other woman breathed in deeply, like someone who was about to jump into a body of water they expected to be cold. Mallory had the odd sense that she was forcing Suzanne to enter against her will, and she had started to turn away when she heard the woman blurt out a response.

"Okay, sure. I'll come in. Thank you."

Suzanne joined Mallory in the small foyer; then the other woman followed her wordlessly to the kitchen, tracing her hand slowly against the wall as they walked. Once there, she accepted Mallory's offer of tea. Instead of moving into the makeshift dining room as Carlotta had done, Suzanne leaned against the counter in the kitchen. The posture reminded Mallory of Joel, which was a welcome thought. The pot she had made for Carlotta was still hot, and she poured it into two cups, adding milk to both after Suzanne confirmed her preference. The entire time, she could feel Suzanne staring at her appraisingly. The other woman looked at her shrewdly as she accepted the tea.

"You have a great body, you know. Is that weird to say?"

Mallory was startled, but she tried to laugh it off. "A bit. But thanks. I appreciate it."

"How old are you?"

Once again, Mallory was off-balance, but it was fun to be in the company of someone so ingenuous. It was clear that the woman had been affected by her return to the home where Sean had been killed and, just as evidently, that she had trouble processing those emotions, so she was focusing on something tangible. Despite the terrible first impression the woman had made in the bar, Mallory's fondness for Suzanne was growing.

"I turned forty in the summer."

"Oh man. That must be a bitch. Four more years for me until that big birthday."

Mallory had pegged Suzanne as much older, given the lines across her face. Alcohol and sadness had taken their toll. Suzanne seemed to take Mallory's silence as disapproval.

"I'm sorry to be so weird. I'm nervous. You seem so sophisticated."

Mallory laughed. "I'm really not."

"It's not just that. I haven't been in here since . . . he died," Suzanne said, forcing out the words.

Her honesty was appreciated by Mallory, who had spent so much time in the months after Graham had passed away pretending that she wasn't thinking of him constantly.

"It must be hard."

Suzanne shrugged nonchalantly, but her eyes betrayed her feigned indifference. Mallory looked at her sympathetically, and Suzanne dropped her act.

"You know what? Yes. It is hard. I really loved him. We really loved each other." Suzanne's tone turned defensive, and Mallory sought to defuse her.

"I lost my husband too," Mallory said quietly.

"I know. I'm sorry," Suzanne said, her eyes widening with sympathy. "I really am. I wanted Sean to be my husband. Even had a dress picked out. I was just waiting for him to ask. I figured he'd have a little more time for me once that case was wrapped up."

Mallory took a sip of her tea.

"Betty told me he was a lawyer. What was his field?"

Suzanne's face brightened. "He worked in criminal law. Private prosecution. He traveled down to Turner for the hearings at the courthouse there every couple months or so. He focused on environmental stuff mainly—corporate negligence. He was really passionate about it. When he talked about it, you would swear you were in the presence of, like, a superhero or something. Real big on avenging the wrongs of our world, you know?"

Mallory smiled, trying not to show that she was unnerved about Joel currently investigating her for a similar charge. "He sounds like a good man."

"He was. He really really was."

"What was he working on when he passed away?"

Suzanne's face darkened. "A cold case that was never properly examined. That's what he said anyway."

"Something environmental?"

Suzanne lowered her voice, as if someone else were in earshot. "No. Well, kind of. It was an awful case. Someone died. Sometimes when he talked about it, he called it a homicide. It was that bad."

"A murder?"

Suzanne took a slow swallow of her tea to draw out a dramatic pause. "That's what he said. But it's not something people around here agree with. At least, not if they think someone's listening."

"Who was the victim?"

"Logan Carruthers's sister."

"Oh, how sad. What happened?"

"No one could save her, the water came in so fast, that's what everyone always says. But Sean thought there was more to the story. Like I said, he was smart."

Mallory's eyes widened as she read between the lines of what Suzanne was saying.

"Logan's sister was Alice Halloway?"

"Yes. Sean was working on a wrongful death suit against the Turner Dam."

Mallory suddenly had a different perspective on the man's obsession with monster memorabilia. Perhaps it wasn't his retirement plan but a way to give meaning to his sister's death. A bell seemed to ring in her ear as she made another connection.

"So Logan was Dean Halloway's uncle?"

Suzanne nodded. Logan was the man who had given Carlotta the house she lived in now. There was much more to him than she had guessed.

"Was Sean hoping to get a settlement for Logan?"

Suzanne's expression turned evasive. "Something like that."

Eagerness eroded her manners. She felt like she had been given a puzzle to solve. "And Carlotta would also have been a beneficiary of a settlement. She was married to Dean, right?"

Suzanne nearly spit out her next words. "That piece of shit."

"Oh." Mallory was taken aback by Suzanne's vehemence.

"Don't get me wrong. According to my mom and, like, everyone who knew her, Alice was a saint. She just raised an asshole for a son. She didn't deserve what happened to her."

"But Dean did?"

"I mean, from what I've heard he was a nasty drunk. My mom told me that Carlotta wore the results of that pretty much every Sunday morning."

Mallory stared at the woman as she tried to formulate a response, and Suzanne seemed to realize she had shared too much.

"Look, stuff like that's not something we talk about up here. People like to let everyone mind their own business. But Sean wasn't like that. Let's just say that some people"—Suzanne raised her eyebrows suggestively, as if Mallory knew who she was referring to—"didn't like him digging around in the past."

The sound of Mallory's phone cut through the conversation, but she made no move to respond, despite the fact that she could feel its electronic tone reverberating in her body. Suzanne looked at her expectantly.

"Aren't you going to get that?"

Mallory knew that it would be strange for her to let it ring.

"I'll be right back."

She walked back to the foyer, where her purse sat in the closet. As she unzipped it and withdrew the phone, the back of her scalp crawled with dread at the thought of who would be on the other end.

"Hello?" she said. She was stunned to hear a male voice.

"Hello, Mallory? It's Ser—I mean, it's Joel. The coroner's come back with a report. I have something to discuss with you. Can I come over?"

"Yes, absolutely," Mallory said.

She was too rattled to ask for more details about what the coroner had told him. Better to talk about it in person. They agreed to his arrival in twenty minutes. Despite the fact that she'd lived in the town for only two days, her home seemed like the most popular destination in McNamara.

When she came back into the main room, she found Suzanne standing in the center of the living room, staring at the large chair in the corner, as Carlotta had.

"Where did you get this?"

"Kylie dropped it off."

"Oh. I thought maybe Joel gave it to you."

"Why would he have done that?"

Mallory's tone was sharper than she intended. The impending visit with Joel had put her on edge, and she hoped Suzanne wasn't suggesting something was going on between them. Suzanne looked down, like she had been slapped.

"I'm sorry. It's hard to see something of his still in the house."

Mallory realized her error.

"The chair belonged to . . . Sean?"

She felt odd at having settled so comfortably in it the night before.

"Yeah. He used to read in it. He liked to look out at the water once in a while, in between turning the pages. He said it helped him absorb the material." She smiled at the memory.

"But why would you think Joel gave it to me?"

Suzanne looked confused. "Well, maybe not give it to you, but just, like, I thought he left it here. What do I know? It's not like we're close or nothing. Joel never liked me much when I was dating his brother."

"The house was empty for ten years. Surely the owner cleared it out before it went on the market?"

Suzanne looked at her closely.

"Joel was the owner of the house."

CHAPTER FIFTEEN

After Suzanne said goodbye with a cigarette-scented hug that was unexpectedly comforting, promising to bring the car back later, Mallory sat on the small front step waiting for Joel. Though the temperature had dropped since her run, she preferred to be outside. After what Suzanne had revealed about the furniture, the house seemed somehow both claustrophobic and unbearably sparse, as if it were waiting to be filled up with the rest of Sean's possessions. She knew that Kylie's intentions were good in bringing his stuff to her, but she couldn't help but wish the woman had let the items stay in storage. She tried to give her friend the benefit of the doubt. Maybe Kylie had been so taken aback by Sean's death that she hadn't been conscious of what she was doing to Mallory. Grief could be dark enough to blind a person even ten years after the fact. Still, it was disconcerting to realize that her home was now furnished with a dead man's possessions. Mallory watched the grass blow back and forth at the edge of the tree line, puzzling through the landscape of her life that was now littered with the pieces of information her visitors had deposited like waves leaving seashells on a beach.

She started with the things she knew for certain. It was an old habit she had developed prior to treating a patient. Often the best way to reach a quick decision was to slow down. Forty-six years ago, in 1974, Alice Halloway had been killed by the sudden flooding of the valley. Kylie's father, Jonathan Shine, had been the one to find her body. Alice was survived by her brother, Logan Carruthers, and her son, Dean Halloway. Five years later, Dean drowned under suspicious circumstances in Loss Lake. Carlotta had been his wife. Shortly after his death, she had been given a new house by Logan. Had she sold the place Mallory now owned? If so, to whom? Somehow, it had ended up in Joel's hands, but he had chosen not to be identified in the property transfer documents. Instead, she had purchased the home from an anonymous seller. At the time, Mallory had assumed it was for business purposes, which wasn't uncommon in Vancouver. Now that she was in McNamara, she was confused by why he wouldn't list his name on the sale when everyone knew who he was. She left that question aside and listed the last facts she had learned. When they were still young children, Joel and Sean's father had been killed, then their mother had died. In 2010, Sean Benson was shot through the window of his home. Her home.

Were all small towns steeped in so much tragedy? She worried the facts like an animal intent on finding meat on a chewed-up bone. Living in a house where a man had died violently was unsettling, especially when there were still so many unanswered questions about the past that she didn't feel comfortable asking her neighbors. Carlotta had suggested more research at the Turner Public Library, and Mallory decided to go as soon as possible. Of course, the whisper network in McNamara was also an option if she could figure out a way to get information without offending anyone. So far, she'd learned more from other people than from Frederich's book. But the idea of questioning Joel about the house where his brother had died seemed heartless. She wanted to stay in his good graces, for several reasons.

As she turned over the information in her mind, she heard tires rolling up her driveway, hungrily crunching the dry leaves and small stones beneath their tread. When Joel's car came into view, she smiled at him through the windshield of his police cruiser. Despite her uncertainty about him, she couldn't deny the excitement she felt at the sight of his face. As he stepped out, her heartbeat raced and slowed like a butterfly being blown and dropped by a strong gust of wind.

"Hello, Mallory." He dropped his eyes immediately after he met hers, as if he too was nervous. "Do you mind if we take a walk as we talk? It's such a beautiful day. I'd like to spend as much of it outside as I can."

His demeanor was miles away from the confident, brusque sergeant who had visited her two days before. She had expected him to bring up the coroner's report right away, but instead he seemed almost shy. Something had changed between them in the forest, and she could tell he felt it too. But underlying her attraction to him was a sense that he wasn't exactly who she'd thought he was. Why had he not told her about being the person who had sold her the house? She stood up and brushed off her pants.

"That sounds perfect."

The two of them moved toward the gate in formation, like they had taken this walk together all their lives. After she unlocked it, Joel took a trail that jogged to the left instead of the one she had run on earlier, which veered to the right. Ferns and brambles stretched their long fingers across the brown earth, welcoming them back into the thick of the forest. After a few moments, Joel stopped in a clearing in front of a large stump. He kneeled at the base and pointed at a small clump of fur.

"Here's the source of that scream you mentioned yesterday," he said.

Mallory looked closer. The white fur was marred by streaks of blood.

"Probably a hawk. Rabbits, especially light-colored ones, are pretty easy pickings around here. They never seem to understand how easy it is to see them from way up in the sky. I suppose no ecosystem could survive without naivete of the ones on the bottom, but still. Always sad to see."

Mallory looked up at the sky, half expecting to see a bird of prey swooping down at her with bloody claws. Instead, she saw thready clouds blowing across the sky in white lines. She took one more look at the poor creature by her feet before they began to walk again.

"You wanted to discuss something?" she asked.

"Yes," he said, pausing to turn back to her. "I'm here as a friend. Unofficially."

She was flattered to see a slight blush on his cheeks as he said the word "friend." Her face warmed in sympathetic pleasure even as her stomach flipped.

"We've got an identification of the drowning victim. We need to notify the family before releasing the name, but apparently she was behaving erratically."

"So it was a woman?" Mallory asked. Her throat narrowed in apprehension and she swallowed hard.

"Yes. Logan Carruthers told me that she'd been in the bar with him for most of the day," Joel continued. "The prevailing theory is that she had a few too many and stopped to cool down at the beach. She was pretty inebriated, which might have been a factor in her death. Nothing points to negligence on your part. The only thing that may come of it is a warning to fence off that path from Main Street to the beach. It's your property now. It should be secured. But don't worry. This should all be wrapped up soon."

Relief rushed through her. "That's so good to hear."

"I thought you'd be happy. You can enjoy the lake now without worrying."

She tried to smile, though her hands were shaking. She was eager to speak of something besides the woman who had recently been identified in the lake. The thought of the recovered body chilled her but not as much as her dread about what still remained below. She rubbed her arms to generate warmth before she spoke.

"Actually, I have been trying to get to know more about the area. Especially the history of Loss Lake."

Joel tilted his head at her. "Our area has had its share of tragedies. But I don't want you getting the wrong impression of this place. I'm sure you've heard about Alice Halloway by now."

"Yes. And her son."

Joel sighed and crossed his arms.

"Dean Halloway's death was before my time on the force, but I've heard some things about the fellow that aren't too flattering."

"Such as?"

"I really hate to speak ill of the dead, Mallory. But basically, he was a troublemaker as a kid who got worse as he got older. His father died in a logging accident, when he was a teenager. After that he raised such hell his poor mother didn't know what to do with him. Apparently, she was even considering military school. That was kind of the only solution back in those days. Anyway, he was seventeen when she passed away, and I guess the whole town rallied around him. No matter what kind of a teenager he had been, he was an orphan. He met Carlotta at a fundraising dinner the town was having in his name. She was from Turner, and they fell in love. They got married as teenagers. Then he died before he reached the age of twenty-two."

It was hard to imagine Carlotta as a teenage bride. "I didn't realize he was so young."

"Yeah, just a kid. Carlotta seemed to tame him for the last few years of his life. There were still rumors of his bad behavior, of course, but nothing like the fights and violence that he'd been involved in before they got together."

"What kind of rumors?"

Joel looked away. "The usual small-town stuff."

Mallory was uncomfortable pressing him for more information. He was clearly tired of the subject. Instead, she changed tack.

"Frederich Menzel seemed to indicate he was experienced enough as a canoeist that his drowning was unlikely."

"Oh, wow. You got ahold of that book? Let me guess, old Logan sold you a copy?"

Joel laughed as Mallory blushed.

"You know, Freddie never met a conspiracy he didn't support. He and Logan have been trying to make money off that story for years," Joel said with a shake of his head. "Fact is, even after getting hitched to Carlotta, Dean Halloway could drink any man in McNamara under the table, and often did. There were rumors he was rough with her. The whole town knew Logan was teaching her how to use a gun. It didn't come as a shock to anyone when his body turned up on shore after he took the boat out that night."

"Do you think Carlotta had something to do with it?"

Joel shrugged. "Like I said, it was before my time. The case was ruled an accident."

A shadow hulked over the forest as the sun went behind a cloud, and Joel's eyes darkened from brown to nearly black.

"We should probably be getting back," he said. His tone turned teasing. "Unless you have more questions about ancient history?"

Mallory knew he was joking, but she seized her chance.

"Just one. Why didn't you tell me that you owned the house?"

Joel looked at her with sharp eyes. "Who did you hear that from?"

"Suzanne was over here earlier."

His features were tight and his voice was strained when he answered.

"Why are you talking to Suzanne about this stuff? She's hardly a reliable source."

Mallory heard the hitch in Joel's voice, but she couldn't stop herself from responding. "Suzanne might be a drinker, but that doesn't mean she can't be trusted."

"Suzanne is a whole lot more than a drinker. Ask her sometime about where she was the day my brother died."

His words were bitter enough to leave a bad taste in Mallory's mouth, but her desire to learn everything she could about her house's former occupant made her press on.

"What do you mean?"

"There were a couple of guys fishing on the lake that afternoon. Sound carries over water. They heard Suzanne and Sean arguing, and, by their account, it was vicious. The last thing they heard Suzanne scream to my brother was that she wanted to kill him. Those two fought like cats and dogs, especially when she was drunk. I had to separate them a few times after they got home from a night of drinking. She was lucky I didn't arrest her."

Mallory instantly regretted letting the woman borrow her car. There was so much she had to learn about the people of McNamara. And about her own instincts in judging a person's character.

Joel rubbed his jaw with the back of his hand. "Sometimes I think that I could have done something different."

"Oh, Joel. It was an accident. You couldn't have stopped it."

"Maybe, maybe not. I was a rookie cop back then with the Turner Police Department. I commuted back and forth every night to work a beat. When I walked in that morning, his . . . body was the first thing I saw."

Joel's words blew away in the wind that swirled through the trees and around them both. She let the whisper of the air fill the silence until the glassiness left Joel's eyes.

"Was Suzanne a suspect?" she asked.

Joel dug his toe into the dirt. "Forget I said anything, okay? There were no suspects. It was a hunting accident, plain and simple. I know Sean wasn't always . . . a good guy. He had been a pain in the ass for a whole lot of people in the town for a real long time. There were plenty of people here who wanted him dead, but no one in McNamara is going to take a shot in plain daylight at the town's lawyer. It's not like that here. It was an accident."

His tone was firm enough to demand an apology from her. "I'm sorry. This is none of my business."

"You're right, it's not. Listen, Mallory. In a town this small, sometimes the police work does itself, and sometimes you have to let sleeping dogs lie. I mean, if we weren't in McNamara, I might look into the reason why a woman from Vancouver happened to drown in the lake within hours of you moving here. I might ask if you knew a woman named Cynthia Rooney."

Mallory's eyes widened. She hoped it didn't look like guilt. She drew herself up to respond.

"I would answer if you asked."

The wind picked up again as they stood in silence. Then Joel's eyes changed from stern to soft.

"I don't need to. You're one of us now. We look out for each other here. There are some things we don't talk about. Okay?"

Tension released from her shoulders.

"Okay."

They locked eyes. He stepped forward until there were only two inches between their bodies. His hand, rough and warm, brushed against her waist before lying flat on the small of her back. He moved forward, and her hips bumped against his thighs. They were so close that she could feel the folds of his canvas jacket halting the flow of her breath. He was so much taller than Graham had been. She looked up and he looked down and in that moment, she couldn't think of anything to do except to kiss Sergeant Joel Benson.

PART TWO

CHAPTER SIXTEEN

Twelve days later, Mallory sat on a padded stool in front of the vanity table in her bedroom. It was another gift from Kylie, who had been making almost daily donations of furniture, household goods, and linens. Joel had brought things over as well—a cast-iron pan and a sturdy coatrack. She hadn't had the heart to ask them to stop. If Kylie and Joel found solace in her using their deceased brother's possessions, she was fine with bowing to their needs. She didn't want to judge them or curtail the way they were working through their sorrow. Since Mallory had moved to McNamara, the cycle of her grief had softened to the point where she could remember Graham without feeling like it would destroy her, but she still struggled to find an appropriate spot for his ashes, which were stored on a shelf in her closet. Losing someone was complicated. Dealing with what they'd left behind was even more so.

She and Kylie met most mornings in the back-room tea shop of Kylie's store to catch up and chat. After a week of their chats, Mallory had begged Kylie to begin stocking coffee. Her younger friend had reluctantly agreed, though she couldn't be persuaded past selling a fifty-fifty mix of decaffeinated and caffeinated. Since the beans had arrived on the shelf, Mallory had been stopped on the street by dozens of McNamara residents so they could thank her for nudging Kylie toward caffeine. Suzanne had treated her to another beef-on-a-bun sandwich the Thursday before. Mallory had begun to find exactly what she was looking for in McNamara: a community of her own. People who protected her.

∼

When Cynthia Rooney had accused Mallory of murdering Graham, no one had stood up for her. Not even her own family. Mallory had been looking out the window distractedly as she pretended to adjust a wreath beside Graham's coffin. She needed to give herself space from the crowd of people who seemed almost eager to give her their condolences. Cynthia had pulled up to the funeral home with a screech of brakes so loud it was audible even with an external wall between them. She was late to the funeral, and Mallory had been hoping she wouldn't show up at all. Since the day Graham had died, Cynthia had been a poisonous cloud of accusing phone calls and bitter emails. Seeing the woman again sent a sliver of fear through her numbed mind.

The gray-painted room reeked of air freshener, as if death were a smell that could be masked with the right blend of floral chemicals. Cynthia had bypassed the guest sign-in and stormed up the narrow aisle between the pews. Her face was reddened with rage and, from the smell of her, last night's vodka tonics.

"Why have you been avoiding me? You should be ashamed of yourself," Cynthia spit at Mallory.

Mallory's stomach twisted.

"I can't talk right now, Cynthia. We're about to begin."

She tried to skirt the woman, but Cynthia stepped to the side to block her. Mallory saw her mother's gaze dart in their direction, then sharply away. Her father was slumped in the second pew, trying to hide his hangover. Several other members of Graham's family stared at them in interest. Mallory wished someone in the room were on her side as Cynthia continued in a voice quiet with anger.

"There was supposed to be a nurse that night, Mallory. I contacted the home-care providers and told them I was going to take care of your final bill."

Cynthia held up her phone and jabbed at it. Mallory couldn't read the small text on the jumping screen.

"I don't know what you're talking about. Now excuse me. I need to take my seat."

"You do know what I'm talking about. Someone canceled his care. And because of that, he died."

The fire in Mallory's cheeks seemed hot enough to swell her skin.

"Get away from me," she muttered.

Cynthia's eyes lit up like the words had been a confession, and she pitched her voice even lower. Their confrontation had captured the attention of most of the front row.

"Admit what you did to Graham. Look me in the eyes and tell me what happened. I know he was sick, but he still had a chance. He was on the transplant list. He could have made it. Maybe you thought it was a mercy. Maybe I'll understand if I hear it from you."

Mallory looked down to avoid Cynthia seeing the silent scream inside her mind. *I owe you nothing.* Cynthia took the break in eye contact as an act of submission.

"If I don't hear it from you, Mallory, and soon, I'm going to the police."

Finally, Sadie, Cynthia's sister, had intervened. Her large body nearly filled the aisle as she bustled toward them. Mallory met her eyes gratefully as the woman clasped her sister's arm and steered her toward a seat in the third row.

"The service is about to begin, Cyn. Let's sit down."

Mallory hadn't heard a word of the eulogy. She had been too busy starting a countdown in her head. As soon as her house sold, she wanted to be as far away from Cynthia as she could be. Somewhere safe. She had nearly succeeded. Until Cynthia had followed her to McNamara and drowned. Joel's confirmation of the identity of the woman in Loss Lake had been Mallory's worst nightmare. His willingness not to dig deeper had been a dream come true. If living in peace meant living with secrets, it was a small price to pay.

Cynthia's accusation could have seemed like nothing more than the empty threat of a grief-addled relative, easy to dismiss, simple to deny, except for one thing. She knew if anyone found out what her relationship with Graham had really been like, Cynthia's words would take on a much greater significance. One that she had to avoid at all costs.

The truth was, Mallory had wanted Graham out of her life.

She couldn't be sure how much Graham had told Cynthia about what was going on in their marriage. A month before his heart problems became evident, after ten years of marriage, with no children and little to bind them but a mutually owned house, Mallory had told Graham it was over. She wanted to separate, amicably and civilly. She was happy to move out and leave Graham the house. It had never really seemed like hers anyway. He asked why she wanted their marriage to dissolve, which confirmed her decision. Having such a different understanding of their relationship seemed reason enough to end it. They had both changed so much in the last decade that there was nothing to connect them other than their certificate of marriage, and that was no longer enough for her.

Despite his initial misgivings, Graham had come around to the idea of them separating fairly quickly, particularly when Mallory assured him that his life wouldn't change much at all. They had been preparing for a graceful divorce when his heart failed and revealed the irreparable damage that had been done to him during the trip that was intended to do good in the world. He had asked Mallory to stay, and she had been unable to refuse. They both knew she wasn't there out of love, but, for both of them, being there was enough. Marriage was more than sex and socializing as a unit. She had agreed to be Graham's partner in life and death, and she knew she had to honor the contract.

Had his body begun to show the signs of its deterioration a year or two later, Mallory might never have known. She would certainly not have been expected to quit her job to care for him. But as it was, their decision to divorce was too fresh to allow her to walk away. No one in their lives—not even her mother—had been informed of their plans. It seemed hurtful to tell them about their separation and Graham's death sentence in the same conversation. So she kept it to herself.

Their marriage had started happily enough. Mallory had been well established as an emergency room nurse. She loved her work and the stability it brought to her life, but the success she achieved had allowed her to focus on the world beyond her work. She had begun to long for a partner. Besides, her mother's constant fretting about her being single had worn on her nerves more than she cared to admit. She was inexperienced with dating, however, and often perplexed by the way her friends and colleagues seemed to meet people so easily. When her friend had suggested a blind date with a single man she knew, Mallory had been happy to accept. Their first date had been pleasant enough to warrant a second. Mallory might not have sensed electricity between them, but she liked the way the older man listened thoughtfully as she spoke about the value of her work. On their second date, it was clear to her how much Graham enjoyed her company, and she decided to enjoy his just as much. Their courtship had been composed of many affable hikes and comfortable dinners. When he asked her to marry him, producing a serviceable ring on a trail in Stanley Park they both found pretty, she could not think of a single reason to say no. So, she said yes.

For many years, she had been lucky to be both married and partnered with someone she considered her closest friend. She found herself offering Graham's opinion in conversations at the hospital so she could work the words "my husband" into her sentences. Graham had seemed just as content with her and the life they shared. He had been happy in his job as an IT manager and immersed in training for his races. Then, about five years into their marriage, Graham had been passed over for a promotion that he was certain he was going to get. He had been angry at first, heatedly searching for another job and going to several interviews. When nobody made him an offer, he stopped his search for a new position and settled into a life of quiet oblivion and underlying resentment.

Every evening, he came home with a list of petty grievances about his job, seeming to hate every minute he spent at it. On the weekends, he declined social invitations, preferring to burrow himself into a small world of sports on television. Since she couldn't bear to spend hours on the couch in front of a monotone man meticulously dissecting decisions in a game she didn't care about, Mallory often found herself alone. When Graham did enter into a conversation with her, his general unhappiness bled into each interaction. The food she made was too spicy or the movie she wanted to see was too weird. Graham had settled for a numbing life, and he wanted her to anesthetize hers as well. The constant droning from the television in the den seemed like the voice of a hypnotist convincing Graham that nothing in life mattered. Even his daily runs offered him no joy. Each time he returned, he complained of new aches in his body. At the time, she had attributed his grumbles to a general malaise and had been impatient with him. Now, she realized that his heart had been straining to keep up with him for years. It was only one of the things she had done to her husband in his last years that made her cringe with guilt. Her grief would be so much simpler if she had truly loved him when he died.

Sometimes, especially toward the end, Mallory had been hobbled by guilt about how much she wanted it to be over. She wondered if Graham felt the same way, but she had never dared to ask in case it reminded him that she was only with him because he was sick. But just because they didn't talk about it didn't mean it disappeared. The unfinished emotions created a slow-boiling frustration that underscored their conversations.

Graham woke up every morning with breath so vile it was impossible to ignore that his insides were decomposing. As he grew sicker, her endless days and nights of caring for him were full of insults. He accused her of taking too long with his medication or deliberately leaving his sheets unwashed. The quiet misery that had infected him in life grew loud and abrasive as he neared his death. Twice, he had hurled his full bedpan across the floor because she'd failed to empty it within seconds of his urination. Once he viciously whispered that it was her fault they had gone to Guatemala in the first place. The trip had been her idea. Mallory had not fought back, though her anger had built like a campfire being fed pieces of dry tinder. No one seemed to notice that she had been anything but the perfect wife. Except Cynthia.

~

She smoothed her simple black dress over her hips, looked at herself in the mirror, and told herself to let go of the past. Both Graham and Cynthia were gone. It was time for her to start over, and a night out with Joel was the perfect way forward. It had been ages since she'd worn anything but jeans and a T-shirt, but Kylie had told her to dress up a little for the annual harvest pageant at the local elementary school, which would be followed by a community social. As Mallory appraised her appearance, she decided a necklace was required.

She took out the jewelry box her mother had given to her as a wedding present, stroking the mother-of-pearl inset into the wooden box in the pattern of a lotus flower with the pad of her finger before opening its lid. As she gazed inside, she was dismayed to see all her necklaces clumped together in a ball of silver and gold strands, much like her own thoughts and miseries wound into each other. It was difficult to tell where one began and the other ended. Untangling them seemed hopeless, but she sighed and picked up the mess of metal, picking at one sparkling chain at a time. She was careful not to pull too hard, lest she make them completely impossible to separate. As Mallory slid one fingernail beneath a delicate gold thread, the entire cluster loosened, spilling smooth, cool necklaces onto her open palm like water. Each piece glittered up at her in clean, elegant lines.

She reached for the most beautiful of the lot. Graham had slipped it around her neck when she was sleeping on the morning of their first anniversary, when their time together was still new enough to feel like a blessing. The pendant was a simple, perfect circle, like the ring that Graham had placed on her finger on their wedding day. She hadn't worn it since she had asked him for a divorce. As she closed the clasp behind her neck, the golden links were like a soft breath on her skin. She smoothed her hair down and declared herself ready just as she heard the thrum of an engine coming up her driveway. Joel had arrived.

CHAPTER SEVENTEEN

Dating Joel Benson came with its own set of conflicts. Kissing him was a salve and a betrayal. When their lips met, it was everything she had wished it had been with Graham. Joel understood things about her that she hadn't allowed herself to show anyone else. They had both been marked by death, hollowed out by grief, and their empty pieces were being filled by one another. But when they pulled apart, she wondered if Graham did still exist in some form and if every part of that form hated that another man's hands were on her now. Especially when Joel's touch made her feel the way it did.

Being with Joel provided her with a clarity she thought she had lost forever. Their long conversations about death and life captivated her. The way he listened made her say things she hadn't realized she was thinking. At first, she had shied away from discussing Graham with him, worried that it would remind him of how recently she had become widowed and how quickly she was moving on. Or worse, that talking about her past would make him wonder if there was any connection between her and Cynthia Rooney. But Joel had encouraged her to tell him about the toll Graham's months of poor health had taken on her. It had helped to speak about him, even if she couldn't tell Joel everything.

Two nights before, when he had taken her to a steaming natural hot spring down a winding trail into the forest, she'd nearly gasped at the sight of his body in swimming trunks as she hurriedly pulled off her own clothes. It had been cold, so she had rushed into the rocky basin, laughing in relief as the naturally heated water engulfed her. Joel slipped in beside her, but the rocks were unstable below his feet and he leaned too far forward as he clambered into the pool. His hand touched her rib cage as he steadied himself. In nearly one motion, she leaned forward and he kissed her. The moment had seemed too perfect to be possible. To their left, she could hear the quiet rush of a small creek that fed into Loss Lake, flowing as gently as her days had since she had moved to McNamara—peaceful, beautiful, and free. When Joel looked at her, it made her feel like everything she had ever done in her life had been right, because it had led to him. He made her forget who she used to be. As his kiss deepened and his muscular body pressed against her, the bubbling of the stream had seemed to rise in a watery crescendo, nearly sweeping away all her inhibitions and reservations about sleeping with him. Then a crash in the forest had startled them into separating.

"Is that a bear?" she whispered.

"Probably," he whispered back.

She had stared at him in horror until his eyes began to dance. He whispered again, this time with such exaggeration that she realized he was pulling her leg.

"You're beautiful enough to bring a bear out of hibernation," he said. "But that sounded more like a deer."

As his truck rumbled outside her door, she walked down the hall and to the front door, where she had left her coat and purse on the foyer table, ready to be collected at a moment's notice. Old habits died hard. Graham had been impatient if she took even a minute too long when he was ready to go. She left the foyer light on, and its reflection glinted back at her from the large window in the living room that was still without curtains despite her best efforts. Kylie had laughed when she'd innocently asked which store in McNamara carried drapes. *None,* she had said, still giggling. *Unless you want camouflage netting from the hardware store.* So purchasing curtains was yet another task to take care of in

Turner when she found time to make the drive, along with having her internet and telephone connected. The bare windows still seemed like hollow eye sockets when the sun went down. She still hadn't been able to fully shake her unease about living in the house where Sean had been killed, though it was becoming the happiest place she had ever lived.

As she jogged to Joel's truck, the air was cold enough to take her breath away. She smiled as she approached, though the bright lights prevented her from seeing inside the cab. She was always smiling around him these days. It seemed impossible not to do so. It wasn't until she stepped up and slid herself into the passenger seat that she could tell how happy he was to see her as well. He kissed her before saying hello.

"You ready for this?" he asked. There was a chuckle underneath his words as he maneuvered his vehicle down her driveway that Mallory found both intriguing and slightly daunting.

"What exactly should I be ready for?"

A week ago, Jonathan Shine had brought Kylie's two-year-old daughter, Aura, into the store during one of their chats. The little girl had announced she was going to be a bush in the pageant. Kylie had beamed with pride before becoming so preoccupied with costuming that Mallory hadn't been able to learn much about what actually happened at the annual event.

"Depends on who you ask," Joel said. "It's been an annual tradition here as long as I can remember. Freddie Menzel's got himself pretty convinced that its roots are deeply entrenched in ancient rituals of gratitude and sacrifice. He directs the play each year, so we are likely in for a bit of a doozy on that one."

Having finished his book the week before, she agreed with Joel's assessment. Though it had started strong, the work meandered rapidly in the later chapters, bringing in everything from the Loch Ness Monster to the Egyptian practice of weighing the heart of the deceased to determine whether one would enjoy an afterlife or a second death. The ideas presented were fascinating, but the prose was so convoluted, it was hard to keep the argument straight. Mallory had been left with as much ambiguity about the Loss Lake monster as she had started with. During her frequent runs along the shoreline, she sensed that the answer to what really lay at the bottom of Loss Lake wouldn't be found in a book.

"Well, at least I finally get to meet the famous Freddie Menzel."

"Oh yes you do. This is his moment to shine. But be careful. One word with Freddie can easily turn into a three-hour-long conversation that you can't escape."

"Noted."

"Then there's Logan, who will use it as a chance to sell miniature monsters or whatever else he's been making these days."

Mallory tried unsuccessfully to keep from laughing. "Oh, Joel. He means well, and I think it's lovely to celebrate the turning of the seasons."

"Yeah, my dad always told me that it was a time to acknowledge the land and be humbled by what the earth provides for us, so there's that. But for me?" He turned to her with a wink. "I always thought that we had the harvest festival because it's too damn frigid to get together at Christmastime."

Mallory laughed again as Joel steered his truck into the small parking lot beside McNamara's only school. Once parked, he walked around to let Mallory out, and the two walked together through a set of double doors that led into the gymnasium.

"Here we go," he said with a grin.

CHAPTER EIGHTEEN

As she stepped into the darkened room, the thick vinyl floor depressed lightly under the heels of Mallory's shoes like a plastic-coated bog. The gym smelled vaguely of sweat socks and chalk. Orange, yellow, and red crepe paper had been twisted and taped at various places around the room. A collection of several dozen wooden chairs faced a raised stage at the far end of the room. To the side of it, as Joel had predicted, Logan Carruthers stood behind a kiosk littered with monster merchandise. He winked at her as she waved. Six tables lined the wall beside the door, nearly groaning with the weight of platters, dishes, and trays heaped with every kind of fall food imaginable: macaroni and cheese, cabbage rolls, bubbling soups, and roast beef and dinner buns courtesy of Tuck and his wife. At the end of the row, Mallory caught sight of more cakes, squares, and tarts than it seemed possible the fifty or so people in the gym would be able to consume. Judging from the piled-high plates, everyone was doing their best to rise to the challenge.

"I didn't realize it was a potluck. I would have brought something," Mallory said to Joel.

"Oh, don't worry. Betty gave you a pass this year because you're new in town. Next year, she'll have you ironing the tablecloths like everyone else."

As if on cue, the tiny blonde-haired woman called to them from across the room. She was dressed in a tailored pink dress that made

Mallory grateful she had worn jewelry. Mallory and Joel picked their way around piles of small gourds and pumpkins that had been scattered around the floor in a decorative fashion that must have seemed less dangerous when the room was well lit. In the dimness, illuminated only by candles, Mallory feared breaking an ankle, but she made it safely into a brief but joyful hug with Betty.

"I am so happy to see you both," Betty said, exaggerating the last word with a suggestive wiggle of her eyebrows. "It's nice when young people find love."

Mallory was glad the room was dark enough to cover her blush. "It's nice to see you too, Betty. You've done a fantastic job."

"Thanks. Listen, I've saved you both"—another eyebrow raise—"seats up front, right beside me. We can talk more after I take care of these neck breakers that Suzanne thought were a good idea. Honestly, I don't know why I thought she'd be any good to me after four p.m."

Betty mimed raising a cup to her lips.

"I'll be glad to help," Joel said. "That's a lot to carry for one woman."

Betty put her hand flat on her chest and let her eyelashes flutter in Joel's direction. "Oh thank you. Mallory, why don't you fix this wonderful man a plate."

She leaned in and noted under her breath, "I wouldn't recommend Carlotta's lentil loaf unless you want to cut off a slice to use as a doorstop."

Mallory grimaced in shared understanding. She still remembered the muffins Carlotta had given to her as a housewarming gift. As she waited in line at the food table, she watched Betty and Joel begin to collect gourds and squashes, laughing like children given free rein at a pumpkin patch. When her turn came, she began by spooning maple-glazed carrots onto two plates. Carlotta walked to the table and took a place in line beside her. The woman looked as severe as always, clad in a dark-gray woolen turtleneck dress that swept the floor. It reminded Mallory of a large sock.

"Good evening," she said.

"And to you."

"Did you help with this festival?" Mallory asked, reaching for a conversation topic that would keep them on neutral ground.

"Of course I did," Carlotta replied. "That's what we do here in McNamara. We help each other."

Mallory sighed as she braced herself for another pitch. Sure enough, Carlotta placed the serving spoon she had been holding back on the table and squared her shoulders to face Mallory.

"On that note, I'm glad to run into you here. I have been hoping that you will reconsider your position on Suzanne and I using your land. The deer are rampant this year, and if we don't keep their numbers low now, all our gardens, yours in particular, will take a heavy hit this spring. I understand you don't want to join us, but I'd be happy to give you some meat in return."

Mallory pictured the stern librarian giving her a dripping package, her hands still red from the butchering. She wondered why Carlotta would think that would make her offer more enticing, particularly after Mallory had told her she rarely ate meat. Mallory tensed her muscles to prevent her shudder from being visible.

"My answer is the same as it was before, Carlotta. Joel and I have been using the trails nearly every day. I don't want to have to worry about getting shot on my own land."

Carlotta shook her head. "You won't have to worry. I give you my word."

"I've made my decision. There must be somewhere else for you and Suzanne to hunt," she said curtly. "Excuse me, please. I'd like to eat dinner before the play begins."

"Of course. Forgive an old woman her ramblings," Carlotta said mildly. "But don't forget my request. It's not just about using your land and saving you from the overpopulation of deer. Allowing me to show you how to hunt might be the only thing that keeps you safe. Winters

163

are long and cold around here. I want you to know how to protect yourself."

Mallory didn't answer. She hoped she was wrong in sensing that underneath Carlotta's words of concern, there was a threat. The suspicions Joel had mentioned about what really happened to Dean Halloway came to her mind. She took a few more items for their plates, but, before she could step away, Carlotta heaped a mealy-looking slice of lentil loaf on both.

"Try this. It's my own recipe," she said with a smile. Mallory looked at it helplessly. It resembled a cross between wet cardboard and tree bark.

"Thank you."

She found Joel at their seats, and the two of them ate their dinner as soft rock played through a set of speakers. Both of them studiously avoided Carlotta's offering. Mallory hid hers under her napkin as she took the plates to the bins that had been set up, grateful that Carlotta was nowhere to be seen. She hurried back as the lights flashed in the gymnasium. The show was about to begin. Betty slipped into the seat beside her as Mallory waved hello to Kylie, who was perched on one knee at the front of the stage, her phone held up and at the ready to record her daughter's performance. Jonathan Shine was in the front row as well. He turned and nodded to them both.

"It's a shame that Doug can't be here," Betty whispered in her ear, low enough that it didn't attract Joel's attention.

"Is that Kylie's husband?" Mallory asked. In all the hours she'd spent with the woman, Kylie had never brought up the man who had fathered her child, and Mallory hadn't felt it right to ask. Betty leaned in again, clearly excited to impart an old piece of gossip to a person who had never heard it. Her mouth was so close to Mallory's ear that it tickled.

"Kylie was never married to him. She met him at a conference down in the city. He came up here for a few months shortly after she found out she was pregnant, but I guess McNamara wasn't a good fit. He left her before she even gave birth to Aura. Poor thing. Good thing she has a wonderful grandfather to take the place of a poor father."

Before Mallory could answer, the auditorium went completely black. In the darkness, someone hit a drum. Its deep bass was loud enough to make Mallory's sternum wobble. Over and over, the noise bounced off the walls of the auditorium. On the tenth beat, when Mallory was almost nauseated from the sound waves, red lights came up on the stage. A small child, dressed in a tattered white dress, wandered aimlessly from one side of the stage to the other. Aura hunched in the corner, decked in layers and layers of fabric leaves, quivering in her attempt to be still. Kylie shifted forward and held her phone up to the stage. Mallory was disconcerted to see the action of the play on the small screen of the phone while the real live version played out on the stage. She focused on the main event as out of the eaves came another creature, dressed entirely in black. For a single strange moment, Mallory didn't register the child as being entirely human. On their head was a giant glossy black papier-mâché mask that had been built in a grotesque exaggeration of a bull's head. Horns as thick as Mallory's forearm protruded from the sides, and a perfect ring in its nostrils caught the red lights and glinted as the child wearing the headpiece wove under its weight.

"The time has come," a chorus of small voices said.

Mallory's attention jerked to the other side of the stage, where a cluster of six children, wearing similar tattered dresses, chanted. Kylie had told her that Freddie made a point of casting every child from the town each year. As she watched, the group of six grew to a number close to twenty, and the small voices grew louder.

"To pick the one," the chant continued. "The one who stands for the many."

Mallory dared a glance toward Betty, who was staring rapt at the macabre performance. She looked over at Joel, whose cheeks were drawn in like he was biting them. Was he upset? He turned to catch her eye, and she realized that he was barely containing his laughter. He nudged her knee and widened his eyes, then turned back to the stage, where the children had begun to chant:

In our town we have a bull.
He eats until his body's full.
Every year we all must fear
That the bull will munch our ears.

The pull of his amusement combined with the strained rhyming began to lift the edges of her own mouth into a smile. There hadn't yet been a moment with Joel when she had sensed that their perception of the world was different. Often, while watching a movie with Graham, he had looked at her in confusion when she'd erupted into laughter, and she had swallowed it rather than ruin the joke by explaining it. But so far, Joel had not failed to understand why she thought something was funny. She slid closer to his body, wishing she were bold enough to let her head rest on his strong shoulder, but she wasn't ready to showcase what was growing between them to the entire town. In the few calls she'd had with her mother since arriving, she hadn't mentioned him either. It seemed too soon.

She touched the gold necklace around her neck. It had been her favorite piece of jewelry for years, which meant she almost never wore it. When Mallory was a child, her mother had taught her to be wary of sharing her most treasured objects with the world. *The more you wear them, the easier they are to lose,* her mother had chided. Later in life, Mallory had heard of a Greek woman spitting on the ground seconds after she held a newborn to keep the evil spirits from discovering the beauty of the child. She had known immediately that the practice came from the same foundation of distrust as her mother's warnings. All her life she had been taught that showing others how much she loved something would make her vulnerable. She concentrated on what was left of the play.

Like Freddie's book, the play spun out quickly, devolving from what seemed to be a childish adaptation of the myth of the Minotaur into a mishmash of Greek myth and a modern Thanksgiving story, where numerous notable Greek gods and figures arrived for a feast. The script steered just shy of suggesting that the young girl would be sacrificed, but the return of the morbid drumbeat and chanting as she was led off the stage was enough to make Mallory uncomfortable.

From that point on, the plot became increasingly garbled, but the main message seemed to be to give gratitude for both the food and protection offered by the king. Mallory was more relieved than enlightened when the group of small actors stood at the front of the stage for their final bow, joined by a thin man with thick tortoiseshell glasses and a wiry white mustache who could be no one else but Frederich Menzel. She clapped enthusiastically to cover up her confusion about the performance. She hadn't known what to expect of the small-town play, but it definitely hadn't been that.

After the play ended, Kylie rushed backstage, her face proud. Mallory smiled at her and waved before she disappeared into the wings. She kissed Betty goodbye, then followed Joel into the crush of bodies, returning the friendly greetings of those around her, many of whom had been introduced to Mallory by way of her coffee bean victory. When they were steps away from the door, Mallory found herself face-to-face with the tall man who had taken the curtain call along with the actors.

"You must be Mallory Dent," he said with a dramatic bow. "How I hope you enjoyed our little evening at the theater."

His voice was reedy with syllables blunted by the remains of his German accent.

"Oh, but I did," she said. "You must have many admirers to thank tonight."

"Pishposh. No one else here has bought my book so quickly upon moving to our humble town."

"How did you—"

"Logan and I have grown close over the years. He keeps me apprised of book sales. Of course, his little library has nothing on the shelves of the Turner Public Library. As a book lover and an aspiring sleuth, you should definitely take the time to visit."

"An aspiring sleuth?"

Frederich winked. "Word gets around, my dear. I suspect you and I have much in common in terms of our curiosities."

Mallory found herself at a loss for words and scanned the crowd to see if Joel was close by. She spotted him involved in a conversation with Logan and realized she would have to keep the conversation going a bit longer for the sake of politeness, despite the fact that Frederich seemed to be veering close to a subject she and Joel desperately tried to avoid.

"I'm not sure I follow."

Frederich winked again and looked around the room pointedly. "Of course, of course. Loose lips, right? I only meant that the lake and its surroundings hold us both in thrall. Why, only last week, I was speaking with a budding marine biologist from Vancouver, who mentioned that saltwater fish had been found on the shores of Loss Lake. You know what that means, of course?"

Mallory shook her head. She was relieved that Frederich was more interested in the monster than the numerous deaths in McNamara.

"Underground tunnels still exist, my dear. Channels to the sea. Maybe whatever is here is going to be able to find its way back." Frederich became surprisingly morose. "Maybe we all will."

She found herself more baffled by the man himself than she had been by his dramatic production. She wasn't sure whether to comfort or question him when Joel arrived back at her side. Instead, she opted for the easy way out of the conversation.

"Pardon me. The last thing I wanted to do was to abandon my date."

Frederich looked at him closely. Mallory thought she saw a flicker of something unfriendly in his eye before he swept Joel up into an embrace.

"Oh, the mighty lawman. What did you think?"

"A masterpiece as we have come to expect, Freddie. You never disappoint. But, if you'll excuse me, I must escort Ms. Dent home."

"Of course, of course. I'm sure I'll see you at the Freeze Feast tomorrow morning," Frederich said. He kissed Mallory on the cheek with gusto, then said, "Don't forget about the Turner library, my dear." His voice was so quick and quiet that Mallory almost thought she had imagined it.

As Joel gracefully steered her away from Freddie's enthusiastic calls of goodbye and into the cold night air, a sense of relief made her fingers tingle. They climbed into the truck, and it grunted to a start. Mallory felt a puff of cold air on her hands and face as the heater blew to life.

"What's the Freeze Feast?" Mallory asked. For a town this small, McNamara had an astonishing number of events to keep track of.

Joel smiled again. "Another one of our traditions. The morning after the harvest pageant, Logan hosts a pancake breakfast on Sled Beach. They go hand in hand. Tonight, we feel grateful for the food. Tomorrow, we give thanks for getting through another year."

She was nervous about the idea of an event on her land, in the same place where a person had died so recently, but she didn't want to allude to the drowning. She kicked herself for not putting up a fence earlier. It would be so much easier to disallow access and close off the area to people than to be reminded of what had happened.

"I'm disappointed that Logan didn't ask for your permission," Joel said. "I suppose he's so used to doing it there that it didn't occur to him. I told him it was no problem back when I owned it. Carlotta on the other hand? She and her lentil loaf are probably best kept on the perimeter."

He laughed softly. In the cold of the truck cabin, it blew from his mouth in a visible puff. Suddenly, in the bustle of cars jostling for space in the parking lot lit only by a single streetlight, her tangled emotions unfurled like the necklaces in her hand. She didn't want to end up like her mother, alone in her marriage, surrounded by possessions she was unwilling to show the world, or like Carlotta, rigidly fixated on safety and security, or like Frederich, stuck in a desperate obsession. She wanted to believe in what life had to offer. For too long, she had been with someone who made her feel like half of who she was. With Joel, she could be everything. Her head was clearer than it had been in months, and it was all because of him. She slipped her hand into his and rested her cheek against his jacket, which smelled smoky and sweet like the flames of a fire lit with cedar.

When he looked down at her, she lifted her face to his and spoke in a low, clear tone. "Joel, I want you to drive me home," she said. "Then I want you to stay the night."

CHAPTER NINETEEN

Mallory opened her eyes to the feeling of Joel's heavy arm lying across her waist. She was on her side, in something close to a fetal position. Joel's body was in a nearly identical position facing her. As her sleep slid away, she realized that her knuckles were curled loosely against his chest like he was a door she was about to knock on. She ran a finger along the inky lines on his skin, tracing the way he had marked his body. Clouds had thickened the sky outside her window enough to make it appear to be dawn, though it was close to 8:00 a.m. Gray light streamed through the window. Joel stirred, and she propped her head up on an elbow as he slowly opened his eyes.

"Good morning," he said.

His smile was lazy and pure. She leaned over to kiss him, careful not to part her lips. Last night had been everything she had hoped it would be. She didn't want to change his opinion of her based on a bad case of morning breath.

"Coffee?"

He chuckled. "You know I'm dating royalty around here now, right? I've been a loyal member of the police force here for seven years, but I am nothing compared to the Lady of the Coffee." He smiled when she pushed his shoulder gently. "In other words, yes, please."

He pulled her toward him, and their bodies pressed together. Her face fit in the angle of his neck as they embraced. His smell made her feel that she had finally found the person she was looking for. She pulled away from him reluctantly.

The only thing that could drag her out of his arms was a hot cup of coffee. He followed her down the hallway and into the kitchen, where she began to fill the carafe with water from the tap.

"You know, I still don't understand why Logan or Tuck didn't start selling bags of coffee out of their places."

Joel grinned. "It's kind of a code around here that Kylie handles the dry goods. Tuck orders in the junk food. Logan supplies the beer. Everyone has their role, you know? No one wanted to step on any toes. We needed a newcomer to arrive and shake things up a bit."

He winked at her. Her body responded as if he had kissed her. She turned back to the coffee maker to hide her desire. As she poured in the water, he walked over to the large window that faced the lake. Unlike her, he seemed to have no qualms about standing so close to where his brother had died. She supposed time did heal wounds, no matter how jagged the scar. The reflection of the skies on the water made it milky and obscure. Mallory saw ice gathering on the edges like a cataract on an aging eye.

"I haven't seen this side of the lake in the morning in a long time," he said.

She looked up, worried that the view was bringing up bad memories, but his face was still passive. Mallory had yet to visit Joel's house. Their dates had all been in public places or in the forest. The attraction between her and Joel had been so strong from the moment of their first kiss. She couldn't trust herself to be alone with him until she was sure she could handle having sex with another man. Last night had proved to be worth waiting for.

"So you and Kylie both live with your father?"

"Sure do. Henry too. But we don't share rooms or anything," Joel said wryly before his tone changed to a more serious one. "After Sean died, my mom and dad asked us all if we wanted to build our own cabins on the property. His property's the same size as yours, one hundred acres right on the lake, a bit west of here. You might have seen his place right on the point."

Mallory remembered the large log cabin she had seen, jutting out toward the lake like a lighthouse. The name of Joel's brother hung in the air between them. It was the first time he had mentioned Sean since their discussion about Cynthia. She spoke carefully.

"It must have been so hard for them to lose a son."

"Yeah, it was, so we all agreed to it right away. He said it made my mom feel better, having us close. He protected her."

"Sounds like it."

He drummed his fingers on the countertop instead of elaborating. Mallory sensed that the conversation was making him agitated, so she offered him an out.

"We don't have to keep talking about it."

"No, it's okay."

"Do you find it difficult to be here?"

Joel took a deep, quick breath while Mallory held hers. Graham would have deflected the question immediately. He had hated it when Mallory tried to explore anything emotional. She readied herself for Joel to snap at her. Instead, he met her eyes.

"Yes, but I'm happy you've made this your home," he said. "It's complicated to remember him."

She wondered if it was possible for death to be simple. "How so?"

"Sean was . . . a difficult man. He drank a lot. Sometimes he got violent, not only with Suzanne but with me too. He was always looking for a fight. I worried about him getting mixed up in something he couldn't handle. After he died, it took me a long time to stop feeling guilty about the fact that there was a part of me that was relieved."

"I know exactly what you mean," Mallory said.

The kitchen seemed to brighten with their shared understanding. Both she and Joel had been left behind to deal with the burden of their fraught relationships. Joel ran his hands through his hair, and Mallory could nearly feel his fingertips on her scalp as well.

"I'm happy to be here with you, though. It wasn't until this morning that I realized I was sleeping on my own bed. I put it in storage when I moved back to my dad's. It was too big for my new place. But now, I'm back again. It's just like it was when . . . I lived here."

"It's . . . a great bed," Mallory said weakly.

"It's almost like Kylie was trying to set us up from the start."

Mallory laughed as the coffee maker beeped to alert them to the welcome arrival of its contents. She poured them each a cup, adding a dash of milk to hers and keeping his black. As she sipped it, she became secure enough to ask him a question that had been on her mind since her conversation with Suzanne.

"Why didn't Logan follow up on the wrongful death case after Sean died?"

"He and Sean didn't always see eye to eye on everything," Joel said. "One of the Turner officers who was working the case let it slip that the two of them had words with each other right before Sean was killed."

"Logan fought with Sean?"

"Like I said, Sean could be difficult," Joel said as he took a large gulp of his coffee. Mallory realized her curiosity had broken the pact between them, but Joel's tone was still easy. "These days, I rarely let myself wonder about what anyone in town does besides me and the most beautiful woman I've ever seen. It's a lot easier to live in this town that way."

He moved toward her for a kiss. His mouth was warm and tasted like roasted coffee beans. He pulled away and finished the last of his cup.

"I'm going to be late if I don't get on the road now, and if I am, I've got to buy Henry lunch."

"You sure you can't duck out and come to the Freeze Feast with me this morning?"

"Sadly, no. Henry will be there to keep the peace, but I'm scheduled to meet with a citizens group this morning in Turner. They're forming a block watch, and they need some advice."

"Okay. Who am I to stand in the way of civilian policing?" she said with a smile.

His eyes glinted with laughter and desire. "Listen, why don't you come over to our house for dinner tonight? I know my dad would love to get to know you better. You play your cards right and I'll even give you a tour of my place."

"How can I resist that?"

"See you at seven," he said with a wink that was enough to make her toes curl.

After he left, she took her almost full mug of coffee to the plate-glass window. As she watched out the window, snowflakes began to fall on the gray landscape, like a shot across the bow from winter itself. The lake swallowed them in a way the ground could not. Before Mallory's eyes, the shore of the lake began to turn white. Her mind wandered as she watched the flakes accumulate. The snow danced across the sky toward the earth, then knitted together on the ground like a thousand tiny stitches in a wool blanket. Their collective presence bleached all color from the world. Mallory's view became a stark study in black and white.

She tore herself away when the feeling of isolation became too great. The sight of the snow-swept shore made her feel like she was on an iceberg surrounded by a deep, black lake. She shook off her alienation and made her way down the hall to shower. It was time to join her friends in celebrating, rather than mourning, the change of the season.

CHAPTER TWENTY

Mallory parked at Tuck's Fuel and Food, then continued on foot down the trail between it and Betty's office. The snow was still falling hard enough to make her wonder if she could manage to get a run in that afternoon before her dinner with the Shine family. Given the way everyone had been warning her about the severity of winter around there, she figured she may have to find a form of exercise that she could do in cold weather. The thought of pursuing an indoor workout plan with Joel made her smile. What she was considering might not burn as many calories as a long run, but it would certainly keep her mood high.

The first thing Mallory saw when she stepped onto the beach was a banner whipping in the wind that had kicked up from the lake. Sand flew through the air with the snowflakes, and she struggled to close the distance between herself and the small group huddled under a white tent that contained a folding table. The uneven ground below its rickety legs made it list to the left, but no one involved in the feast seemed to notice or mind. Logan was standing by a small hot plate, flipping pancakes onto white Styrofoam plates covered with flecks of dirt. She spotted Suzanne, Betty, and Henry in the midst with two men she had never met before. Henry was bolting down the pancakes while keeping an eye on the ropes holding the banner. The others were chatting softly.

As soon as she got close, he called out a hello. "Mallory. I heard you're coming to dinner tonight."

She was pleased that Joel had shared it with Henry so quickly. "I'm looking forward to it."

"Grab a plate, dear. Logan's got plenty of pancakes for you." Betty shuffled her toward the older man while Henry took a step toward the flapping banner to inspect it more closely. Under her breath she whispered, "Keep an eye out for Suzanne's new friends. Apparently they're in the area for deer hunting. She met them at Logan's last night. They all stayed quite late from what I heard."

Betty raised her eyebrows to indicate her disapproval, then shooed Mallory toward Logan, who slid two pancakes onto her plate. They smelled sweetly artificial, and Mallory spotted a large bag of pancake mix beside a bowl. She edged off a piece and bit down. It crunched in her teeth.

"Frederich told me you enjoyed his book," Logan said. "You should stop by after the feast. I have a few more items you might be interested in."

Betty scolded him with a gentle pat on his arm that suggested affection between them. "Now, now, Logan. She's here to celebrate the freeze, not to buy anything."

Mallory smiled gratefully at the woman, though she still wasn't sure exactly what the feast was intended to do.

"What are we celebrating today? I hope it's not a polar bear swim," she joked. Instead of laughing, Logan and Betty stared at her in disbelief.

Betty answered first. "Swim? Well, I wouldn't recommend that in this lake."

Mallory was taken aback by the dread in her voice.

"I thought it was safe?" Mallory said.

"It's not," Betty said. Her mouth was set in an expression Mallory could only call prim. She seemed offended at the very suggestion of something so improper. "This feast is to honor the power in the lake. We must respect it. When the lake freezes over, it brings a peace to

McNamara, a closing of the year. We are here to acknowledge that, even if others are just here for pancakes."

She swept her eye over Suzanne and her two friends. Mallory wasn't sure how to respond to Betty's grand statements. Logan seemed to sense her discomfort.

"There's a lot to get used to around here, Mallory, but it will make sense soon enough. I know they all tease me, but I'm not selling this monster stuff for my bank account. It's a kind of offering. A tribute."

"To the monster?"

"To the power," Betty said, nodding firmly.

"I didn't realize that you both . . . believe in the stories," Mallory said carefully.

"We would be absolute fools not to," Logan said solemnly.

Betty clasped her hand and squeezed. Her skin was as soft as fine linen. "But you know that. You read Frederich's book. We must honor what's here."

Mallory worked up the courage to ask about something delicate. "I don't mean to be rude, but I did read about Dean Halloway. His death seemed suspicious. Do you think the monster killed your nephew?"

The folds around Logan's mouth deepened into a frown. "Let's just say there have been plenty of deaths along this shore. Like the recent drowning right over there. Impossible to explain. Unsolved. Mysterious."

Mallory grew cold as the man met her eyes. She and Joel had a tacit understanding not to speak about the death of Cynthia Rooney. It was disconcerting to hear her death bandied about by Logan, but his expression was placid and unaccusing. It seemed the drowning of Graham's cousin was just one more myth to add to the folklore of Loss Lake.

"Well now, this food is going to go to waste without somebody to eat it." Betty's voice was saccharine again. She turned to the rest of the group at the far end of the table with a loud call, pitched to be heard over the gathering wind.

"There's plenty more pancakes, everyone. Come one, come all. We don't call it a feast for nothing."

She placed a light hand under Mallory's elbow and guided her a step away from Logan.

"He doesn't like to talk about his nephew much. He cared for Dean very deeply. It was difficult for Logan to say goodbye."

Mallory realized how clumsy her question had been. Of course Dean's death had been hard on his uncle. Still, she had one more question that she hoped Betty would not consider too rude. She knew it was best to let sleeping dogs lie as Joel had cautioned her, but her analytical nature made it difficult to leave a loose end untied.

"The only reason I ask is because, after Dean died, Logan became the beneficiary of any settlement that might have come out of the Turner Dam accident. Suzanne told me it was what Sean was working on when he died. Was Logan involved in the lawsuit?"

Betty's face hardened, and Mallory worried she had overstepped. Just then, Henry responded to Betty's call, brandishing his empty plate. Logan piled on another stack of pancakes, and Betty laughed merrily. Mallory sensed that she was happy to dodge her question.

"Henry Shine, I've never known anyone with an appetite like you in all my life."

Henry laughed. "It's cold out here. I've got to keep my heat in somehow, especially if I'm going to try one of those ice pops Logan made."

He pointed toward the edge of the table with his fork. Mallory saw an open cooler with a dozen or so handmade popsicles on display. There was no need for ice, as the temperature of the air was hovering close to zero degrees. A hand-lettered sign read "Monster Pops $5." Mallory took a step closer and saw that inside each cone of ice was a molded plastic figure of a monster. Again, it was gray and wormy, similar to other versions of the monster she had seen from Logan, but notable in this particular application given how deeply unappetizing it made the offering. Even if she had desired a frozen treat in freezing conditions, she wouldn't have picked a Popsicle that looked like it contained a preserved slug.

"Want one?" Logan said.

"No, she doesn't. Hey, Mallory," Suzanne interrupted. The two hunters had left her side, and Mallory saw them stumbling down the path back to Main Street. Mallory guessed that now that their bellies were full, they were ready to sleep off the effects of the night before. Since Suzanne's eyes looked as fuzzy as her syllables sounded, Mallory hoped she would make a similar choice. Instead, she lurched toward Logan. "Two pancakes. But no monster pops, okay? It's bad enough that you try to sell that junk all over town. But not my gas station, hey, Mal? I made sure of it. I was like, come on, we don't need more plastic shit everywhere. Right?"

Logan spoke affably despite Suzanne's insults. "Sure thing."

Betty tsked under her breath as Henry squared his shoulders.

"And then it's probably time to call it a night, right, Suzanne?"

"I'll call it a night when I feel like it, Henry." She drew his name out unnecessarily.

She held out her plate to Logan, then began to eat a pancake with her bare hands. After a few bites, she wandered toward the cooler and set down her food so she could pick up two snow globes.

"Like, what even are these, Logan? Why do we pretend there's something in the lake? There's no flipping monster here. Just a bunch of evil people. Right, Henry?"

"Cool it, Suzanne," Henry warned.

"Or what?"

She shook the two snow globes toward each other mockingly, but her movements were misjudged and the two collided. Mallory's jaw dropped as the thin glass shattered upon impact. Water and glass and a thread of blood flowed from Suzanne's hands. Her eyes widened; then Mallory heard the snap of a rope behind her. The banner cracked violently as the wind pulled it loose. Its length thrashed toward them. Mallory ducked, then rushed to Suzanne to help stem the bleeding. Henry and Logan tried to secure the rope as the banner kicked and twisted in the wind. The waves of the lake were cresting with caps as curled as an elderly fingernail. The entire scene had become menacing enough to make Mallory's throat tight, but she fought her panic and brought her training to mind as she turned Suzanne's hand over. There were several cuts, one deep enough to look like it still contained a shard of glass.

"I need to clean this wound. I've got a first aid kit in my car," Mallory said.

"I'll come with you," Betty said, taking the stumbling woman's other elbow. Suzanne's skin was the same bleached gray as the low, heavy clouds above them.

"Get her home." Henry grimaced as he tightened his grip around one of the ropes tied to the banner. It snapped again as the wind gusted, which seemed like a warning, so Mallory hustled the two women toward the trail. As they walked, the snow began to come down harder, falling fast enough to obscure her view. It seemed as though there wasn't enough space between the flakes to breathe, like the snow would soon fall fast enough to bury them. She felt nearly suffocated by the eerie press of the storm. Despite Logan and Betty's intentions, Mallory wasn't sure if the Freeze Feast had honored something supernatural or invoked it.

CHAPTER
TWENTY-ONE

The storm eased around noon, shortly after Mallory dropped Suzanne off at her trailer with instructions to sleep. Back home, she made a cup of tea and moved to the front window to watch the snowflakes turn to drops of water on the eaves above the large window as she stared at the lake. The temperature had risen, and the heavy wind was scattering the melting snow across the beach. Despite her knowledge of what had happened to Sean in the spot in which she was standing, it was the place in her home where she thought best. She was troubled by the conflict between Logan and Betty's admonishments and Joel's memories of swimming in the lake with his brothers and sister when they were young. Had the two older people built up the danger in their own minds to make sense of what had happened to Logan's nephew? Or was Loss Lake really so perilous? The idea of a large body of water that no one swam in filled her with sadness.

Though her own parents hadn't bothered to plan family vacations, she had loved Graham's stories of his annual summer trips to the cottage with his family and cousins. Graham, Cynthia, and her older sister, Sadie, had been close as children and teenagers. Graham had albums of pictures bathed in the orange-yellow light of 1980s photography. Once he had confided that the lake cottage had been the site of his first kiss—with Cynthia. He had laughed off Mallory's disgust at the idea of him making out with his relative.

"Oh, Mallory. It was an innocent kiss. You didn't have brothers or sisters or close cousins. It's a different kind of relationship, especially when you're a kid. It's not like we were in love with each other. It was more like putting on a play. Don't make it weird."

But it had been weird, especially when she saw the way Cynthia had acted after his death, like something had been left unfinished between them. She distracted herself by leafing through Frederich's book again, but the dense prose failed to offer any answers.

Hours later, by the time Joel's headlights flashed in the window of the front room, the snow had almost fully melted, leaving behind a cold damp that worked its way under her skin as she stepped from her house to his car. He kissed her and she settled into the passenger seat. He smiled at her as he revved the engine.

"You look pretty enough to make me feel like a teenager, Ms. Dent."

"Are you sure it's not the fact that you're bringing me home to your father?"

"Maybe. But that lipstick isn't helping me calm down."

As he pulled back onto the main road, they chatted about the Freeze Feast disaster. At the intersection where Suzanne's trailer lolled on the corner, she uttered a silent hope that Suzanne had sobered up enough to take care of her hand. Joel signaled right. This was the first time Mallory had driven away from town instead of toward it. She clasped one hand in the other to calm her nerves. Despite her teasing, she too felt the tremor of adolescent nerves. Jonathan Shine had seemed to offer his tacit approval of their date the night before at the harvest festival, but this was the first time she was going to be formally escorted into his home.

They followed the line of the dark forest west. The edges of Joel's headlights blurred into the darkness as they drove along. A driveway appeared that looked identical to hers, and they turned up it. The road grew steeper and narrower as they followed it. She had glanced at the map in Frederich's book to glean that the Shine property was almost a mirror image of hers: a long, rectangular-ish piece of land with a thick band of forest lining the front and a long stretch of lakeshore along the back. Unlike hers, however, the land here rose in elevation on the northwestern edge to form a granite cliff above Loss Lake, where she had seen the house. In the narrow beam of the lights from the truck, the trees loomed in front of them, almost appearing to lunge forward as they bounced along the bumpy road. She wondered if Carlotta ever pestered the Shine family to allow her to hunt on their land. The thought of it made her feel uncomfortable. Would the woman have the gall to make a request about guns to Sean's family? It was hard to put it past her, given the persistence she had shown with Mallory. Half a mile up the driveway, Mallory saw another dirt road veering out to the left. Joel told her it was the turn to the rest of the property, where the other cabins had been built.

As they pulled up to a large log house with windows lit up like eyes full of laughter, Mallory rolled her shoulders to loosen them. Once stopped, she gathered the two bottles of wine she had brought with her and exited the truck. Despite her nerves, she was looking forward to seeing Kylie and Joel with their family. She hoped this night would lay the blueprint for many more to follow. Joel held out his arm as he came around the truck, and they walked together to the log home perched on the granite beachhead. Though the ground was nearly bare of snow, the fallen leaves had been frozen by the earlier precipitation. They popped beneath her feet like shards of glass until they reached the stone-laid path that hugged the edge of the steep slope.

Over the cliff, she could see the glow of her kitchen light about two miles down the beach. It was both comforting and disconcerting to realize her home was so visible from the Shine home. The uneven rhythm of waves crashing on the beach below provided a dramatic soundtrack to their movement. The force of the wind made Loss Lake sound as powerful as an ocean. When they reached the short staircase that formed the entrance to the log house, their footsteps echoed on the wide wooden steps. She paused to look at the intricate construction of the exterior walls. Each huge log had been notched carefully to make room for the one laid below it, like the wood was cradling itself. It gave an impression of solidity and comfort. Joel pushed open the front door, and they walked into an entryway that led into a large sunken sitting room. Kylie was seated at the bottom of the small staircase that led down to the rounded seating area, speaking happily to her dad. She raised her hand and cried a hello as Mallory and Joel made their way over to her.

"Welcome to our home," Jonathan said with an extended hand. Mallory reached out with a thank-you. He shook her hand once, firmly.

"You drink whiskey?" he asked.

"That sounds perfect," she said. Jonathan nodded to Joel, who stepped over to a bar table set up by the fireplace on the far wall. The wood crackled invitingly as Mallory took a seat beside Kylie.

"Your daughter did a fantastic job in the play last night," she said with a smile.

Kylie beamed in a combination of amusement and pride. "It was a big moment, for sure. We've heard a lot about it today. Watch out, Broadway. She's pretty tuckered out today, though. Despite her best effort to stay up for you, I had to put her to bed an hour ago."

Mallory laughed. "Next time," she said.

"I'll tell her you said so," Kylie replied.

Joel returned with two tumblers full of amber liquid, and Jonathan raised his glass. "To new friends," he said.

The toast was as warm as Mallory's first sip of whiskey. Her shoulders relaxed as the fire danced across Jonathan's face. She was grateful to be in the company of people she liked so much.

"So you're from Vancouver?" Jonathan asked.

"Yes. I was born there. This is the first time I've lived anywhere else in my life," Mallory said.

"How are you adjusting to our small town?"

"She loves it!" Kylie declared, elbowing Mallory gently in the ribs.

"At least now that she can buy coffee," Joel said. Kylie mock-glared at him as Mallory answered Jonathan.

"I do love it," she said. "I feel like I'm finally home."

Mallory was immediately embarrassed at her sentimentality and glanced at Joel to see if he was rolling his eyes, the way Graham would when she got overly emotional, but Joel's face was neutral. Jonathan nodded once in understanding.

"That sounds like what my wife, Dee, used to tell me. She was a city girl too, until I convinced her to come to the wilderness. Of course, she still liked to go back from time to time. She said she could never find the right pair of shoes in Turner, and she was very particular about shoes."

His eyes softened as he thought of her. Mallory experienced a pang of unexpected guilt. Betty Barber had said Dee died five years ago. She wondered if she would think of Graham as fondly after so many years had passed. Especially as Joel slipped his hand over hers, making her fingers tingle as much as the back of her throat.

Then the front door flung open with a gust of cold air. She couldn't help but smile as Henry bounded into the room like a puppy, not bothering to take off his jacket. His cheeks were even redder than they had been in the blustering wind of Freeze Feast. He grinned when he saw her, then enveloped her in a hug that smelled like winter.

"Mallory! We meet again! It's been so long!"

Mallory went along with the joke. "Have you missed me?"

"Desperately," he said with a theatrical bow. His over-the-top flirting was something only a younger brother could get away with. Joel cuffed him lightly on the shoulder as Henry rose.

"Now that Henry's home from work, we can eat," the older man said.

Jonathan's words seemed to cue up her senses. Mallory smelled roast chicken, and her stomach rumbled in anticipation. The three siblings and Mallory followed him out of the sunken living room to the back of the house, where a long cedar table ran the length of the east wall. The wood was the color of honey. Two benches, each carved out of single logs that had been planed down to make a flat surface, stretched alongside it. She couldn't resist touching the tabletop. It was as smooth and warm as running her hand down Joel's back. Jonathan noticed her tracing the length of the table before she sat.

"A remnant of my logging days," he said as Kylie, Henry, and Joel brought the food to the table in a routine choreographed by time. "I used to bring home the lumber that the mill couldn't use, if it was waterlogged or too knotted up for their saws. I hated the idea of wood being wasted. Nothing is a mistake."

She realized that Jonathan must have carved the elegant chairs at the back of Kylie's store as well. Mallory smiled in response to his statement, though disloyalty clenched her stomach. The idea of everything happening for a reason meant that fate had led her to McNamara. It was exactly what she had been thinking since the first time Joel had kissed her, but admitting that her husband's death had been what sent her down the road she was always supposed to be on wasn't something she could say out loud. At least not yet.

As they placed the last of the serving dishes on the table, the rest of the group sat down. Mallory was pleased to have Joel slide in beside her, close enough so their legs touched, like he had always been there. Her mouth watered as she looked at the platter of roasted chicken, the stack of golden corn on the cob, the perfectly smooth brown gravy, and the inviting bowl of green salad. Comfort food, which was perfect, given that she was now comfortable enough to crack a joke as Henry dived into a mountain of mashed potatoes.

"Thank goodness you arrived," she said. "Joel was convinced you had run off with Ms. Becker."

Though she had met McNamara's police secretary only once, Joel had told her that Henry had a crush on her.

"Oh, is that right? Is that what the old biddies are saying about me?"

Mallory laughed and looked sideways at Joel. "Well, one of them at least."

"I don't know what the latest gossip is about you, Henry, but I did see you taking an awfully long time to help her issue those dog licenses."

"I think she's lovely," Kylie said, her eyes sparkling as she took her younger brother's side. "She has a fondness for extra-dark chocolate, if you ever need to know."

"That is information I'll be storing away in this steel trap of mine," he said with a wink. "Not because I need it right now, but one never knows when tidbits such as those will come in handy."

"I'm a lucky sergeant to have such a dedicated deputy," said Joel.

"Indeed you are." Henry leaned forward with his elbows on the table. His expression turned serious as he looked back and forth between Mallory and Joel. "Unfortunately, I was late for a reason that's a lot less pleasant than a certain Ms. Becker."

Joel picked up on Henry's tone and responded in kind. "What do you mean?"

"Mallory, I hate to tell you in this way, but as I was driving back home, I took a cruise around your property as part of my rounds. And who did I find but Carlotta and Suzanne walking around your fence line. Both of them had rifles. They were trying to get in."

Mallory was grateful that Joel had helped her level out the high ground he had used to get into the property the day they had met in the forest. Because of him, she knew the property was secure. Still, her confidence didn't stop irritation from nipping at her at Carlotta's relentlessness.

"Will that woman never give up?"

"Probably not. If I'm honest, it made me furious to see them like that."

Kylie looked at her younger brother. Worry painted the faint lines on her face with a deeper brush. "Are you okay?" she asked.

Henry shook his head. "Don't bring up ancient history, Kylie. I was doing my job."

"Did you give them a warning?" Jonathan asked.

His eyes were full of concern for the possibility of his son reliving his past trauma as well, but behind it, Mallory saw something that looked like anger. She remembered Suzanne's slurred accusations in the bar and Kylie's explanation. She knew she wasn't the only one at the table thinking about Sean.

"I did. Carlotta was pissed, but she's lucky she didn't get the full trespassing charge."

"Good," Jonathan said. "But be careful, Henry. That goes for all of you. We all know the danger of guns being in places they don't belong."

Mallory wasn't sure if she was imagining it, but she thought she saw a sheen in his eyes. The idea of Jonathan being overcome by the memory of the tragic death of his son was more than she could bear.

"Is there anything I can do? The last thing I want is for anyone else to get hurt the way Sean did."

At the mention of his name, each of the four people around her stiffened. Even Joel wouldn't look in her direction, and she realized she had broken the unspoken agreement they had again. This time, he didn't seem so willing to forgive. She kicked herself for her inability to leave a problem unsolved. He didn't want her to mention Sean, just like she didn't want him to mention Cynthia. For the first time that evening, she became an outsider as Kylie met the eyes of both her brothers, then her father, before turning to Mallory.

"We try not to mention his name in the house," Kylie said. Her voice was close to a whisper, as if her father wouldn't be able to hear the words she uttered next. "It's too hard for Dad."

"Of course," Mallory said, cursing herself for letting her curiosity overcome her common sense. She had to remember that some things were best left unsaid.

CHAPTER
TWENTY-TWO

Joel's headlights painted white lines across the front of her house as they returned with full stomachs and the lingering happiness of spending an evening in pleasant company. After her faux pas, the Shines had worked hard to make her feel just as welcome as she had upon arrival. Now it was late. Joel shifted into park and looked in her direction. She moved over and leaned into his warm chest, feeling overcome by a wave of anticipated loneliness.

"Are you sure you can't stay?" she said when they ended their good-bye kiss.

"I wish I could, darling, but I've got an early meeting in Turner. So early that I shouldn't even be up this late," Joel replied. "Someone kept me awake last night with her feminine wiles."

He punctuated his sentence with a yawn that made Mallory laugh.

"Okay, I get it. Sweet dreams."

"Tomorrow?"

"Absolutely."

She slipped out of the truck, bracing herself for the stark difference between the cozy cab and the cold, dark night. Sure enough, the air was frigid enough to feel solid in her nostrils. Joel's truck growled behind her like a protective animal as she made her way up the path to her front door. When she opened her door and turned back to Joel with a wave of farewell, he gunned his engine to leave. The sound was comforting and startling as it ricocheted off the trees behind them. She watched the truck lumber down her driveway, its taillights bouncing in the blackness, leaving her alone.

Once inside, the house was nearly as cold as the darkness had been, and she scolded herself for forgetting to turn on the heat, though she was grateful that she had left the kitchen and foyer lights blazing. She was uneasy entering the empty house at night, but she dismissed her anxiety as nothing more than the remnants of the whiskey and her ill-advised mention of Sean. The group had easily moved on from her gaffe, but the thought of the way she had nearly undone her agreement with Joel had lodged in her mind like a fish bone at the back of her throat. The sooner she could accept the history of the house in its entirety, the sooner it would feel like her home. She told herself to let go of her mistake. It had been a long day, but a good one. She knew she had made a good impression on Joel's father. As she was leaving, he told her that she was welcome anytime. Over his shoulder, Kylie and Henry had mugged their agreement with exaggerated thumbs-up.

She slipped off her shoes and walked straight to the thermostat beside the plate-glass window, greedily cranking the dial to the left until the comforting hum of forced air began. With a sigh of pleasure, she stepped directly onto the heat register and let the tiny air currents swirl around the soles of her feet. The warmth coaxed ticks and creaks out of the house as it filled the room, reminding her of the soothing sounds of the Shines' fireplace, which had underscored their after-dinner conversation in the main room. It had started with Henry asking her eagerly if she had yet caught sight of the monster in Loss Lake.

"No, I haven't," she had said with an indulgent smile.

Seated between Joel and Henry on the long couch that faced the fire, full of good food and easy conversation, she was content and calm, though it was evident that even the waning hours of the evening were not enough to dampen Henry's exuberance. He exuded excitement like a small dog being taught to sit still. Joel placed his hand on hers and squeezed gently.

"Don't worry, you will," Henry said.

She laughed. His words indicated a longing for the event she didn't share. "I'm not sure I'm looking forward to it."

"As it should be," Jonathan said from a large armchair close to the stone fireplace. His face was lit by the flickering flames. His serious tone changed the mood. Betty and Logan's certainty about the monster flashed through her mind, and she wondered how many people in McNamara really did believe the monster was lying in wait in the depths of the lake and whether Jonathan Shine was one of them.

"Dad saw the monster," Henry said. "He was one of the first people here who did. He used to tell me about it when I was a kid."

Mallory remembered the story he had told her the first night they met about the despised man his father had known who had disappeared before the eyes of his crew. The gravitas and nobility of Jonathan Shine made it more difficult to dismiss.

"Only because you begged him for the same story every night," Kylie teased.

"I witnessed something that was unexplainable," Jonathan said with a warning deepening his voice further. "I've never called it a monster. But a man died in front of me that day in a way that has troubled me ever since."

Henry looked down as if chastened, but the gentle nudge of his elbow against Mallory's ribs was enough to indicate that he was nothing of the sort. She sensed Joel's eyes on her, and she turned her head to see a questioning look on his face, making sure she was okay. She leaned into him, touched at his concern.

"What do you think happened?" she found herself asking.

Jonathan fixed his eyes on her. Even in the half-light, she could see they contained a depth of emotion. Sadness, uncertainty, and something that looked like fear. She regretted her question, hoping she hadn't offended the man with her curiosity or, worse, dredged up another memory he didn't want to relive. Again. But then, Jonathan's expression opened up, as if he had decided she was worthy of knowing about his life.

"There had been a storm the day before, and another one was coming in fast. That wasn't unusual for the shoreline in October 1973. That year, we worked through the rain all autumn long. We were wet and cold so often I hardly remembered what it felt like to be dry. But on the day I'm talking about, it wasn't raining. The air was dank and thick, like whatever was coming wasn't good. I don't know if that's what made him do it, that feeling that hung over us, but I never knew why he did anything. He was a terrible boss and a worse man."

Mallory recalled what Henry had said about the poor man's wife as Jonathan paused in thought. When he began again, his voice was low and rumbled in his chest.

"In any case, he decided to take a swim. Maybe someone dared him, maybe he thought it would impress us, or maybe he needed a bath. When he jumped into the water, everything got quiet. I stopped what I was doing and walked down to the edge of the shore, and I wasn't alone. We all felt it, that oddness. The farther he swam out, the stronger that feeling got. Then the calm water started to bubble. Just a little at first. It wasn't a wave or an eddy. It looked like a whirlpool, but it felt like something else. Something I can't explain."

Jonathan rubbed his hand across his jaw. He seemed to be miles away from them, stuck in the past. The fire snapped and shifted, one log tumbling onto the others as its core burned through. The sound seemed to jolt Jonathan out of his memories, and he cleared his throat.

When he spoke again, there was no trace of the uncertainty that had framed the story.

"We listed the death as a logging accident, and maybe that's all it was. The water around a mill yard is unpredictable. Logs get wedged underneath the surface and come shooting up in strange ways. Anyway. It's best to be cautious, Mallory. Don't swim unless you're prepared to face the unexpected."

His advice about entering Loss Lake made her feel more conflicted than she had before.

"I'm not much of a swimmer, and these stories are not inspiring me to pick up the sport."

"That's wise," Jonathan said. His expression was unreadable, but his words were kind.

Joel had risen from the couch. "It's good for Mallory to know our history. Now, I think it's about time for me to call it a night."

Jonathan stood as well. His tall frame silhouetted against the fireplace behind him obscured his features and made him look like a shadow.

"There's one more thing. I'm still not saying I believe in a monster, but the night of the flood, something unforeseen came into this valley. Betty, Logan, Carlotta, and everyone else who lived through it remembers the way the animals went quiet before the water came down. Poor Alice was the only one in the direct path of the water. Sometimes I think that her death drew something impossible to understand to this valley. I don't know what was unleashed that night, but I do know that Loss Lake began in a way that nothing ever should."

Jonathan's children and Mallory all paused for a beat. What he was saying added another layer of depth to Logan's and Betty's earlier words. She had never considered that Alice's death could be the key to the mystery of McNamara.

"I spoke with Betty and Logan this morning at the Freeze Feast. They both seemed completely convinced that the monster is real."

"Are you sure he wasn't trying to sell you those crappy snow globes?" Henry joked.

No one laughed. Only the crackle of the fire responded to Henry's words. Joel cleared his throat pointedly.

"Now, now, Henry. We've always been taught to respect our elders," Joel said. "But this is a conversation we can finish on another night. It's about time for me to get this lovely woman home. Early day tomorrow."

Joel and she had said their polite goodbyes. On the ride back, he hadn't mentioned anything further about the monster, and she had followed his lead, though she was interested to know what he thought. It seemed safer for the time being to let Joel lead the conversation rather than risk saying the wrong thing again.

But now, Jonathan's words lingered as she rubbed the sole of her foot absentmindedly against the ridges of the vent. Unlike Betty and Logan, Jonathan didn't seem to believe definitively in a monster. Yet there had been something in his voice that indicated he still struggled to make sense of what had happened to the man in the logging camp and all the deaths that had occurred since. Mallory contemplated leaving her foot-warming station to fix herself a cup of tea to calm her mind before bed when another sound edged past the low-level whir of the heating system.

Unlike the quiet murmurs of the house, the noise was rough, jarring, and repetitive. It sounded like footsteps on icy ground. Mallory froze like a frightened rabbit, though she knew her stillness couldn't save her. She held her breath, willing the disturbance to be imagined, a figment of her fatigue and her incomplete confidence in being alone in the house. Instead, it came again, slower and lower this time, like the movement was being adjusted to avoid detection. The decrease in volume was more unsettling than the louder sound, which could have been made by a large animal walking by. She had to assume the presence moving toward the plate-glass window at the back of her house was human. Someone was outside who didn't want to be heard. And they were coming closer.

Crunch. Crunch. Crunch. The footsteps continued. Mallory felt as if the pebbles under the intruder's feet were being lodged under her skin. She looked at the large window. Why hadn't she made a trip to Turner to buy curtains? Within seconds, she would be visible. Exposed. The night sucked away her ability to see anything but a distorted reflection of the chandelier swimming in an oily pool of blackness. From outside, it was different. Whatever—whoever—was outside would have a perfect view of the room. Of her. The light was supposed to protect her. Now it was her greatest threat.

Crunch. Crunch. Crunch. They were close now, at the corner of the house. Only one more step and there she'd be, paralyzed in the corner, waiting like prey.

Blood roared in her ears. She lunged for the light switch, hammering the old-fashioned levers down with the flat of her hand hard enough to make her wince. Suddenly, she was in the darkness. Her breath came fast and hard as she moved quickly to the back door, twisting the stubborn dead bolt into place. The lock protested, then thudded as it finally hit home. Mallory paused. The footsteps had stopped. Had the intruder left? Or were they biding their time? Then Mallory remembered.

She hadn't locked the front door.

The footsteps began again, as if the prowler could read her thoughts. Quicker this time. Mallory shrank into the shadows as a dark shape moved past the glass window. *Crunch, crunch, crunch.* The person moved to the back door. The only light in the room was the clock display on the stove in the kitchen, beaming steadily through the gap between the countertop and cupboard.

The footsteps stopped. In the dimness, Mallory saw the round knob turn an inch to the left, then an inch to the right, squeaking slightly. Panic clenched her throat, but she forced her shaking legs to move toward the front door. With each controlled step, her muscles quivered. She edged her way back through the dining room, into the foyer. The pounding of her heart blocked out the sounds from outside as she moved. Finally, she was a step away from the door. Her mind screamed that the intruder must have raced around the house, but she kept her movements slow. She had no gun, no weapon, no training as a fighter. Her only way to stay safe was to stay hidden. *You can do this,* she thought. With one smooth move, she stretched forward and turned the dead bolt. Her lungs compressed in relief as she stepped away from the door. She strained her ears. Her eyes fixed on the doorknob as she anticipated another ghostlike rotation. A second passed, then two. Mallory heard her own heartbeat. Nothing happened.

She counted to sixty, then one hundred and twenty, then all the way to three hundred, pausing after every minute to listen for the sound of someone outside. She couldn't tell if the silence was an end or a beginning. Finally, she let herself breathe. The blood began to flow freely through her body again, and Mallory's fingertips tingled with its renewed presence. She made her way back to the dining room to try to determine whether she was actually alone. She kept her steps soft in case she was not.

In the moments she had been standing at the front door, the moon had come out from behind the clouds, and a trail of night light now spread across the floor of the living room. The faint illumination was enough to allow her to see there was something different about the plate-glass window. Her view of the dark waters of the lake was now partially obscured by a dark square in the center of the glass. It looked like a note. She sucked in her breath so sharply it hurt. She knew she had to turn on the light. She had to see whatever or whoever was there. She forced herself to the standing lamp by the armchair, half crouching behind it as the plastic ridges of the switch dug into the pads of her fingers. She steeled herself, then turned the dial to its brightest setting, blinking against the white glare that filled the room. She retrained her eyes to the glass, half expecting an evil face to be smeared up against it, hungry for just this moment, when they could finally see exactly where she was and how they would get her.

But instead of a human or monster, all Mallory saw was a piece of paper with four block letters crowding each other to form a word that spread from edge to edge.

BANG.

CHAPTER
TWENTY-THREE

The darkness turned to dawn like a healing bruise. Mallory had tossed and turned for hours in a state in between sleep and waking. Her sheet was twisted into a rope under her feet as she rose to a seated position. It was too early to call Joel, but she had left it for long enough. She needed to tell him about the intruder. Last night, she had struggled with whether to wake him in the middle of the night when she knew he had an early morning. Eventually, she had decided to struggle through the long, dark hours alone. Every minute of her insomnia had driven home how important he had become to her. Only he could explain how something so threatening could happen in a place where she was supposed to be safe. Besides, he was the sergeant. He would know how to investigate this properly. She couldn't stop thinking of Henry's description of chasing Carlotta and Suzanne from her land prior to arriving home for dinner. Could one of the two women be to blame? Or both? Were they trying to scare her into allowing them access to the forest?

Her stomach heaved in disappointment as the first ring was interrupted by the sharp click that indicated a redirection to his voice mail. *He must be on the road already,* she thought as she let the sound of his recorded voice speak, though she knew it was probably useless to do so. He had warned her that reception could be dicey between Turner and

McNamara. She left a quick message, hoping that her voice sounded calmer than she was, then slid out of bed. She had to see Joel. She had to go to Turner.

She dressed hurriedly in jeans and a thick sweater. She wasn't sure if the chill in her body was coming from the fog that clogged the sky above Loss Lake or the fear that had oozed from her body all night in the form of sour sweat. Once clothed, she walked down the hallway toward the front door. Her heart jumped irregularly in her chest when the back window came into view. She forced herself to examine the paper, which she had decided to leave plastered to the glass the night before. After all, it was evidence. If there was any possibility of finding the person who had done this, she was willing to live with their foul message pasted on her window for the time being.

Upon closer examination, she couldn't find anything conclusively damning. The paper was plain white, standard size, with no smudged fingerprints screaming to be identified. The letters, written in thick black marker, seemed deliberately generic, like the culprit had traced each from a poster hanging in a preschool. She took a few photos of the paper and the window with her phone. Already, the tape had started to peel at the edges as drops of condensation slid alongside it. She swallowed hard when she turned her back on the window, dread creeping up and down her back like the word was watching her. She double-checked the lock on the back door, pulling it hard to ensure the dead bolt would hold, then retrieved her purse from the small table in the foyer before letting herself outside. She locked the door tightly behind her, once again making sure the lock had slid into place.

Once outside, Mallory was surrounded by stillness. The low clouds acted like a cover over a birdcage, muffling the usual songs that came from the trees. The light seemed muted, scared to emit more than the lowest level possible. Mallory couldn't shake the sense that something was following her as she stepped quickly to her car, breaking into a trot when she was a few feet away. Once inside, her rapid breath clouded the windows as her trembling fingers pressed the button for the internal locks. Mallory knew it was irrational, but the sharp click of all four doors being secured was reassuring.

The heater blew cold air until she was halfway down the driveway. At the same time the gusts became warm, a scattering of snowflakes landed on her windshield, disappearing the moment they touched the glass like rocks thrown in a deep lake. Graham used to say that a road always looks different when you're leaving home than when you're returning, which seemed more true as Mallory drove to Turner than it ever had. She barely remembered the turns and bends in the highway she had taken to get to McNamara. It looked unfamiliar enough to make her second-guess whether she was on the right road.

She breathed a sigh of relief that steamed the windshield when she finally saw a highway sign indicating she was on the correct route. As the miles passed, the snowflakes gathered strength, collecting in white lines on the edge of the road. Mallory was too distracted by her worries to register the meaning of the accumulating clouds. Someone had threatened to kill her the same way Sean had died. Despite her unspoken promise to Joel, she had to figure out what his death had to do with her life—and fast.

Once again, she went through the facts. Sean had died from a bullet through the window while reopening an investigation into criminal negligence on behalf of Alice Halloway and her living beneficiaries, which included Logan Carruthers and Carlotta Gray. Suzanne had insinuated that it was why he had been killed, and she had been cagey about Carlotta's and Logan's involvement with the lawsuit. Betty had avoided her question about whether Sean had been working on behalf of Logan. Was she crazy to think that the lawsuit had something to do with Sean's death? After all, Suzanne was hardly the most reliable authority. And who was the plaintiff? She didn't even know who had owned the Turner Dam. Frederich's book had mentioned some of the employees had stayed in McNamara after the collapse. Could one of them have been protecting their former employer?

On the other hand, maybe the threat had nothing to do with Sean at all. Her earlier suspicions about Carlotta reared up again. Carlotta had been increasingly aggravated about Mallory's decision not to allow her to hunt on the land. Henry Shine had seen Carlotta and Suzanne near her house hours before she had heard the prowler. Joel had told her the two of them had a tumultuous relationship and Suzanne was prone to violence. She knew that Carlotta and Suzanne were close. Were the two women capable of issuing a threat like the one taped on her window? Or worse?

Mallory tried to shape the facts into a story with a clear conclusion, but all she could come up with were more questions. She was missing something, and she hoped she would find it in the Turner Public Library.

On the outskirts of Turner, she followed a series of signs to the city center and found herself on a main street that looked like a larger-scale version of McNamara. The storefronts were frosted like gingerbread houses, and Mallory realized that the snow was accumulating quickly. She cruised up and down the street in search of the police station. The fear that had made her bold was now starting to seep from her body like water from a wrung wool garment. All of a sudden she was tired, and she angled into a free parking spot by the side of the road. She pulled out her cell phone and dialed Joel.

No answer again. Mallory left another message, then stepped out of her vehicle. She hadn't eaten breakfast or bothered with coffee. She could pass the time in a coffee shop until Joel called her back and ask around for a local shop that would sell her the thickest curtains she could find. She knew covering the window wouldn't keep her safe, but at least it would leave her less exposed.

As she stepped out of her car, the inch of snow on the ground licked at the frayed stitching of her boots. Her socks became damp immediately, and she shivered into the winter coat that had been sufficient for chilly days in the city but seemed too thin for the current conditions. She was woefully unprepared for the bite of the wind as the snowflakes batted against her face like pestering insects. She looked at the building directly in front of her. A freshly painted sign that read "Turner Public Library" was placed in a whitened lawn. Tufts of grass leaned in her direction, begging not to be engulfed by the falling snow. She decided to enter. She would grab something to eat later. Maybe there was something more she could learn about the history of McNamara that could help her solve the puzzle of Sean's death. She couldn't forget the look in Jonathan Shine's eyes when he had spoken of the night the dam had failed. She wanted to know more about what had happened, and, from what Carlotta and Frederich had said, this might be the only place in the world she could do so.

The Turner Public Library exterior was remarkably similar to its counterpart in McNamara, down to the stain of the brick, but the building was at least twice the size. Inside, the library couldn't have been more different. Unlike the plain yellow walls in McNamara, this library was covered in adornments that Mallory could never imagine Carlotta selecting. In each corner of the entryway, macramé weavings were hung, interspersed with dream catchers, brightly dyed textiles, and Nepalese prayer flags. The library walls were painted a deep shade of orange, evoking album covers and afghan blankets from the 1960s. She scraped her wet boots off on a mat that was emblazoned with a smiling toadstool and made her way into the main room of the library.

Behind the counter was a beaming older man with white hair pushed back from his forehead by a pink tie-dyed scarf.

"I was about to tell you that I'm closing up early. But I've been expecting you, Mallory Dent."

Mallory blinked. Had her reputation really gotten as far as Turner?

"I'm sorry, have we met?"

"Let's just say we have a friend in common, sister." The older gentleman motioned for her to come forward. "I hear you're into history."

He reached under the counter without breaking eye contact with her, then placed a book flat on the counter, keeping his hands pressed against the cover so she couldn't make out the title. Mallory walked closer, feeling both curious and annoyed. Though the man seemed friendly enough, his overly dramatic approach and embroidered chambray shirt made her think they'd soon be talking about chemtrails. The wetness from her boots' leaking seams was beginning to numb her toes, but she tried to be polite.

"I'm so sorry. I feel a little lost."

The older man nodded like she'd said something profound. Now that Mallory was within two feet, she could smell the faint sweetness of pot mixed with patchouli. She wondered if Carlotta had to work with this fellow closely. She experienced an uncharitable longing for a chance to observe their staff meetings.

"We're all a little lost up here," he said. "I'm Wolf. Frederich told me you were coming."

Mallory nearly kicked herself for not realizing which McNamara resident was most likely to be friends with a man like Wolf.

"Of course. He's a lovely man."

"He is indeed."

Mallory smiled as Wolf paused, seeming to need a moment to ponder the depth of his feelings for Frederich.

"Is that book for me?"

Wolf spoke solemnly. "Best book about this area that's ever been written."

He flipped it over, and Mallory hoped her face didn't reflect her disappointment at what she saw. Frederich must have paid for a paperback of his work to be produced in addition to the blue hardcover she had purchased, which was why she hadn't recognized it. This book was less flashy—a simple black cover with the title in white.

"I've already read that one," Mallory said. "But I wouldn't mind—"

"You haven't read this version. Trust me."

Mallory's forehead creased in disbelief, but she accepted the book when he held it out. If it was a reprint, maybe there was something additional in it that would be helpful—a piece of information that could help explain why someone was threatening her.

"You've got ten minutes to read it, but you can't take books out of here without a library card. Sadly, those cards are reserved for Turner residents because even our library systems seem to think we need rules about, like, disseminating information," Wolf said. "I'll be closing early today. I'm out of here, man. This storm is going to hit hard. If you're planning to head back to McNamara, you should get back on the road now."

"Storm?" Mallory had assumed the snow would follow a similar pattern to the day before—flurries in the morning that were nearly melted by the afternoon.

"Oh yeah. This one looks like it's going to hit hard and fast. Sure hope you've got winter tires. These early ones are the worst. They're calling for a foot of snow by noon."

Dread rippled through her stomach like spoiled milk.

"Thanks for letting me know."

She didn't want to stay any longer than necessary to humor the man. He seemed sweet, if overly invested in what was probably only a tweak or two that Frederich had made between his self-published editions, but she dutifully brought the book to a study carrel in the corner. Before opening it, she looked out the window. The sky was now completely white. The snow was falling so quickly it made the landscape move before her eyes like static on a television screen.

She turned back to the book and let it fall open to a page that had been marked with a dog-eared corner. Scrawled notes covered the edges around the typed words. She suspected Wolf was the only person who had examined Frederich's work to such a degree until she looked closer.

The handwriting contained references to legal cases, mostly precedents of criminal negligence. One line read: STATUTE OF LIMITATIONS DOES NOT APPLY TO INDICTABLE OFFENSES. It was underlined heavily. The blocky letters matched the writing she had seen on the grocery list left behind on the shelf in her house. Mallory flipped to the old-fashioned card in a small envelope pasted to the inside cover. She slid it up to read the name of the last person who had checked out the book.

Sean Benson.

She turned back to the counter, knowing she had to try to borrow the book, but Wolf was nowhere to be found. A quick glance at the clock told her she had seven minutes left until he planned to close the library. There was no photocopier in sight. Her curiosity bubbled like a shaken soda can as she looked back down at the pages. In the margin, Sean had scrawled:

A corporation can be held accountable for negligence if "directing mind" of company can be shown to be responsible (e.g. if the board was made aware of faults in dam and chose not to repair them—MUST PULL BOARD MEETING MINUTES). If, however, an individual hid information, they would be at fault. DID HE KNOW ABOUT THE CRACK? Did engineer sign off on safety report? Did he act "carelessly or with such reckless disregard for the safety of others as to deserve criminal punishment"? OR WAS IT THE COMPANY?

Sean's notes went on to detail the case of a ferry crashing off the west coast several years before. Mallory recalled the story—it had been big news in Vancouver when the ferry operator had been found personally responsible for the accident due to his leaving the bridge during a tricky passage. Was Sean suggesting the same outcome could be possible in McNamara? Mallory scanned the next section, which was both dog-eared and heavily annotated, to try to figure out the name of the engineer that Sean was talking about. She had only skimmed the staff list the first time she read the book, but she remembered Frederich including a description of the personnel who had been running the dam the night of its collapse. Sure enough, the page had also been annotated by Sean. Circled in a thickening ring of ink was one name.

The head engineer had been Logan Carruthers.

Mallory gasped. Alice's brother and the uncle of Carlotta's husband had been the person responsible for securing the dam. Sean had been investigating the very person she had thought would be the one to receive a settlement. She stood up so quickly that the legs of her chair whined against the floor. Wolf was still nowhere to be seen, and she had less than a minute left before he had threatened to close. Without further thought, Mallory did something she had never imagined she would do. She slipped the library book under her shirt and walked out into the snow that was beginning to change the shape of the world.

CHAPTER
TWENTY-FOUR

She had been in the library for less than half an hour, but when she returned to her car, it was covered with two inches of snow. There was no time for curtains or booking an internet technician today. The librarian was right. She had to get home. While the engine warmed up, Mallory called Joel again. Like before, she was immediately directed to his voice mail. He had not been this hard to reach before. Nerves prickled her neck. She didn't like the idea of him being out in a storm, and she hoped he was on his way home as well.

Her tires slid like sneakers on an ice rink as she tapped the gas to maneuver out of her spot. Within seconds, her lower back was damp with sweat, and the muscles of her fingers were cramped around the steering wheel. When she had first been learning to drive, her mother had hired her a driving instructor. Back then, she had paid more attention to the spit gathered at the corners of his mouth than his advice about driving in the snow. She was a teenager who lived in a city where it snowed once a year. What did she care about turning into a skid? But now, twenty-four years later, she realized she should have been paying attention. Sometimes the most important lessons are introduced too early.

On the way to Turner, it had taken her just over an hour to drive the seventy-five miles from her doorstep to the library. She had been lost in her thoughts the whole way. Now, though her mind kept trying to circle back to the idea of Logan and Sean, she couldn't spare a moment of attention toward anything but keeping her car on the road. The wind huffed snowflake-laden air from one side of the road to the other, shaking her car with the force of the blows. Fifty miles from the outskirts of McNamara, the storm worsened. She was terrified to push her car faster than a crawl. The snowflakes drew closer and closer together. Clumps of snow surrounded her, the flakes sticky enough to form their own snowballs as they came down. The wind whipped against her, jerking the steering wheel under her hands. For a brief moment, her visibility cleared. What she could see was worse than what she couldn't.

All around her, the world was white. Unbelievably so. The road had nearly disappeared under all the snow. The rapid accumulation made it impossible to tell where the edge of the road was, so she veered closer to the middle. The last thing she wanted to do was let her tires dip into the soft ground at the side of the road. She had to stay on the road.

She wasn't sure if the weak glow of her headlights was visible to anyone in the oncoming lane. She could barely see five feet in front of her own vehicle, and she was now on the stretch of road she hated the most. Until the turnoff to McNamara, the road undulated like a snake clinging to the edge of a cliff above the fifty-foot drop down to Loss Lake. There was no guardrail. The plunge to the water was high enough to kill. The eroding shoulder seemed to crumble with the hollow weight of the snow. Was this where she would die? A dizzying free fall, then an icy plunge into Loss Lake? On her first pass through the section, the day she had arrived, the steep cliff had made her nervous. Now, with the snow silently pelting her car, she was absolutely terrified. Her fear felt physical, like a heavy hand pressing on her chest.

The storm gathered more force. It looked like she was driving in a cloud. She couldn't see anything except white snow and shadows. The back of her throat was painfully dry. Even if Mallory had thought to pack water, she wouldn't have dared to reach for it. She breathed in and out, repeating the only thing she could think of. *You can do this. You can do this, Mallory.* The car bucked under her hands, and she tapped the brakes out of reflex.

It was a mistake.

The back end of her car spun. Her stomach swooped in the same nauseating circles as the vehicle. She was locked in a sickening figure eight, careening inches from the edge. Lake, ditch, lake, ditch. The two views flashed like a slideshow. She had no control. No way to help herself. The steering wheel slithered back and forth in her hands. Loss Lake loomed, then retreated. The car dipped. Her tires slipped. There was an echoing whomp of impact. Her head hit the side window with a hollow thump. Then everything was quiet.

She blinked hard, though it made her head hurt more. The world was a white tunnel of a car lodged on its side in a snowbank. She hadn't gone over the edge. She was not falling from a cliff into the unforgiving waters of Loss Lake. Her car was in the ditch. She had been spared. For now. The snow pressed against every window. It was as porous as a deadly sponge cake. Her breath was ragged. It was the only sound besides the hissing of snow or internal fluids melting on her engine. Her vision doubled, then tripled in a woozy haze as she tried to free herself from the seat belt digging into her collarbone.

She jammed her half-numb fingers into the unlocking device, ignoring the stab of the impact on the tips. Finally, it released. Gravity slammed her against the driver's side window. She struggled into a seated position. The door mechanism dug into her tailbone. She gingerly touched the left side of her forehead. It was tender, and already she could feel a fleshy egg shape rising, but she was experiencing no nausea or dizziness. She blinked hard and counted to one hundred, then back, which reassured her that her head injury was minor. She had been right to drive cautiously. Any faster and she would be dealing with a concussion on top of everything else.

She scanned the cab of the car for signs of her purse. All the bits and pieces that had collected in the vehicle since the last time she'd cleaned it lay strewn around her. Crumpled receipts, gum wrappers, and, inexplicably, a pink pencil eraser littered the haphazard interior, but there was no sign of her bag. She jammed her body in the gap between the front and back seats and scrounged around the floor. Finally, she found it, mercifully zipped up and intact. Inside, her cell phone was tucked safely into a side pocket. Her relief diminished as soon as she saw tiny letters reading "no service" on the top of the screen. Fear from last night pooled with her current panic. The toxic mix began to eat at her empty stomach. She was miles from McNamara and even farther from Turner with no phone, a car stuck sideways, and outer garments designed for a fashionable two-minute dash from the train station to someplace warmer. Since Graham had died, Mallory had thought often of how she would eventually go. She had never imagined it would be like this.

She hated making mistakes. As a nurse, her errors could be the difference between life and death. And though she had been good at her job, no one was perfect. She shoved herself back into the front seat. Her mind started to work against her. Ugly thoughts popped up like growths, some big, some small. The largest malignancy was Graham, always Graham, but she stubbornly refused to think about her husband as she worked the latch of the passenger-side door, trying to force it open against a burden of snow. Another memory from her early days of nursing surfaced. She had been treating an older woman complaining of both a headache and chest pains. The woman had been insistent that she couldn't answer any of Mallory's questions while her head pounded. Mallory had been eager to fulfill the duties of her job. Too eager. Without consideration, she had doled out two aspirin tablets to the woman. Just before the patient had tipped the small paper cup to her lips, an older nurse on staff lunged for it.

"What are you doing?" Mallory's coworker said under her breath after telling the patient they were unauthorized to deliver any medication without a doctor's orders.

Mallory's cheeks were burning so hot it was difficult to answer without bursting into tears. "She said she had a headache."

"Okay," the other nurse said, taking pity on her as she motioned to join her in the hallway, out of the patient's earshot. "You remember about nonsteroidal anti-inflammatories, right?"

Mallory had agreed miserably. "They can increase the risk of heart attacks."

"Yes. Acetaminophen only from now on, okay?"

Mallory had been grateful to the woman. It was a mistake she never made again. Sometimes, being scared was the only way to be good. She rubbed her hands to warm them and release the darkness of the past. She had gotten through nursing school, the first dire years of her position, and all the other trials her life had contained. She could get through this. With difficulty, she braced her feet on the uneven contours of the door and stood to open the passenger-side door. The weight of the snow and the unusual angle made the door like the hatch of a submarine. She pushed hard enough to make her forearms ache.

It opened a crack, then a few inches, then enough to wedge her head and shoulder out. As she climbed through, she kept a part of her body propping it open to ensure it didn't slam down again. Her thigh pinched between the frame and the door as she wiggled. Once out, she found herself staring at the three-foot-high ditch between her and the road. Already, the marks from her tires were being filled in by the falling snow. With her cell phone held above her head like a beacon, she jumped down. Icy lumps found their way under her waistband. She slogged through the deep drift to get back to the main road, clawing at the snow with one hand as her cheap boots tried to gain purchase.

In the other, she kept her phone high to protect it. Finally, she reached the firmer surface of the road.

As she walked down the highway in a fruitless search for a signal, the trees around her moaned like members of a Greek chorus. The wind whipped the waves of the lake below the edge of the far side of the road. Her body's response was heavy and slow. Parts of her shrieked against the cold. Parts of her were numb. The sounds funneled into one muffled roar of misery as she realized she could die on this lonely road. Her heart nearly broke as she realized her only chance was to turn around. How could she have left the house without a pair of mittens?

Struggling to retrace her steps, Mallory muscled her way back into the car, blowing on her chapped hands to try to thaw them as best she could. She huddled into herself, wrapping her arms around her legs. She wasn't sure if she should turn on her car. What if something had been damaged in the crash that led to her being poisoned by carbon monoxide? Her jeans were damp now from the ill-advised walk in the snow. Her breath whitened the inside of the windshield and windows as it froze around her. She wasn't sure how much time she had left. Could she last hours in below-zero weather? A day? She cursed herself for not shoving a granola bar or a bottle of water into her bag. The storm couldn't last forever. She could wait it out. She hoped.

Then, below the howl of the wind, Mallory heard something. A low rumble that turned into a familiar growl. Was she imagining the grinding of ice beneath heavy tires? There was no way to see out of the snow-covered windows. She stood up. Her hand scrabbled at the cold plastic of the handle, pushing at the door with the top of her head to earn another sharp pain to add to her collection. But it was worth it. She heard his voice coming through the small opening.

"Mallory? Mallory? Are you in there? Are you okay?"

"I'm here!"

In an instant, the weight of the door vanished and she saw a strong arm clothed in a tan jacket reaching in to pull her up against him. His warmth, his smell, the fact that he was there overwhelmed her, and she sobbed into the chest of the man she had met less than a month before. In that moment she could have easily confessed she was in love with him. All the fear that had racked her brain and body dissolved into adoration as he murmured into her hair. Finally, she broke away. His face was dotted with melting snow that seemed to be dissolving due to the warmth of his smile.

"You're safe now, Mallory. I've got you."

CHAPTER
TWENTY-FIVE

There was no chance of getting a tow truck out in this weather, Joel assured her. It was best to go home together in his four-wheel drive, then deal with her car after the storm broke.

"The most important thing is to get you home," he said as she raised the small cup from the top of his thermos to her lips, sipping at the dark, sweet coffee he had brought for the road. "No one should be out in this weather. Why are you here?"

Mallory quickly filled him in on what had happened the night before. As she spoke, Joel's knuckles whitened on the steering wheel in a way that had nothing to do with the danger of the storm that continued to rage around them.

"Did you see the prowler?"

"No," Mallory replied. "But the note was still there when I left. I took pictures too."

"Good thinking. This snow is probably going to wipe out any physical evidence around your house. But I'll see what I can gather."

"I think it has something to do with Sean, Joel."

Joel frowned, and Mallory's stomach clenched. "I don't know about that. We need to be thinking about what Henry saw last night. I'd like to talk to Carlotta and Suzanne first—make sure they're not trying to bully you into letting them hunt. Sometimes the simplest answer is the right one."

His voice was calm, but Mallory sensed the same tension in him that arose every time she brought up Sean. She curled her legs onto the bench seat of the truck, trying to position the dampest parts directly in line with the air from the heater. Despite the blowing snow that kept snaking its way across the road and the lingering aches in her neck and head, the anxiety that had been twining its way through her nervous system since she'd first heard the prowler was starting to unfurl. She didn't want to press him on a subject that made him uncomfortable immediately after he had saved her life.

"Yes, that sounds like a good next step. How was your morning?" she asked.

He rubbed his jaw and smiled ruefully. "Honestly? I thought I was the one who was going to come home and regale you with awful stories. In the middle of my meeting, I got called onto the scene of two different accidents this morning. No fatalities, but everyone was pretty banged up. You were lucky to get out with only a couple bruises. This storm isn't going to end anytime soon."

An unfamiliar fright swirled around in her stomach. In Vancouver, the few snowstorms she'd been affected by had been inconveniences, not crises. There were trucks that came to push the snow away and trains she could use, all without her having to think of whether she would be safe. But this storm was different. Not only had she been forced to leave her only means of transportation on its side in a ditch, but she had no idea when it would be possible to get it out. The wind rattled the passenger-side window in its frame. For the first time since she'd arrived, she understood what everyone in McNamara had been trying to tell her. There were things here that could kill her if she wasn't careful.

Being with Joel was the only thing that kept panic from consuming her. He drove like a man who had navigated many storms in his life. His movements with the steering wheel and brakes were measured and calm. They shared a sandwich from his lunch box as his tires dug solidly into the sweeping layer of snow. Mallory was grateful for each mile they completed. She couldn't imagine trying to drive this without him. Eventually, Mallory spotted the turn to McNamara. The wind blew sheets of snow around the sign like it was trying to trick them into missing it. She sucked in air as the back end of Joel's truck wobbled during the turn, but he accelerated smoothly through it.

Though it was a Monday, every storefront except Kylie's looked dark through the piles of snow that had collected on the sidewalks and eaves. It was just after lunch. Had everyone gone home early? She spotted a small group of children being escorted by the principal, Mrs. Rose, away from the school. Their snowsuits hampered their movements, making them look like they were trying to walk on the moon.

"Looks like a snow day," Joel chuckled. "Best day of school all year."

"Or days," Mallory said with a smile. "This might be a snow week."

"Bob will get out here soon, but yeah, if it keeps dumping like this, he'll be busy for a while."

At the end of the road, Joel turned, slower this time. Mallory held her breath, but this time, the truck's wheels stayed true. They made their way back to her home, passing the spot where Mallory knew Carlotta's house was, though she couldn't see a glimpse of it in the whitewashed air. Farther down the road they turned again. Her body was loose with relief as the truck drove up her driveway. She was almost home. Then she remembered the prowler from the night before. The thought of spending a night alone in the house without knowing if they'd be back again made the muscles in her neck spasm.

Snow tugged at the tires like a dog trying to direct its owner away from danger. A high-pitched whine came from the undercarriage as the treads sank deeper and the truck ceased to move. For a moment, their wheels spun without purchase on the powdery snow. The snow stopped. A strange sensation came over Mallory when she saw the lake, almost as if it were tugging them toward it, like a magnet. Joel increased the pressure on the gas pedal and the truck lurched into unsteady forward momentum. It began to snow again. Mallory wondered if she'd imagined the glimpse of water urging them onward during the pause in the storm.

Around the final curve, Mallory spotted her small house fuzzed by a thick layer of snow, and she breathed in a sigh that seemed to draw oxygen down to the tips of her toes.

Until she saw the car parked in the driveway.

CHAPTER
TWENTY-SIX

She recognized the vehicle immediately. It belonged to Sadie Rooney, cousin of Graham, older sister of Cynthia. The roof of the car was coated in at least four inches of snow. Sadie had been here for long enough that her tracks were covered.

Joel interrupted her thoughts, and she jumped. "Are you expecting company?"

He turned off the engine as she said no. The door of the car opened the moment the truck engine stopped, and Sadie Rooney stepped out. Unlike Mallory, Sadie had prepared for the blizzard. Not only were there chains on the tires, but her wide frame was clad in a bright-orange puffy down jacket. She looked nearly radioactive in comparison to the barren, bleak landscape.

Sadie beamed and waved enthusiastically at Mallory and Joel in the truck, even though Mallory was doubtful the woman could see them inside.

"Old friend?" Joel asked. He had been staring at her since they'd pulled up, but she couldn't take her eyes off Sadie. It wasn't that she hated the woman. She just never wanted to see her again.

"More like an unexpected relative," Mallory said.

His head cocked in the same way it had the first time they met, when she'd been certain he was about to arrest her.

"This is a terrible day for a social call. Did you know she was coming?"

Mallory shook her head miserably as lines of concern scrolled across Joel's forehead.

"Are you okay?" he asked.

"I'm fine," she lied. "Bad memories, that's all."

"We can do this," he said, even though Mallory was nearly certain that he wouldn't feel the same way after he spoke with Sadie.

He placed his hand flat on her forearm. The weight of it, combined with his words, got her moving. She half stepped and half slid out of the car. The soles of her boots were still wet and her feet were still cold. The snow had fallen deeper here than on the highway. Even if she hadn't crashed on the side of the road, Mallory wasn't sure her car would have been able to plow its way through. Sadie seemed unperturbed by the drifts. She bounded through the snow toward them. Flakes caught in Mallory's eyelashes as she tried to smile.

Mallory had met Sadie only twice before Graham's funeral: once at their wedding and once at his fortieth birthday party. She lived several states away and worked as a receptionist for a large firm that manufactured party goods. Mallory had always been left with an impression of a woman who was happy to be charmed by the world but not too concerned with the details of how things came to be. Her social media feed was full of aphorisms about living, laughing, and loving, often emblazoned over jewel tones or picturesque landscapes and anonymously authored.

"Mallory!" Sadie cried as she wrapped her in a hug. Her jacket compressed under Mallory's face. It felt like being embraced by a down pillow. "I've been calling and calling. Must have been a hundred times with no answer. You're a hard woman to get in touch with. Thank goodness I finally spoke with your mother. If she hadn't passed on your address, I would never have realized you had decided to move here. I wouldn't have been able to look you up."

Mallory gritted her teeth. She had forbidden her mother from doing exactly that. As Sadie continued, her tone shifted to sadness.

"I came up to see where it happened. Find some closure, I suppose. You must have heard about Cynthia?" Sadie's eyes welled up.

"Yes, of course I did. My sympathies. It happened shortly before I arrived in town. I haven't had a chance to send a card."

She looked at Joel, who extended his hand. She could tell by the way he wouldn't turn his head to meet her stare that he knew exactly who Sadie was talking about. His radar was up. She tried to act as if it were perfectly fine for him to learn what the connection between her and Cynthia Rooney really was, but her thoughts were flying like the snowflakes in the sky. She wasn't sure, however, if what they had been building could withstand the things she had never told him.

"Sadie, this is Sergeant Joel Benson. Joel, Sadie."

The lines on Joel's forehead deepened as he shook Sadie's hand.

"Nice to meet you. I am sorry about Cynthia. She was your . . ."

He trailed off, and Sadie obligingly filled in the blank.

"Sister."

Joel dipped his head once, like she had confirmed a known fact. The gesture made Mallory's stomach drop.

"I believe I spoke with your mother on the telephone. Maria Rooney?"

"Yes, that's her. She was devastated to hear the news about Cynthia, but she said you were kind. It's nice to meet you as well. Despite the circumstances, of course." Her eyes were deep with sorrow. "I needed to come back here, you know?"

Mallory tried to nod and change the subject simultaneously.

"How did you know where to find me?"

Joel cleared his throat as Sadie blinked at her. Mallory realized her words were rude, but it couldn't be helped. Anticipating her mother's tendency to bow to pressure, she had given her only a post office box number—no street address. It would have been difficult for Sadie to get to her house, yet here she was. Sadie took the question in stride.

"Well, when I didn't hear from you, I remembered that I had dealt with a lovely real estate agent several years ago when I arranged the family reunion at the cottage. We didn't have enough room for everyone, so she helped me coordinate accommodations. You and Graham couldn't come, remember?"

Mallory silently cursed Betty Barber while hurrying to distract Joel from Sadie's response.

"Oh, yes. We were on our honeymoon."

"That's right. We missed you. It was a lovely time."

As Mallory looked at Sadie's eager expression, she realized there was no way not to invite her inside. Despite her down jacket, Sadie was trembling as the wind needled at them.

"Well, we've found each other now. Would you like to come inside?"

She accepted, and Joel volunteered to help Sadie with three carrier bags and a huge purse from her car. He kept focused on his task, despite Mallory's attempts to catch his eye. She even grabbed a bag from his hand, but he gave it up without glancing her way. She shifted it to get a better grip and heard the distinct clink of bottles.

At the door, Mallory fumbled with frozen fingers to get the key in the front door, terrified that she would drop it in the drift of snow on the doorstep. She was unused to the action of turning a key in a lock, though it had been only three weeks since she had done so. Finally, the tumbler clicked apart, and Sadie and Joel followed her inside and slipped off their boots and wet jackets. Mallory fussed with hanging them up carefully on the coatrack, brushing off the unmelted snow as she slid them over the spare hooks. She hoped her action would draw Joel's attention to the item he had given her—a reminder of the trust they shared, even if she hadn't told him about Cynthia.

Joel led the way into the house. Mallory followed with Sadie on her heels, relieved to see that the awful four-letter sign had dropped from view. She wasn't sure how she would have explained that to Sadie. Nearly a foot of snow had blown up on the sill outside. It pressed against the window like sand inside an hourglass.

Mallory and Sadie settled at the dining room table as Joel went to look at the window. Mallory was touched that he was still willing to investigate the prowler. She hoped it wasn't only professional obligation. The sky was the color of wet concrete. Still, the snow fell. Mallory could feel it wrapping around the house like a cold blanket. She looked at her watch and was amazed to see it was only 1:00 p.m. Her body ached from the accident. Fading adrenaline clouded her thoughts. It seemed nearly impossible to navigate the complexities of her relationship with Sadie in her current state. She needed something to clear her head.

"Tea?" she asked.

Sadie shook her head. "I'd rather a toast to my sister, if it's all the same to you."

Before Mallory could answer, Sadie pulled a corkscrew out of her purse and set to work on one of the bottles of wine she retrieved from her bag. Joel walked to the back door. He kept his back to her as he spoke.

"I'm going to check on that window, Mallory. I'll only be a minute."

Mallory tried to catch his eye, but he kept his back turned. "I appreciate that." She looked back at Sadie. "I'll get glasses."

She heard a resounding pop from the bottle as she selected three wineglasses from the back of her cupboard. It was much too early for her to have a drink, but she was too tired to insist on anything else. Kylie had brought over a set, and they were dusty from disuse. She pulled a dish towel from the rack and wiped them clean.

When she returned, Joel was kicking off his boots at the back door. He shook his head at her to indicate he'd found nothing. She held his eyes but couldn't read his expression. His face was as guarded as it had been the first time they'd met. They joined Sadie, who seized the glasses and poured them each a generous serving of wine, ensuring that her own glass was the fullest of the three.

Sadie took a deep gulp of the contents of her glass before raising it to eye level.

"To my sister," she said. "To Cynthia Rooney. May she rest in peace."

Mallory took a small drink and was unnerved when Sadie raised hers again.

"And to Loss Lake," she said. "The place she loved more than anywhere else in the world."

CHAPTER TWENTY-SEVEN

Joel's body stilled at the second toast. Mallory looked across the table, which had been another gift from Kylie. For the first time since Sadie had arrived, she could see a clear emotion on his face. Anger. He stared at her for a fraction too long before he raised his glass. In his eyes were questions she had no way to answer. Their sips were a tenth of Sadie's, who was nearly halfway through her portion. Almost immediately, the wine deepened the general rosiness of the habitual drinker that had already been present on her cheeks and nose. She sniffed.

"I'm sorry for your loss," Joel said, setting his wineglass on the table. Mallory knew he wouldn't have another sip. Though his shift had technically ended, there may be more problems in the area caused by the storm.

"As am I," echoed Mallory.

Sadie seemed to hear the sincerity in their voices—the sound of people who understood loss. "Thank you. That means a lot."

No one spoke as she wiped a tear from her eye. Mallory changed the subject to the most banal thing she could imagine.

"It's a shame you arrived during the storm," Mallory said. "It's such a pretty landscape."

"Oh, yes, I've always loved it up here. So did Cynthia."

Too late, Mallory realized she had invited in the very subject she was seeking to avoid. Joel pushed his chair back, then leaned forward with his elbows on his knees. Mallory was impressed by the way he used his body to inspire intimacy even though his eyes had turned hard as a predator's.

"I have been wondering what prompted her to drive all the way up to McNamara. You mentioned that Cynthia loved this area? What was her connection to McNamara?"

Mallory fought her desire to slump down in her chair.

"Oh, we spent every summer here when we were kids. My family had a cottage. Graham came with us too, right, Mallory?"

She nodded grimly, though Joel didn't take his eyes off the older woman.

"Cynthia and Graham both loved it. In fact, he used to talk about it even more than her. I always thought they'd both eventually buy property up here. Now I suppose it's too late."

Mallory's stomach flipped as Sadie looked down morosely. Joe glanced at her and then back to Sadie, who was topping up her wineglass.

"I hadn't realized that Cynthia was so familiar with the area. Is the cottage you mentioned earlier still in your family?" he asked.

"Sadly, no. My father sold it when I reached my twenties, and us kids wailed. But you know, it was his decision. We had to let it go. None of us were really in a position to use it at that point."

Sadie finished her glass and looked hungrily at the one Joel had left nearly untouched. She set her elbows on the table and shifted her weight into a half slump, unconsciously mimicking Joel's posture.

Joel pushed his glass toward Sadie. "Would you like to have mine?"

She took it happily. After another drink, she reached over to touch Mallory's arm. Her thoughts flowed as fast as the wine she was consuming.

"Mallory knows how much McNamara meant to all of us. Graham told me once he had never been happier anywhere else. I assumed that's why you moved here, Mallory. To be close to him. Or at least his memory."

Joel met her eyes. For the first time since they'd kissed, she wished he hadn't. There was a hostility in them she had never seen before.

"Is that the reason you came here, Mallory?"

His tone was as sharp as a razor's edge. She could feel anger radiating from him, but its source was difficult for her to place. He hadn't seemed bothered by the discovery that she was related to Cynthia. Instead, it was her husband's connection to the area that was setting him off. She was careful with her words, hoping to avoid upsetting him further.

"There were many reasons, but yes, Graham spoke of Loss Lake often. He said it was pretty."

Joel looked at her with a frown. "Pretty?"

"Yes," Sadie echoed. "Pretty and so peaceful, you know. We all loved it here. Just the perfect way to escape the city. Like camping but with power."

"So nothing drew you here but your husband's memories?"

"No, there were several reasons—"

Joel cut her off. "And Cynthia happened to be here for nostalgia as well?"

"I'm not sure what you're asking—"

This time, it was Sadie who interrupted.

"Cynthia had her own reasons for being here. You know I never believed what she said about you, right? I want to clear that up now. She was like that. Always standing up for Graham."

"Yes, she was," Mallory said, keeping her eyes locked on Sadie. Joel was already angry with her. She doubted this line of conversation would lessen his rage. She took another drink even though her stomach pinched as she swallowed. She wanted to divert the conversation, but she couldn't figure out how to stop Sadie from saying what she didn't want Joel to hear. Her mind was as blank as the snow. Joel spoke up.

"Did your sister know Mallory was up here?"

This time, he didn't attempt to disguise the note of interrogation in his voice as he stared determinedly at Sadie, who took another drink before answering. The only thing Mallory could hope for was that Sadie herself would shut down the conversation. She knew Sadie didn't like to speak badly of anyone. Apart from Cynthia, most of Graham's family had avoided conflict at any cost. It was why she'd been able to escape Cynthia's accusations without consequence. Until now.

Sadie waved her hand to dismiss Joel's questions.

"Oh, that's over and done with now. Everyone handles losing someone in different ways."

Joel straightened up and flashed a smile at Sadie.

"Absolutely. You're absolutely right about that. But I wonder if Cynthia had a reason to come to McNamara besides reliving memories. It's so important for us to keep accurate records in our case reporting."

The idea that the purpose of the conversation was administrative rather than inquisitive put Sadie at ease. She glanced at Mallory with a reassuring smile, then turned to Joel. Mallory cringed. She knew what was coming.

"Oh, sure. The last time I spoke with her, she told me that she deeply wanted to have another conversation with Mallory. I'm guessing your mother helped her out as well." She looked at Mallory again. "When I found out you had moved here, I assumed at least part of the reason she drove up was to try and do that. It's a shame the two of you never got a chance to speak."

And just like that, she was revealed.

CHAPTER TWENTY-EIGHT

She practically had to run to keep up with Joel as his long legs tore through the house. Even the breeze that blew in his wake felt furious. He stormed out the front door with her following close behind him. She reached out to catch his arm. He turned on his heel to face her, jerking out of her grasp. The anger distorted his face and made it closer to monstrous than she could have imagined possible.

"I should be taking you down to the station. You know that, right?"

The snowflakes fell heavily between them, making the distance seem greater. She still hadn't changed into dry clothes, and the return to the storm sent ripples of discomfort through her. Her body screamed to get back inside, but she knew that if she did, she would lose Joel forever.

"I didn't do anything wrong."

"Lying to a police officer is a crime, Mallory."

"You never asked me if I knew her. You said to let sleeping dogs lie."

She regretted the words the moment she said them. They made her sound guilty. Joel's eyes narrowed with disgust.

"I thought you understood what I meant. You seemed capable of so much more. I thought this place meant more to you than closing a circle with your dead husband."

"What?" She'd thought he would be angry about her obfuscation. Why was he bringing up Graham? "I don't understand."

Joel's face was full of both incredulity and scorn.

"Did you see her that day?"

"I had no idea she followed me up here. Not until . . ."

"Until what?" Joel snapped. "Don't lie to me again."

Mallory was too overwrought to be dishonest. Besides, Joel deserved to know the truth.

"I did pull over at Sled Beach. I stopped before I turned into town. I was trying to get my bearings, to look at Betty's map. I wanted to stretch my legs, so I got out of the car and walked to the water. It looked so lovely that day."

Joel snorted.

Mallory was taken aback by his reaction to her words. The lake had been pretty that day—beautiful, in fact. The water had sparkled like it was dancing with the sun. The moment had been perfect until she heard the grunt of a car pulling in and stopping behind her. She hadn't turned around. Back then, she was used to ignoring the presence of others as she had in the city—the politeness born of proximity that allowed people to find space in close quarters.

But the raucous call that had come at the same time as the car door slamming suggested anything but civility. Though she had never heard her name shouted with such raw emotion, she recognized the voice immediately as Cynthia Rooney's—the woman she had traveled so far to escape. Cynthia was the reason she had told her mother not to give out her forwarding address to anyone. Especially not this woman, who must have followed her all the way from Vancouver.

Mallory had never hated anyone before that moment. The ugly emotion was almost beautiful in its purity. She had wanted nothing more than for Cynthia Rooney to die. Mallory remembered the tears burning in her eyes as she raced back to the car.

She turned her attention back to Joel.

"It's not what you think."

"What happened to Cynthia, Mallory?"

"I don't know," Mallory said. The words seemed too big for her tongue to handle. "She yelled at me. She was so angry."

Cynthia's face had been almost purple when she spoke.

"She . . . accused me of killing Graham. She said I had done it on purpose—that I had canceled the home nurse and withheld his medication so he would die. That I was taking the easy way out."

Mallory spoke in a dull, low tone. She had played Cynthia's words in her mind over and over, but it was still so difficult to say them out loud. Cynthia had known about the trouble between them. She had gone through Graham's diary and found out he had met with a divorce attorney. It all seemed so damning when Cynthia said it out loud. Joel was looking at her like she was a suspect. She felt sick.

"She believed I killed him."

Joel looked deeply into her eyes. Apparently, he didn't like what he saw, because he tossed his head in anger.

"Did you come here to relive the past, Mallory? His past?"

Mallory was confused by the question.

"I came here to find peace."

"Or so you've led us all to believe. You made it seem as if you were called here, but now I see that the only reason you came here is to take a trip into your husband's memories. You're not ready to move on from him. You're not ready for any of this. Did you know Cynthia Rooney was following you? Did you lead her here?"

"No," Mallory said. She was confused by his accusations, which were coming in too fast for her to process. "I had no idea. It's like what happened to Sean. An unsolved accident. Something we have to leave behind us."

"Do not bring my brother into this."

"But it's the same thing."

"It's not the same at all. I went to work one day and then I came home and my brother was dead."

"That's exactly what happened to me, Joel. I left a woman standing beside a lake, and the next thing I knew you were knocking on my door to tell me she had drowned."

Joel's face was colder than the wind.

"You better not say another word to me, ma'am, or we'll have to get this on the record."

"Ma'am? Are you serious?"

"It's how I address strangers."

"I'm not a stranger, Joel. You know me."

"How can I trust a word you're telling me?"

"Joel—"

He turned toward his car, and Mallory's heart sank.

"Joel!" she called again.

He looked over his shoulder, and she was hopeful until he spoke.

"The roads are going to be too bad for Sadie to get back into town. You might as well ask her to spend the night."

"Here?" Her heart leaped. "But what about the prowler? I don't think it's safe for either of us."

Her plea landed on deaf ears. Before she had finished speaking, Joel turned his back. He pulled at the handle of his truck, wrenching it open, before speaking to her without changing his position. Every word cut through her like an icicle falling into a snowdrift from a great height.

"You'll be fine," he said.

She watched as the truck struggled back down the snowy drive. Snow flew out from behind his tires like a wintry cape. She tried to make herself believe he was right.

CHAPTER
TWENTY-NINE

Sadie was even drunker than Mallory expected when she returned. She blinked blearily as Mallory approached, her head resting loosely on her elbow propped on the table. The second bottle was on the table. Close to half of it was gone. The storm had darkened the entire sky to charcoal. Mallory sat down heavily. She was so exhausted she wasn't sure how she would ever be able to rise from the chair again.

"Did your . . . your friend leave?" Sadie said. Her words were too round, like she couldn't figure out when they ended.

"Yes."

She thought about Joel's wheels spinning furiously in the soft snow. She wondered if his tracks were already covered.

A minute passed in silence. The corners of Sadie's mouth drooped down in an almost clownish expression.

"Two deaths, back to back."

Tears rolled down her cheeks. The other woman's grief got caught up in Mallory's guilt about Graham, Joel, and Cynthia, forming a ball in her throat that made it hard to swallow.

"I'm so sorry, Sadie," Mallory said. Her tears fell too.

She grabbed a box of tissues and offered it to the woman, who smiled at her gratefully. As they both dabbed their faces, Sadie picked up her glass of wine and clinked it against Mallory's with a rueful smile. Her eyes were redder, but her gaze seemed more focused. Sadness seemed to have sobered her up. Mallory smiled back and took a large sip of her wine. This time, the drink was welcome in her body.

"I know how much she wanted to see you," Sadie said. "From the way she was talking, I think she wanted to apologize."

"Apologize?" Mallory was stunned.

"Of course, doll. Cynthia was so full of fury about Graham dying, but she was starting to get through it. It wasn't about you. Sometimes death makes people angry. She couldn't let him go—kept pestering him to try experimental therapies to heal his heart damage."

"I didn't know that."

"Cynthia was like a dog with a bone when she wanted something. And she and Graham were so close when they were kids."

Mallory tried not to let her face show that she knew exactly how close they had been. She must have succeeded, because Sadie continued.

"But we all knew how Graham was doing, Mallory, and how hard you worked to help him. None of the rest of us blame you at all. I thought Cynthia was starting to see our side of things."

Mallory wiped away another swell of tears. She had never thought she would be forgiven by Graham's family. The feeling that the others believed her capable of withholding care from Graham had been grinding at her like a piece of sand she couldn't remove from her eye. Though Mallory was comforted to learn that Sadie suspected no wrongdoing, it made deceiving her all the more difficult. There was so much more to Graham's death than she could explain. Sadie lived in a house where the writing on her walls implored her to fight less and cuddle more. At Mallory's wedding, Sadie had told her that she preferred to think the best of people because anything else was too complicated. The reality of what had happened to her cousin was impossible for Sadie to comprehend. To hide her emotions, Mallory took another slug of wine.

Sadie smiled peacefully. Delivering the message of forgiveness seemed to have relaxed her. She grabbed the bottle of wine to top up Mallory's glass. Mallory took another drink in thanks. The alcohol burned a trail from her tongue to her empty stomach. She knew Sadie liked to drink, but not alone. If Mallory was going to fully return to her good graces, she needed to match her glass for glass, but she couldn't do so without food.

"We should eat something," Mallory said.

"I brought cheese!" Sadie said with glee as she reached beside her.

Mallory hurried to gather plates. The two women set up a feast of cheese, bread, and olives, all of which Sadie pulled from her bag like a drunk Santa. Mallory lit a few candles on the table as the two of them dug in. Now the room was dark enough to suggest evening. The buoyancy of wine floated her along the steady river of Sadie's inebriated musings about McNamara's scenery and garbled gossip about members of Graham's family Mallory wasn't sure she'd ever met. When the second bottle of wine was finished, Sadie didn't hesitate to open a third. Mallory made a sound halfway between a moan and a cheer as Sadie refilled her glass. The two of them chatted until that too was nearly finished. Though Mallory was drunk, she could tell that both of them were struggling to understand any line of thought, their own included.

Finally, Mallory excused herself to go to the bathroom. She rose on unsteady legs, using the walls on each side of the hallway as a guide to the toilet. As she peed, thoughts bounced around in her mind like drunk drivers in bumper cars.

After tonight, she wouldn't have to worry about Cynthia or Graham anymore. Unless . . . what was she forgetting? Yes, Joel. Unless Joel decided to look into Cynthia's death now that he knew she'd known the drowned woman. He had been so angry when he left. Why? Something about Cynthia? That didn't seem quite right. She tried to follow the thought, but it lurched away from her. There were things she needed to figure out. It had to do with Joel. Mallory made a rubbery frown as she thought of him storming off. There was only one solution. She had to talk to Joel. She pulled out her phone and dialed his number, clearing her throat as it rang in the hope that it would help clear her head. Voice mail. She hung up without leaving a message.

She washed her hands, then wandered back into the hallway. *Blankets,* she thought. *I'll make sure Sadie has blankets.* She walked into her bedroom and closed her eyes, trying to remember where she'd placed the stack of quilts Kylie had brought. Her equilibrium wobbled. When she opened her eyes, the soft folds of her bed seemed to beckon. She lay down. It was good to let the weight of her head sink into the pillow's depths.

She woke with a start. Her mouth seemed to contain a layer of paste that was cementing her tongue to the roof. Sharp prongs of pain throbbed against the front of her skull where dehydration was slowing blood flow. The necessary fluid in her body was struggling to move like sludge through a narrow pipe. She rolled over, which was a mistake. Nausea accompanied the aches in her muscles. She rubbed her temples. The tender spot on one side was an instant reminder of her car accident. She lifted her head more slowly, which earned her a tolerable swoop of queasiness. The house was still and dark. No indication that Sadie was awake.

The filtered light coming from the window projected a square from a clouded moon that was only a shade lighter than darkness. She pushed herself to sit up on the bed, knowing she should check the time and Sadie, but alcohol was still traveling in her system like an unwanted guest. Their conversation from hours before began to play indistinctly in her head. Anxiety crept in and began to mix with the alcohol as she tried to recall her exact words. What had she said about Graham? Had she told Sadie too much?

Mallory heard a sound that froze her already stiff body into a rictus of fear. Footsteps crunching in the snow. Someone was outside.

Again.

Anger licked at her fear as she crept off the bed and half crawled, half belly slid out of her bedroom. Her breath rebounded between her mouth and the floor, making it impossible for her to hear whether the footsteps were getting closer or farther away. She went over her actions from the previous evening. Terror seized her. She hadn't locked the front door. Or the back one. Whoever was outside was going to get in.

Crunch. Crunch. Crunch.

It sounded like they were close to the front door. All they would have to do was turn the knob gently. This time whoever it was wouldn't even have to worry if their bullet was going to cut through the glass. They could shoot her in the chest. And Sadie too.

Crunch.

Panic pounded through her body like a car alarm. She jumped up from her position on the floor, sprinted to the front door, and slammed the dead bolt. Then she raced to the back door to do the same in jerky movements that seemed like a replay of the night before. Only when the dead bolt was safely lodged did she allow herself a moment to pause, bracing herself for another footstep or sound. All she could hear was a series of wet snores and her own panting. The house was so dark.

No more footsteps. Had she scared off the intruder? Or were they waiting, poised like a snake about to strike?

She tiptoed into the living room and saw Sadie sleeping on Sean's old chair, her head lolling on her chest. Guilt at the woman's uncomfortable position wormed its way through Mallory's fear. She had passed out, leaving Sadie to fend for herself. So much for playing the good host. Mallory cocked her ear again, listening. Nothing.

Between Sadie's snores and the lingering alcohol, she was able to summon the bravery she hadn't had the night before. She wasn't alone. The house was secure. Mallory breathed in deeply, then crossed the room and cupped her hands to the icy glass of the window where the note had been. Mallory's teeth chattered, a reflexive snapping that made the bruised part of her head throb.

But the view contained no hint of malice. Instead, she saw a clearing night. The reflection of the moon whispered on the lake. Though still partially screened by the remains of the clouds, a small line of its light played on the rolling surface, just enough to brighten the purely white landscape. The storm had ended. The lakeshore and surrounding trees were draped in what it had left behind. Mallory breathed out the breath she had been holding. She tilted her head again and listened hard in the space between Sadie's rhythmic snorting. Nothing but the tiny tick of Sadie's wristwatch.

Mallory wondered if the combination of her argument with Joel, the fear surrounding the accident, and the fact that there was another person sleeping in her house had triggered her to imagine the same sounds as the night before. She was about to turn away when something on the ground caught her eye.

Where the snow stretched out to the lake had looked smooth and uniform, but on closer examination, she could see depressions in it that formed a soft and repeating set of footprints. The slide of the powdery snow had filled in some of the hollows, but it was possible to make out the series of holes where someone's feet had been. She knelt down to get a better angle on the damage to the otherwise perfectly flat landscape. As she followed the line of steps with her eyes, her breath came in and out like a scared dog's. Nearest the window, the footprints were turned toward her. Whoever had been out there had been trying to look in.

Another line of footsteps headed back to the shore of the lake. She could see where the feet had been placed, one after another, all the way down to the water's edge. She stood on her tiptoes, straining to see the end of the trail. There was no break in the progression. The footsteps went down to the place where the water met the land. Then they disappeared.

CHAPTER THIRTY

The physical discomfort she had experienced the night before had been only a hint of what was to come. Her hangover arrived in force sometime between her second encounter with the prowler and sunrise. Shortly before waking, she dreamed of gulping ice-cold glasses of orange juice, one after another, like shots at a bachelorette party. The pain in her head increased alongside nausea as she struggled into a seated position. Her eyes seemed too dry to close, and her body was both sweaty and chilled. She wasn't sure what was worse: her compromised state or her despair at the idea of facing Sadie in such a condition.

Mallory stood up and walked down the hallway. A bubble of saliva rose in her throat, followed by another, like a length of liquid rope trying to gag her. She swallowed hard and cursed herself for making this day more difficult than it needed to be by drinking so much the night before. She forced herself to review the things she had to do the way she used to grill herself on the human anatomy during nursing school. First, she had to say goodbye to Sadie and send her off believing everything was as it should be. Then she had to find Joel and apologize for Cynthia. And Graham. And whatever else he had been angry about. The list would have been arduous even if she were in perfect health. As it was, she was uncertain she could make it through the next hour without vomiting, let alone navigate the complex relationships before her, but she had to try.

As she entered the dining room, she misjudged the position of one of the chairs, and it bumped painfully against her hip. She cursed under her breath as she headed to the spot where Sadie had been sleeping. But when she got close enough to see the heap of blankets, she realized there was no one underneath them. Sadie was gone.

Mallory looked behind her, as if she had missed the woman bustling around. But the kitchen, dining room, and living room were empty. She walked back down the hall to peer into the second bedroom and the bathroom. The doors of both were open, but there was no one inside. Mallory was alone in the house. Her scalp rippled. She felt like Sadie was about to jump out at her from a closet or burst out from behind the shower curtain. It was silly, but not enough to leave either area unchecked.

Nothing. The house was silent.

She returned to the front door and realized it was unlocked. As she opened it, a skiff of snow blew in from the two-foot-high pile leaning against the door, like it had been impatiently waiting to be invited in. The flakes were cold enough to burn the tops of her feet. She scanned the periphery outside her house. The driveway was covered in a thick layer of snow that resembled mold on an orange. She looked from side to side. Sadie's car was nowhere to be seen, but there was a set of tracks dug deep into the snow. Her mouth dried with worry. Where had Sadie gone?

Mallory closed the door to block the cold wind. As she walked back, she scanned the surfaces for a note from Sadie or an indication that she planned to return. But the woman's purse and carrier bags were gone too. Even the wine bottles had disappeared. Only the tire tracks and the unlocked door indicated that Mallory hadn't spent the night alone. What would have compelled Sadie to leave without a goodbye? Once again, she scolded herself for drinking so much and sleeping in. She had ruined her chance to have one final sober conversation with Sadie. As much as she'd been dreading it, it was critical to ensure that

Sadie would take a message of good faith back to her family. Maybe she could call her. Her thoughts were cloudy. She needed coffee.

After she filled the carafe and set the coffee to brew, she used the history on her phone to find Sadie's information. It was the only number that was listed more often than her mother's. No answer. Then she tried Joel. No answer. She knew he wasn't at work, so he was likely intentionally ignoring her call. She swore under her breath as she realized, without him, she had to find a number for the tow truck on her own. But how could she do that without the internet? She had made an enormous error in judgment in not having it installed sooner.

She tried to wash down her panic with a drink of coffee. What if her calls weren't getting through either? The endless ringing could be a sign that the phone towers were down. She had planned to get a landline in case of this kind of emergency. Now, she had no phone, no internet, and no car. She was stuck in a place where someone kept returning every night. Even the heat of the coffee wasn't enough to prevent the chill from traveling up her arms at the thought of the footsteps leading to the lake. She tried Kylie. Maybe her friend could pick her up later or arrange a tow truck from the store.

No answer.

Unease churned in her already tender stomach. The coffee wasn't helping. She set down the cup and tried to figure out a way to get her car back from its position on the side of the highway. She had never felt so isolated. The days were so short here, and it was already close to eleven. She had slept most of the morning away and missed the only ride to town available.

She peered out the window. The skies were dull, like a layer of dust had coated the atmosphere. The snow might start again any minute. She had to find a way to get her car back. She had to walk to Carlotta's.

She left the kitchen. Carlotta's house was less than a mile away. If she started now, she would have at least five hours before the sun set. She had no other choice. Besides, Carlotta had often told her that the people of McNamara helped each other out in times of crisis. It was time for the woman to prove it.

She changed into the warmest clothes she could find, wishing she hadn't tossed out her old ski pants during her purge of the house after Graham's death. It had been difficult to think straight about what the future would hold. As a safeguard, she texted her plan to Joel and Kylie, hoping the messages would get through. Back at the door, she pulled on her boots, still soggy from the day before, and slung her purse over her shoulder.

Despite its powdery appearance, the snow was shockingly cold. Her cheap boots were immediately submerged in a layer of wet slush beneath the fluffy surface. The wind nipped at her with icy teeth. As she walked, the freeze from her feet and face spread quickly to the rest of her body. Her feet ached in a way that reminded Mallory of the case studies of trench foot she had been assigned to read in nursing school. The soldiers had walked for miles as their flesh rotted away beneath them. If they could keep going, surely she could make it. Her sore muscles protested at the plowing motion, but she pressed on.

Within minutes, her pants were soaking wet up to the knee, sticking to her shins like a soggy Band-Aid. After ten more steps, her thighs were protesting as much as her feet. She hadn't realized that walking in deep snow was going to be so difficult, but she steeled herself to continue. Until she got her car back, she was trapped. After last night, that was the last thing she wanted to be. Her breath grew ragged in her chest as she slogged on. The frozen ground was as bleak as her looping thoughts about the prowler.

What did the person want from her? There had been no threat last night, no lettered sign indicating she was about to die. Were they searching for something? The strap of her purse dug into her shoulder. She realized the book with Sean's notes was still in there. Was that why the prowler had returned? The librarian had appeared to be colluding with her, but what if it had been a trap? Maybe Joel would know what to make of everything. If he ever forgave her.

For now, she would have to figure it out by herself. Why had someone threatened to kill her the same way as Sean had died? Mallory went through the story one more time with the inclusion of the new information she had received the day before. Sean had been investigating reopening a case of criminal negligence against the Turner Dam. Initially, she had assumed that Logan was in favor of the effort since he and Carlotta were the next of kin to Alice Halloway and the likely recipients of a settlement. But now she knew that, as the head engineer at the dam, he might actually have been found at fault, perhaps even personally responsible for the damages. Sean could have been building a case against Logan—not for him.

Mallory was confused about who would benefit from a settlement against the Turner Dam. Could Sean have been working for Carlotta? But why would she betray Dean's uncle by pursuing a lawsuit in which he might be named? Logan Carruthers had given her a new house after Dean had died, which suggested they were close. Her conversations with Suzanne and Joel about Dean being a violent man sprang to her mind. Carlotta had said that she learned to shoot to protect herself and that Logan was the one who had taught her. What if Dean's death hadn't been caused by the monster at all? Perhaps Carlotta had grown tired of her husband beating her and killed him herself. If Logan had known about the murder, he might have blackmailed her into helping him get rid of Sean. Or maybe the two had colluded to get rid of both Dean and Sean. Maybe the reason Carlotta was so eager to get back onto Mallory's property was to get rid of evidence they had left behind ten years ago.

She sucked in a breath. The cold air seemed more solid than her theory. She had no real evidence to suggest that the deaths of Alice Halloway, Dean Halloway, and Sean Benson were related. It was only a hunch. Alice had died in 1974, Dean in 1979, and Sean thirty-one years after that. No one else in town seemed to think they were united by anything but the spooky supernatural force that surrounded Loss Lake. Still, Mallory couldn't shake the feeling that, somehow, they were all connected. What was she missing?

When Mallory reached the main road, her toes were frozen together in an immovable lump. She trudged onward, her feet heavy with pain. Every step was like needles digging into her bones. *You can do this,* she told herself, hoping it wasn't the mantra of the hypothermic. She was panicked at the thought of freezing to death but even more so at the thought of turning around and burying herself in an isolated place with no way to contact anyone. Joel was so angry at her he might not bother to check on her, and she knew Kylie was working today. At best, Mallory wouldn't hear from her until past dark. Who knew what the prowler had in store for her tonight? Time was running out.

After many painful minutes, she finally saw the peak of Carlotta's roof. A plume of smoke billowed into the sky like a fox's tail. She knew it might not be safe to ask Carlotta for help, but she didn't know what else to do. Her toes dragged against the icy ground. She had put herself in danger by going outside so unprepared. Again. The conditions were cold enough to kill her. She had to get to a shelter. She forced herself to put one foot in front of the other.

Then she heard an impossible sound. A low thunder coming closer, loud and dangerous. Her stiff neck twinged as she raised her eyes toward the lumbering vehicle approaching her like a polar bear hunting a seal.

At first, her heart leaped at the sight of a truck similar in size to Joel's until she realized it was darker in color. It rolled to a stop about five feet away from her body, close enough for Mallory to smell the hot oil burning through the engine. Snow sloughed away from its tires.

Behind the steering wheel was Logan Carruthers.

CHAPTER
THIRTY-ONE

Standing still made Mallory's body shake, especially as the wind picked up and the tree branches began to clatter in time with her teeth. The truck was directly in front of her. If Logan accelerated unexpectedly, he could run her over and no one would know. The idea was absurd. The elderly man had never been anything but nice to her. She stepped around the side of the truck and walked toward the driver's door.

An article she had read once came to her mind. It had explained that killers capitalized on people's unwillingness to be impolite. Especially women. She tried to dismiss the dark thought as the man unrolled his window.

"Hello, Mallory. Can I interest you in a ride to town?"

As usual, Logan's tone was folksy. Was she imagining that the warmth didn't reach his eyes? He continued, "Too cold out here to walk. I was looking for you."

The words froze her blood even more than the frigid water soaking her useless boots.

She willed her voice not to shake. "Why were you looking for me?"

"The officer sent me. He said you might need a lift."

So Joel had tried to help.

"Joel asked you to come?"

Logan blinked slowly.

"No, no. Not Joel. Henry. He told me the cell phone lines were down and you had a car off the road. I've got one of the only landlines left in McNamara at the bar. You can call from there. So come on. You getting in?"

Mallory hesitated. She was cold, exhausted, and dehydrated. Every physical part of her was screaming for the comfort of the heater's breath on her body. It was almost overpowering, imagining slipping off the soggy leather of her boots and the thick, wet masses that had become her socks. Maybe it was safe. She had no real proof that Logan had anything to do with Sean's death.

"You coming?"

Mallory didn't move. If she was right about Sean being murdered, the man in front of her might be the one who had done it. He could have crept around her house the last two nights. He might want her dead. But Henry knew Logan was coming to meet her. Surely Logan wouldn't try anything if he was the last person known to have seen her. She took a deep breath. The cold air ate at her lungs.

"What's the holdup?" Logan asked. "You need me to carry you?"

He softened the words with a smile, which Mallory didn't return.

"No, I'm fine. Can you take me to Kylie's instead?" Mallory asked.

Logan spoke impatiently. "Sure, sure, but I can't get you anywhere if you don't get in."

She walked around the front of the vehicle. Once she made it around the side of the truck, Mallory ducked down, digging painfully into the snow to find a palm-size rock to keep in her hand during the drive.

When she climbed into the front seat, her body pulsed as her frozen nerves came back to life. The warm air blew on her face, and she leaned forward gratefully.

"Ready. And thanks."

"Anytime, Mallory. Remember, we take care of each other up here."

She realized that the words might mean something different to Logan than they did to her. In a pack of wolves, antisocial behavior was punished by fighting, sometimes even killing, the errant wolf. Did Logan and Carlotta consider what they had done to be for the good of the town? Dean had been violent, and so had Sean. Had they killed them to keep the peace?

As Logan shifted the truck into drive and began a complicated U-turn to get them back to town, Mallory stole a glance. The brim of his baseball cap was as frayed as the cuffs of his boiled-wool plaid jacket. It was so similar to Carlotta's that it might have made Mallory laugh if it hadn't reinforced her theory about their close connection—and what it might have meant for Sean and Dean. She clenched the rock with the small muscles in her fingers as he turned onto the main road. Suzanne's squat trailer was so covered in snow that it looked like a marshmallow. She shifted uncomfortably as the truck rolled through the drifts onto McNamara's main street.

"Bad luck," Logan mumbled.

"The storm?"

"Bad luck you going off the road from Turner," he said. "You've got to be more careful around here, Mallory. There's a whole lot of things that are different than in the city. You'll learn."

Mallory was silent. She willed the truck to move faster.

"Good thing Joel was around to save you yesterday. But he might not be there next time," he said.

His words seemed to contain a threat. She shifted the rock to her left hand and clasped her right around the door handle. Her heart pounded as they passed the library. Almost there.

"You hear what I'm saying?" Logan asked.

His patronizing tone sharpened her frustration into a pointed reply.

"If everyone takes care of each other, why have so many people been killed here?" she said, feeling fire flash out of her eyes.

She regretted the words as soon as she spoke them. The rock dug into her fingers as she prepared for him to lash out at her, but Logan only nodded in agreement. He seemed almost sad.

"Things are different in McNamara," he said. "The night the flood came in . . . it changed everything."

Mallory braced herself for a confession. Instead, Logan seemed to realize what he was about to reveal and deflected his own thought.

"I can't explain it to you. It's just something you're going to have to learn to accept. If you can't, well . . . maybe this isn't the right place for you after all. We're all family up here."

Family. She realized what she had been missing. If Alice Halloway had other descendants, they would be able to reopen the lawsuit against the owners of the Turner Dam and possibly Logan. They might be in danger too. She had to find them. Taking a huge risk, she asked another question.

"Do you have relatives around here?"

Logan didn't answer as he eased into a slow stop. Again, she clutched the rock. But when he replied, he seemed despondent rather than angry.

"Now that is a real long story," he said to the windshield. "You sure do ask a lot of questions."

She kept her eyes on him, willing him to speak. But he remained silent, facing forward. After a minute that seemed to last five, he finally broke the tension between them. "You can call a tow truck from here. I'll open early for you."

She looked out the window and realized that instead of taking her to Kylie's, Logan had driven her straight to his bar. She slid down from her seat as she pushed open the heavy door, dropping the rock with a soft thud she hoped he hadn't heard. Logan walked up the snow-covered sidewalk to the bar's entryway. When she didn't follow, he turned. His eyes squinted against the bright light of the snow draping every surface around them.

"Come on, Mallory. I've got what you're looking for in here."

His eyes seemed hollow. It was one of the strangest expressions she had ever seen, too uncomfortable to hold for long. She averted her gaze. Through the window, she caught a glimpse of the pub's interior. What she saw made her suck in her breath. The gun above the bar was missing.

She turned on her heel and ran.

CHAPTER THIRTY-TWO

The icy bumps and blowing drifts of snow made her knees knock together as she sprinted away from the old man. Despite the slippery terrain, she kept her pace fast enough to ensure he wouldn't be able to follow. Her heart thudded in her chest. Where was the gun? Had Logan Carruthers been planning to kill her? He could have. The bar was empty. It wasn't scheduled to open for hours. Maybe Henry hadn't sent him at all.

Seeing the lights behind the display outside Kylie's store nearly made her sob in relief. Two days ago, she had helped Kylie lug dozens of the pumpkins from her truck, fresh from the carving contest at the school. The heap of tumbling pumpkins had seemed playful. Now, the eight inches of snow topping them made them appear more like macabre elves. Their empty eyes watched her as she pulled open the glass door and stepped inside.

"Hey, hon," Kylie called from the cash register. A long roll of paper was spooled around her arm. Kylie grimaced at it as Mallory walked toward her, but her lighthearted expression turned to concern when Mallory failed to smile.

"Are you okay?"

"Kylie, I need your help."

"Of course!"

Mallory's body wilted in relief. She would start with the simplest problem.

"Can you call me a tow truck?" Mallory said.

Kylie nodded vigorously. "Oh God, yes. Joel told me what happened with your car. I was going to come check on you after work. Why didn't you call?"

"I did. It just rang and rang."

Kylie's forehead wrinkled up as she shook her head. "Sounds like the lines are down. I haven't heard a thing from anyone. Then again, I guess I wouldn't if no one's phones are working. It hasn't been real busy."

She made a sweeping gesture toward the empty aisles in front of them.

"You're my first customer of the day. Most people laid in their supplies before the storm hit. My dad's at home with Aura. He told me not to come in today, but I'm glad I did. You look like you've seen a ghost."

Mallory smiled weakly, flexing her fingers to try and relieve them of the dull pain.

Kylie continued. "You're soaking wet! Did you walk here? Let's get a cup of tea into you while I get in touch with Bob. He's likely going to be out on the roads right now, but I'm sure he'll come to help as soon as possible. We'll be able to bring your car home before it gets dark. It's not too damaged, right? Joel said your car's in the ditch on its side, but Bob might be able to right it and get it on its way."

Mallory filled Kylie in on the accident as her friend led her to the cozy nook in the back, settling into her usual spot as Kylie prepared tea. Sitting there made her realize that even though there was someone creeping around her place after dark, she had friends here too. Kylie smiled as she reached for the tea bags rather than the jars containing her less traditional ingredients, giving Mallory a thumbs-up.

Mallory slipped off her dripping jacket and sodden boots as Kylie hummed away in the corner. Then she wiggled her toes in her damp socks to increase their circulation. She knew she had to rescue her car, but the idea of going back into the wintry world outside the door filled her with dread. Kylie approached the table with two steaming mugs in hand like a Saint Bernard on a mountaintop. Mallory thanked her for the large cup, then gingerly pressed the tips of her fingers against the side of it to heat them up without scalding the wrinkled, sensitive skin.

"How did you get here?" Kylie asked after they'd both taken a sip.

"Logan Carruthers."

"Really?" Kylie's curiosity made her voice rise. "How did that happen?"

"He told me that Henry sent him."

Mallory's eyes filled with tears at the thought of the danger she had escaped.

"Oh, hon."

"I feel crazy, Kylie. I've had a prowler at my house threatening me for two nights in a row. A friend of mine came to visit last night but left this morning without a trace. Joel is furious at me. And I'm terrified that Logan killed Sean. That he's the one behind everything."

"What? Oh my God. Slow down. You're traumatized by the car accident. Who came to visit you? Why is Joel angry?"

Mallory wiped her tears away hard enough to make her face sting.

"None of that matters. I mean, I'll explain it later. The important thing is that I get Joel to read these notes. We need to find out what really happened to Sean."

"Notes?" Kylie's expression became guarded. "Sean was killed by a hunter, Mallory."

"I know, it all sounds insane. But look."

Mallory pulled the book from her purse. It opened to the page that identified Logan as the chief engineer of the Turner Dam.

"Holy crap," Kylie said softly as Mallory filled her in on her theory about Sean. "My parents never told me that Logan worked at the dam. He must have opened the bar right after the flood."

"That makes sense. He would have needed another source of income—especially if he was worried about his own liability. Plus, Joel mentioned that Logan was seen arguing with Sean right before he died. Kylie, I'm worried he's dangerous."

Kylie's eyes were wide with apprehension, and Mallory realized that hers must be the same. She could feel an unfamiliar sting at the edges, as if too much air was getting in.

"We need to talk to Joel. He'll know what to do," Kylie said.

"Oh God. He's so angry at me. I'm not sure he'll want to help."

"What happened with Joel?"

Mallory wanted to tell Kylie everything about Cynthia, but she couldn't risk losing the woman's support. Instead, she lied.

"We fought. I wasn't myself yesterday. I was worried about my car and getting it home, and I didn't think he was taking me seriously."

"Oh, hon. I can only imagine how stressed you were. It doesn't sound like a big fight, though. I'm sure he's forgotten by now."

"I hope you're right," Mallory said. "But I think the last thing he's going to want to do is help me."

"Whatever is happening between the two of you won't matter to him right now. Trust me. This is bigger than that. We look out for each other up here."

Mallory willed herself to share Kylie's confidence. Maybe if she could help Joel understand what had really happened to his brother, he would allow her to tell him the whole story of what had occurred between her and Cynthia.

Kylie stood up to grab her coat and shut down the store, promising she wouldn't be more than a few minutes. Mallory grew restless as she waited, listening to her friend hum something that sounded suspiciously like Enya as she moved around the store. She flipped through the pages of Frederich's book. Maybe there was more to learn.

A loose piece of paper fell from the middle section of the book. Mallory flattened it out on the table. It was a chart, specifically a family tree, written in Sean's characteristic plain block letters, as meticulous as the grocery list she had found weeks ago. Excitement flared in her mind. She hoped it included the unknown relative of Alice who was working with Sean.

At the top was a box with Alice Halloway's name. A dotted line connected her to Logan Carruthers, indicating their relationship as brother and sister. Her adrenaline surged as she looked at the name to the left of Alice's—her husband, Tom Halloway, the man who had died in a logging accident when Dean was a teenager. But strangely, there was a wavy line connecting Alice to another man. Jonathan Shine. *Was Sean indicating an affair?*

Mallory leaned in until the paper was six inches from her face.

The line between Alice and Jonathan led down to Dean. Mallory squinted at it closely, certain she was reading it wrong. The chart seemed to show that Dean Halloway was the offspring of Alice and Jonathan, not Alice and Tom Halloway. Which meant Dean had been Jonathan Shine's son.

Mallory gasped. Carlotta Gray was listed beside Dean, but no children were connected underneath the two of them. Once again, a wavy line on the other side of Dean's name led to a woman named Jackie Benson. Dean had been having an affair as well, which had produced two sons. Between Jackie and Dean were two straight lines leading to the names Joel and Sean Benson. Mallory dropped the book to the table with a quiet thump. If this chart was correct, Dean Halloway was Jonathan's son and Joel's father. Joel and Sean were related to Jonathan Shine by blood. Joel had been adopted by his own grandfather.

Her mind raced. She remembered Betty telling her that Joel's mother had moved away from McNamara with her two sons shortly after the *death of their father*. Betty had never mentioned a name, but if their mother had left town when both boys were small children, it lined up with the date of Dean's drowning. Maybe the story about another man sweeping Jackie off her feet had been invented to save face for Carlotta. But if Betty knew about Dean's infidelity, Carlotta likely did as well. Which gave her a whole new reason for wanting Dean dead.

This built her case against Logan as well. If Dean was the biological father of Joel and Sean, they were the rightful recipients of any settlement that came from a lawsuit against the Turner Dam and its employees. What if Sean had not been pursuing the lawsuit on behalf of another person but for himself?

She had to tell Joel.

Kylie exited the back room, her jacket already on. Mallory jumped up to join her. She was too shell-shocked to speak, but Kylie didn't seem to notice as she turned off lights, switched the sign from open to closed, and locked the main door behind them. As she worked, Mallory kept worrying. Something still didn't make sense. *If Joel was the only surviving relative of Dean Halloway, and Sean had been killed to end the lawsuit, why would the murderer have left Joel alive?*

Kylie whistled under her breath as the two women walked to her truck.

"Man, I haven't seen an early snowfall like this in years."

Mallory tried to shake off her distraction. "But everyone kept telling me winter comes early here."

"Sure, but it's not usually this bad in October," Kylie said. "Last time it came in this hard was back in 2010." She spoke dreamily, lost in thought. "It snowed us all in then. So deep they had to close the road from Turner. No one could get in or out for days."

"That was the year Sean was killed."

Kylie stopped in her tracks. Her body went rigid for a long moment. Her face was as white as the snow that surrounded them. Mallory looked at Kylie in horror.

"If the roads were that bad, how did the hunters get here?" Mallory asked.

"We should go," Kylie said hurriedly.

"Joel told me he was working in Turner that night. He said he drove back in the morning and found Sean dead in the house. How did he do that if the roads were closed?"

PART THREE

CHAPTER
THIRTY-THREE

The two women drove in silence. Kylie had clammed up the moment they both got into the cab of the truck, telling Mallory that there was nothing more she could say until they talked to Joel. Unlike the fear-laced tension between her and Logan, the space between them seemed like a balloon inflating with questions. *Where had Joel been that night?*

Her mind whirred as she considered what it meant that Joel and Kylie had both lied to her. Then she realized there was only one person who they would cover for. He had been right under her nose the entire time.

Henry Shine. Suzanne had been accusing him of the crime all along. He and Logan seemed to be close. In fact, she had seen them together more often than she'd seen Logan with Carlotta. And hadn't Logan told her it was Henry who'd sent him today? The pieces fit together except for one thing. Motive. What reason did Henry have for killing Sean? And why would he work in collusion with Logan against his own family?

As the snow-weighted trees bowed down to them on either side of the highway, Mallory realized why Joel had been so angry at her for keeping the truth from him about Cynthia. She was now furious at him for his own omissions and obfuscations. Loving someone meant telling them the whole story, not sealing up some parts in the hope they'd never find out. A strange thought came to her. At least now, they were even. Maybe, after the dust settled and they both got to the bottom of each other, there was still a chance they could make a life for themselves. Together.

There was a yellow glow in the window of the log cabin when they pulled up. It was a smaller version of the main house, where Jonathan lived. The snow had gathered, soft and deep, on the angles of the roof and rafters. The piles were lit by reflection from inside, making Joel's house look like a cottage in a fairy tale. Mallory's anxiety rose and she stiffened on the seat. Was she really about to accuse Joel's adoptive brother of killing his biological one? And worse, point the finger at Joel for helping to cover up the crime?

"He's inside," Kylie said. "Do you want me to come with you after I check on Aura? I'll just be next door."

Mallory took a deep breath. It was Joel. He had to have a reason for what he had done.

"Of course not. I'll come by after we talk," she replied.

Kylie agreed. They both knew this was a conversation that had to happen between Mallory and Joel. Mallory got out of the truck and walked up the cleared path to the front door. It had been cleanly shoveled, as if she was expected. The entryway to the wood cabin was three steps up from the ground, and she walked up slowly, letting one foot settle beside the other like a bride in a wedding march. Her unhurried gait allowed her to take in the detail of the construction. The house was easy to admire. Even with the dusting of snow, she could see the honeyed grain of the polished wood beneath her feet. The railing in her hand was made of a knobby stick, sanded to a texture as smooth as glass. Like Jonathan's home, the logs that held this place together had been notched perfectly, each indentation formed to fit with the other. The cabin had been made with love and care, honoring both the wooden beams that formed it and the people who would inhabit its space. She took another deep breath and reasoned with herself. Despite her misgivings, she was safer here than any other place she had been that day. Joel was a good man. He would understand why she had left things out of her story, as she would for him. She had a reason for misleading him. He must have as well.

She knocked on the door, wincing when her skin came into contact with the cold wood. The door opened almost immediately, and Joel stood before her in the doorway. His cheeks were flushed from the heat of the woodstove that enveloped her the moment she stepped over the threshold. He was wearing a charcoal-gray pullover, pilled from many washings, and his hair was tousled at the back, like he had just pulled off a knit cap.

"Mallory," he said. His voice was husky.

Inside, the cabin was even more beautiful—an entirely open space with a bed in one back corner and a rough-hewn table and chairs in the other. An armchair and a love seat were positioned on her right-hand side. The pattern was identical to the chair in her home. Mallory realized it was a matched set. To her left, there was a closed door, which likely led to the bathroom. Along the back wall, Mallory could see a simple hot plate and countertop with a sink. The open fireplace, which stood in the center with a low bench all around it, danced and crackled, lending golden sparks to Joel's brown eyes as he regarded her. Mallory wasn't sure she had ever seen him look more handsome.

"I've been worried about you," he said at the exact moment she spoke.

"Why did you lie to me about being in Turner the day Sean died?"

"Mallory, that is—"

He couldn't finish his sentence. She interrupted him.

"Did you know that you and Sean were related to Alice Halloway?"

"What?" he said.

His face became wary.

"What was Henry doing in the forest that day?"

Instead of knitting them together, her words were a force that was pushing them apart. Joel took a step backward, then another, until he was standing about three feet from the fireplace. She stayed in place by the door, knowing that after she finished, she might no longer be welcome, wondering if she was at that moment, if Joel was just too stunned to kick her out. His expression was unreadable. She wasn't sure he was taking in what she was saying.

"I know that you and Sean were the beneficiaries of the settlement he was pursuing. I think Logan killed him so he wouldn't be held accountable for the settlement. And I think"—it was almost too horrible to say—"I think Henry had something to do with it."

Joel looked away. Mallory wasn't sure if the gesture was one of frustration—or an admission of guilt.

"What aren't you telling me? Joel, Logan's gun is missing. He doesn't like me digging around in the past. He could come after me next. Or send Henry."

"That's not possible."

"Did you know what Logan was planning to do? Kylie told me you were in McNamara that night. Not in Turner."

He jerked his head toward her. When their eyes met, a spark passed between them, big enough to light them both on fire. Then he turned away again. The movement was sharp and reflexive. She followed his gaze to the corner of the room. It was dark, but the flicker of the fire revealed a tall shape propped up in the corner.

Logan's gun. He spoke again before she could find a reason for it to be there.

"I thought you understood. I thought that's why you came."

"Understood what? Why do you have Logan's gun? Where were you the night Sean died?"

Joel stared with blank eyes. His face tightened like he was wearing a mask of the person she'd thought she knew.

"Do you really want me to answer that?"

"Yes."

Joel took a step toward her.

"I was here. We all were."

The words sank into her stomach. Henry, Joel, and Kylie had been involved in what happened to Sean.

"I heard about the trouble Cynthia Rooney caused for you at the funeral. I know what she was trying to do to you."

The abrupt subject change put her on the defensive.

"If you knew about her, why were you so angry when Sadie told you who she really was?"

Joel shook his head angrily. "I've known who Cynthia Rooney was since the day after you got to town. Of course I looked into her death. A woman drowning in the middle of the day moments before you moved to town? It was suspicious. I'm a good cop, Mallory. I needed to know who you really were. But I couldn't let Sadie know what I had done. That I covered it up for you."

"Covered what up?"

"Her death, Mallory. I know you lured her here. I know you understand the power of the lake even if you came here for more frivolous purposes. You have it in you. You can be one of us."

Joel's pupils reflected the dancing of the flames.

"What are you talking about? I didn't do anything to Cynthia Rooney. There was nothing to cover up."

"You don't have to lie anymore. Even if you did come here because of your husband, I know I was right about you. You feel the power of the lake. You're part of McNamara now. We look out for each other here."

The familiar phrase had become ominous.

"What do you mean?"

"You and I are the same, Mallory. Like Kylie and Henry and everyone else. We are willing to do what we have to to protect the people we love. The others here understand. Nobody wants to hurt each other. When someone tries to hurt us, we all fight back."

All this time, she had misunderstood what everyone had been telling her. Mallory was sickened as she considered who Joel was referring to. "We" meant more than one person. It might even mean the whole town.

"What are you talking about?"

"Stop pretending. I know you. You've done it too."

"What do you think I've done?"

"Sean was like Cynthia. All they cared about were themselves, what they thought they deserved. He was greedy. She was punitive. They both had the power to destroy everything and everyone we loved."

"What are you saying?"

Joel looked her dead in the eyes. Something ugly and powerful pulsed between them.

"We both have blood on our hands. I killed Sean like you killed Cynthia."

He paused. She hated the shape of him that was appearing before her. He looked like a monster. "And like you killed your husband."

CHAPTER THIRTY-FOUR

Mallory stared at Joel in shock. He wasn't wrong about her. But he wasn't right either. What had happened between her and Graham was something no one else could understand.

She was a nurse. She should have been prepared. But watching him die wasn't like it had been in the hospital. The long months of Mallory caring for him had worn on them both, turned them into the worst of what they were. But on the last day of his life, something changed.

Gone were the rages and the petty insults. In their place was acceptance unlike anything she had ever seen. He became the man she had first married, before he had let pettiness overwhelm his spirit, before his illness had made him rage against the world, his body, and her. He didn't have to tell her he had come to peace with her and with whatever was about to come next. She could feel it. Still, it didn't make it easier to watch.

Over the course of the last day of his life, Graham's skin had turned gray. At first, the color was easy to dismiss as a trick of the light. It wasn't until the temperature of his skin cooled too that it had become undeniable. Then each of his breaths began to take more effort than the last. For hours, she sat by his side, reading aloud, then watching his favorite movie when he couldn't focus on words anymore. But their laughter wasn't enough to drown out the unbearable countdown of those thick sets of breath.

When the movie ended, he had turned to her.

"I am so tired," he said. His tone was tender and kind.

"So am I."

Then they both wept. It had lasted for a long time, the longest Mallory could ever remember crying. Just like the moment she had shared with Sadie, their wordless tears had released what they had both been holding on to.

He asked her to tell him the story of her worst mistake in nursing. The time she had nearly incapacitated a woman's weak heart by administering aspirin. Reciting it had been almost like a dream. When Graham asked her to retrieve the bottle of the same type of painkillers from their medicine cabinet, it felt smooth and false in her hands as she gave it to him, like a prop in a play. Graham took a shallow breath before he spoke. His lips so chapped. No matter how much balm she slathered upon them, she couldn't convince them to heal.

"It's over. I don't want to do this anymore. One more day, two. It's not worth it."

She had nodded. The movement was loose, as if she were drunk.

"Are you sure?" Mallory had said.

"Yes."

The silence between them seemed sacred. Her husband was wearing an expression she had never seen before. She could describe it only as peace. The out-of-body sense she had been having throughout their conversation heightened into euphoria, like a weight had been lifted from her shoulders.

"I love you, Graham."

"I love you, Mallory."

And she did. In that moment, she had never loved him more. With great care, she walked to the bed and placed a cool hand on the side of her husband's face. He looked at her with the same wondering eyes she had seen on their wedding day.

"Good night."

"Good night, Mallory."

Her tears had been nearly enough to obscure her vision of the bottle of pills that Graham still held in his hand. Once upstairs, she made a call to the home-care nurse, telling her they would not require her services.

~

There was a time she had thought that Joel would be able to understand the mercy she had given her husband. And the one Graham had given to her. But now, the man standing in front of her was unrecognizable.

"I didn't kill Graham."

"Don't worry. I'm the only one who knows. Sadie doesn't have a clue."

Mallory's heart thumped in her chest.

"You spoke with Sadie about me? When did you see her? Where did you take her?"

Mallory was terrified on behalf of the woman who had cried with her last night. If Joel had been willing to kill his own brother, what had he done to Sadie?

"After last night, I had to make sure I was right. I came by this morning."

"What did you do with her?"

Panic bubbled up inside her. Joel no longer offered protection. Instead, his eyes were cold with the threat of harm.

"She's safe, Mallory. I didn't hurt her."

His voice was soothing, but Mallory didn't believe a word he was saying. Sadie was in danger.

And so was she.

Joel continued. "I would never hurt someone who didn't deserve it."

He moved forward a step. She had to regain control of the situation. Keep him talking.

"So Sean . . . deserved it?"

Joel looked down and then up. Mallory was relieved when she realized his eyes were wet with tears. If he was crying, he had to feel remorse. He had to know that what he had done could not be justified.

"I didn't want to hurt him. I tried to teach him how to appreciate what he had. But Sean was never happy with anything. He always wanted more. When Jonathan and Dee took us in, I knew we had finally found a family. Our mom was a drunk, especially after Dean Halloway drowned."

"Your father?"

His face twisted in unresolved hurt. "Dean Halloway was never a father to me. But then again, neither was the man my mom married. My mom moved us away, told us that we could start a new life, but I hated it in the city. She was always out. I had to take care of Sean, until my mom died."

Mallory did fast arithmetic in her head. Something about what Joel was saying seemed off. "Joel, you weren't even four years old when you left McNamara. How on earth can you remember all this?"

"Jonathan saw it all, Mallory. He told me. We could have stayed here so easily. Dean left us the house, you know. He told my mom it was to take care of us, me and Sean. But my mom was selfish. She didn't want to stay in the same town as Carlotta."

So that was why Logan had given Carlotta a house. To make up for his nephew's awful actions. Not only had he beaten her, but he'd left her homeless after his death. Was it possible Carlotta had seen Dean's will? Knowing that he had left their property to his mistress would have provided more motive. Mallory circled back to her original theory.

"Did your mom run away from McNamara because Carlotta killed Dean?"

"What? No. Carlotta didn't kill Dean. She was barely out of her teens. She hardly weighed a hundred pounds. She couldn't drown a grown man."

"So Dean's death was an accident, then?"

Joel shook his head, which sent waves of frustration through Mallory's body. She was still missing something.

"Dean got what he deserved."

Mallory's thoughts were like angry wasps inside her head. "So somebody did kill him?"

Joel's expression turned incredulous.

"You really don't understand anything at all, do you?"

"No, I don't. Help me!"

"Dean drowned. Just like Cynthia." His mouth was firm and his eyes were dark.

"Cynthia's death was an accident."

"Or was it a judgment?"

The air grew still. Inside the fire, a ball of sap popped loudly enough to make Mallory jump. Joel smiled in the way she had once loved. The way that used to make her feel safe.

"Joel, I don't understand."

"I think you do, deep down inside. Dean Halloway was a terrible man. He beat Carlotta. He used my mother like she was nothing. And he killed Alice Halloway."

Her jaw dropped.

"What are you talking about?"

"When the water started rising, Jonathan went to Alice's house to save her. He drove through a river rushing up around his tires to get there. The whole valley was drowning, but he couldn't let a woman he had loved, the mother of his child, die. But instead of a woman clinging to life in a flood, he found her dead with a gunshot in her chest."

"Dean killed her?"

"Yes. She could never control him. He was wild, even as a teenager. Apparently she gave up and started drinking with him just so she knew where he was at night. They kept a loaded gun in the house because it was so remote. Every once in a while, a bear or cougar would come too close to the farm. They were on the outskirts of town. Things like that happened. That night, their conversation must have got heated. Everyone in town knew that Dean had a temper that couldn't be controlled. Alice ended up shot. Jonathan thought he could help her when the water started rising. But it was too late. She was dead in the kitchen."

"Oh my God."

The answers she had sought for so long were coming at her faster than she could process. Dean had murdered his own mother?

"So you see why it had to happen the way it did. Jonathan waited for five years for Dean to get on the water. He knew—they all did—that the lake meant something. Something was drawn here the night Dean killed his mother. The flood was unleashed to give it a home."

Mallory stared at Joel in horror as he continued.

"When Jonathan sank Dean's canoe, he was waiting for the lake to make its verdict on whether or not Dean deserved to live. Jonathan had seen the monster off the coast. He knew what would happen to a man with an impure heart. And sure enough, Dean died exactly the way Jonathan knew he would. He was a strong swimmer, but he sank like a stone. And we all know why."

"You think . . . your grandfather administered justice to your father by . . . letting him drown? You believe that?"

"Jonathan let justice take its course. Dean was a good-enough swimmer to get to shore. Innocent people don't die in Loss Lake, Mallory. You should know that by now. This is a place where people come to be judged, whether they know it or not. If you're telling the truth about Cynthia and you didn't bring her here on purpose"—Joel's mouth curled unpleasantly, indicating what he really believed—"then you should know the lake sees more than a human can. His death proved that Dean was guilty of a lot of things. More than you can ever comprehend. Cynthia must have been too. She would never have died if she wasn't."

She tried to get back on solid ground. Joel's beliefs about Loss Lake were hard to take in.

"But why would Dean do that to his mother?"

Alice Halloway had died in 1974. If it was true that Dean had been responsible for her death, he would have killed her when he was sixteen years old.

"Who knows? Best I can figure, drunken rage," Joel said with a grimace. "All I know for certain is that his evil deed was what caused the dam to break. When the water filled the valley, the monster arrived. Dean brought the monster here. Evil to evil. The curse of matricide. He killed his own mother. When she was murdered, the act was powerful enough to break the dam."

Mallory didn't recognize Joel. He looked like a religious zealot singing about the devil. She tried to bring him back to reality.

"This doesn't make any sense. The dam was faulty."

"There's something powerful here, Mallory. No matter how much you deny it, I know you feel it too."

Mallory didn't know how to speak to the stranger in front of her. She was desperate for facts, not supernatural rhetoric. "But why didn't Jonathan report how Alice really died to the police? Why keep it a secret all these years? Why let it be blamed on the Turner Dam? Dean should have gone to prison."

"He couldn't let Dee know where he'd been that night, that he'd rushed out to save a woman Dee was already suspicious of. McNamara is a small town. People talk. His affair with Alice was common knowledge. Even though it ended before he and Dee were married, she got wind of it."

"So Jonathan covered it up to protect his marriage, then killed his own son for retribution?"

"It was a fair trial. He let the lake decide. Besides, at the time he didn't know for sure that Dean was his son. All he had was Alice's word, and by his account, that wasn't worth all that much. She was a fast woman. She was married to another man. And she was a drinker. She used to come to the logging camps on their days off. Twelve years older than Jonathan, so it was hard to think it could be serious. Jonathan was sixteen when they met and only eighteen years old when she got pregnant. He was considered a man at that age but hardly ready to father a child."

"So he didn't support Alice?"

"He was just a kid. She was married to Tom Halloway. They didn't see each other much after Dean was born. It was for the best. Then he met Dee, and they got married. Everyone thought the matter had been put to bed. Until Sean started digging into places he shouldn't have been looking."

"Did her husband believe he was the father of Dean?"

"I have no idea. He drowned in the ocean off the coast when Dean was a teenager, like Jonathan said when you came over for dinner the other night."

Another piece in the puzzle. Alice's husband had been the man who beat his wife and laughed about it to the crew. Mallory's heart ached at the life Alice had lived.

"You know how insane this sounds, right?"

Joel looked at her with wounded eyes, but she felt no emotional response. Had she ever really loved him? Or was she just terrified of being alone? Maybe she was more like her mother than she'd realized.

"It was only when Sean started going through old medical records to pull out blood types that it was confirmed Jonathan had fathered Dean."

"That's when Sean drew the family tree," Mallory said to herself. Joel didn't seem to hear.

"He interfered when he shouldn't. That confirmation about Dean was hard for Jonathan to take, but he had to accept it. The lake had made its decision."

"So none of this has anything to do with the settlement from the Turner Dam? But who's been threatening me?"

Joel took a step toward her and she winced. His expression registered hurt, then anger. When he spoke, his voice was low and urgent.

"You were getting ahead of yourself by asking so many questions. I needed you to slow down. Until I was sure you really understood."

Mallory hadn't thought Joel could shock her any more that night. His words left her as winded as if she had been punched in the stomach.

"You were the prowler?"

"I was the warning."

The man she'd thought she loved had been terrorizing her.

"But how did you . . . why did you make it seem like the footprints disappeared into the lake?"

"There are ways. The lake deserves your loyalty. I needed you to learn to respect where we are. The world we live in."

"But that's why I wanted to learn about Sean's investigation."

Joel snorted. "Sean didn't respect anything. Sean just wanted money. He didn't care who it hurt. Sean was greedy. He never appreciated what Jonathan and Dee did for us. He didn't realize the value of their care, didn't remember what it was like to live with a drunk for a mother. There was no one in the world like Dee. Nobody like her. We all knew it. That's why we wanted to protect her. After my mom died, when we moved in with the Shines, finally, we had parents who actually cared."

"Grandparents."

Joel nodded, the corners of his mouth turning up like he was pleased that she was finally following along.

"It's the same to me, grandfather, adopted father. It doesn't matter. Even before Sean got the medical records, I respected Jonathan as an elder. Then I learned that he's my blood and he was Sean's as well. And you don't betray blood."

"Jonathan killed his own son! How can you love Jonathan and hate Dean?"

Joel looked at her sadly. She had disappointed him again.

"Jonathan didn't kill his blood. He left it to the lake. He sees me as an equal. A man he can trust. I understand Loss Lake like he does. Like I thought you did too."

The way Joel spoke about Jonathan was eerily reverential. Did he believe that Jonathan had bestowed a great honor upon him by indoctrinating him into his macabre belief system? She had to understand what had happened to Joel's brother.

"Did Jonathan speak to Sean about all this as well?"

"No, that was me. I thought I could trust Sean. When he started looking into the history, I took him aside. I told him the truth, that no amount of money was worth hurting Dee. But he didn't see it that way."

He sighed heavily. "I tried to make Sean understand. Dee was the best mother we ever had. The only mother, really. Jonathan loved her with all his heart, and so did I. She was from the city, like you. He knew she had the strength to keep our bloodline going. He and a couple of other logger buddies went down to see the sights during the breakup, and Jonathan ended up meeting her. He fell in love. She was only twenty when she moved up here. Jonathan never wanted her to know about his . . . indiscretion with Alice. It was over years before he met her, but he knew she would be devastated to learn that Dean could be his son. He couldn't bear the idea of hurting her so badly. Especially when Dean turned out the way he did. What Sean was doing would have destroyed everything Jonathan had built. It would have hurt so many people."

"But didn't Jonathan hurt Alice when he refused to support her? Or acknowledge his son?"

Joel's eyes narrowed.

"He had to choose. We all did."

Mallory looked at him carefully, realizing what he was saying.

"You and Kylie and Henry?"

Joel frowned. "This has nothing to do with them."

"But they knew."

"Not until later. The Turner police were looking into Sean's death. I needed an alibi. So Kylie told the police we'd gotten stuck together on the highway on the way home. That the two of us had stayed the night in the truck waiting for them to open the road again. She said that by the time we got back to McNamara, it was too late. She doesn't know anything besides that. She understands enough not to ask."

Joel stepped toward her again. His eyes were cold and his body was tense. Mallory knew better than to disagree, though she was heartbroken to hear of her friend's culpability in her own brother's death.

"So, if Jonathan decided that only Loss Lake and whatever it contains could exact justice on Dean, why did you shoot Sean? Why didn't you wait until he came to the lake like Jonathan did to his son?"

Joel's expression darkened further. "Sean would never set foot in that lake. Even when we were kids. We used to tease him about it. But that day, it was no joke. I asked Henry to try to convince him to go in. Sean had a real weakness for Henry."

So that was why Suzanne had seen him in the forest. She had been right to accuse him of knowing more than he admitted.

"We walked him down to the shore, but he fought like a demon, then ran back to the house. He thought he couldn't be touched in there. But he was wrong."

Mallory felt sick to her stomach.

"Have you swum in the lake, Joel?"

He looked proud. "I have."

Mallory's voice was quiet. "Have you gone in since Sean died?"

Joel's head shook from side to side. *No.* A flicker of doubt danced through his eyes.

"So you can decide whether someone lives or dies, but you can't let the lake judge you?"

"Can you let it judge you, Mallory? Are you ready to be truly seen?"

I didn't kill anyone, Mallory wanted to scream at him. But instead, she reached behind her, slowly so he wouldn't catch on. Or worse, lunge for the rifle in the corner of the room.

"You and I are the same, Mallory. I can step into that lake and come out again. We didn't kill for greed or out of anger. We are clean. You did it for love. Just like me. I did it for Dee. You did it for Graham. Sometimes, loyalty requires sacrifice."

"We are not the same."

Then she turned the door handle sharply and fled.

CHAPTER
THIRTY-FIVE

She didn't have a car. She didn't have a plan. She didn't know if her boots would hold together long enough to get her home. The soles had peeled away from them, and after flinging herself down the steep trail that led to the beach, they were both flapping like the tongue of a sprinting dog, splashing icy melted snow up at her. But she had to try. She had to find Sadie.

The beach was covered in mounds of snow that had frozen on top but not underneath, rendering the surface sharp but unstable. Mallory lurched from bump to bump, feeling her hips rattling in their sockets. The lake stretched in front of her, dull and gray as an unpolished knife. She slid and stumbled to keep her balance. With each step, she became more and more convinced that she was not alone.

Then, breaking the hush of the waves, there was a sharp cry. Joel was behind her, calling her name.

She leaned forward, letting her momentum carry her past the point of balance as she pushed herself over the humps and heaves of the snow. She pounded her heels into the snow hard, using her legs like pistons. Joel had six inches on her, but she was a runner. She had been training for this day for years without realizing it. She had to get away. She had been wrong about him. He had been wrong about her.

She was not a killer.

~

One month before, sweaty and excited by her close proximity to McNamara, she had stopped at the patch of sand to get her bearings, as she had explained to Joel. She was new in town and not skilled at reading maps in unfamiliar locations. Once, she had gotten lost in Barcelona, much to Graham's irritation. He had waited for two hours for her to return from a quick walk around the corner. She had thought that getting her bearings before driving to her brand-new house would take only a moment. Until Cynthia arrived.

The moment the woman slammed the door of the unfamiliar car, Mallory had become nauseated. She moved to her car, wanting to put a shell of metal between herself and Graham's cousin, who had clearly gone crazy enough to follow her more than a thousand miles north to the place that was supposed to set her free.

"No, no. Leave me alone. You have to go—" Mallory had said, halfway into her car before Cynthia spoke.

"You need to own up to what you did. You canceled the nurse. You knew how sick he was and you let him die!"

Mallory had stopped, frozen midcrouch between the seat of the car and her standing position outside it. No one could hear her now. If Cynthia was going to kill her or hurt her, she had no choice left but to tell the truth. She straightened her body, steeled her spine, and looked into Cynthia's wild eyes.

"Graham asked me to do it."

Cynthia's anger came at Mallory with such force that she took a step back, but she never dropped her gaze.

"He was too sick to keep going. Graham accepted the end. He wanted to do it on his terms."

Mallory had been stunned to see the hate in Cynthia's eyes melt into grief. Pure, wild sorrow filled her eyes. Suddenly, roughly, frighteningly, she grabbed Mallory. But instead of clawing at her, Cynthia pulled Mallory into her arms. Mallory had been overcome by shock at being embraced instead of attacked. Fumes of alcohol wafted from Graham's cousin's body when she hugged her back. Cynthia's tears ripped choking sounds from her throat as she cried and cried. And like that, Cynthia forgave her. It had seemed so simple at the time.

When it was over, Cynthia had smoothed down her hair. Her face was lined with rivulets of black makeup.

"I must look a mess," she said.

Mallory had laughed along with the other woman. "A little."

"God. I didn't expect it to be so warm up here. Maybe I should go for a swim. You know, for old times' sake. Graham always used to say that this was a place where a person could get clean. Really clean. I've held on to so much pain, so much hate, for so long. It's time to let it go."

"Graham used to tell me that too," Mallory said. It was what had drawn her to the small town on the edge of the large lake.

Cynthia smiled sadly.

"You need to get to your new home. You won't hear from me again. Unless you want to."

Mallory wished she had stayed to watch Cynthia enter the water. Maybe she could have helped with whatever happened. Instead, she had left, as the woman asked. In her memory, Cynthia's face would always be smeared with the blackness of her tears.

~

The sand at the water's edge was partially exposed. The waves had licked away some of the ice and snow, like a cat removing an unwanted splash of water. There was a lane there for her to run. She veered toward it. The ice broke under her feet like glass. Several shards poked into the holes in her boots.

Joel's footsteps crashed behind her. Her breath coursed in and out of her lungs painfully.

And then she saw it. Her house, the place that was supposed to keep her safe, to protect her and let her erase the past. A faint light from the kitchen beckoned her forward, and she drove her heels even harder into the frozen sand, forcing her quads to move faster and dig deeper. If she could get home, if she could leave Joel behind, maybe she would know what should happen next. If she turned Joel in, would he turn on her? Would he reopen the file on Cynthia? Would it matter if she shared what she had learned about him and the Shines?

"Mallory!" Joel called again. His voice was raw.

With each stride, the sight of her house grew clearer and the lights flickering around her grew brighter. Too bright. Traces of red and blue flashed through the trees. This was not just the light from her window. It was something more official. The opaque fog drifting from the lake made the entire length of the beams visible as they pulsed on and off. Mallory stopped as three people walked out from the spaces between the trees. Two police officers were approaching with stern expressions on their faces. They were flanked by a large woman.

Sadie Rooney.

Joel caught up. Mallory flinched as he came close, but he didn't grab her. Instead, he doubled over, trying to catch his breath, choking out words between gasps.

"Mallory . . . you have to . . . listen to me."

She pointed. "They're looking for me, aren't they?"

Joel closed his eyes slowly. "I escorted Sadie to Turner. I dropped her at the coffee shop beside the police station. She said she wanted to help you get a tow truck, and I told her the police could call one."

Mallory knew that Sadie spoke freely and trusted everyone. She must have let it slip that Cynthia had drowned while seeking out a woman she had accused of murder. Of course the police had come knocking. But this meant Joel was in trouble too. He had covered up the suspicious case for her. Joel had been right after all. In the eyes of the law, they were the same. Neither of them was innocent. But that did not mean she was guilty.

The police spotted them. She could hear them call to each other, their voices frantic and excited, as she turned her back. Sadie was crying her name over and over, as if it would get her attention. As if anything she said could be as compelling to her as the lake. In the low afternoon light, its surface was as dark and smooth as velvet. At the edge where she was standing, ice had gathered like sleep in the corner of an eye. Her foot was so close to the slow suck of the water.

She remembered what Joel had said. *Innocent people don't die in Loss Lake.* She thought about the way he considered her to be like him: a killer, a human who had taken a life. It was so close to the way she had regarded herself up until the moment she had moved to McNamara. Now, she wasn't sure how much death stained her soul. She didn't feel like a murderer. But she didn't feel clean.

She *had* chosen to come to McNamara because of the stories Graham had told her. The stories about a creature that could weigh a soul. Unlike Joel, she hadn't wanted to avoid blame by pinning her crimes on a legend, a myth, a monster.

She had come to Loss Lake seeking absolution. Now it was her time to be judged.

You can do this.

Mallory didn't hesitate a moment longer. She plunged her leg into the icy water and let the lake decide.

ACKNOWLEDGMENTS

This is a tough section to write because it took so much to get this book into the world, and I leaned hard on those around me as I tried to write through my own fog of grief. Like Mallory, I was lost. Unlike her, the people who helped me were kind and true and, so far, have assisted me in avoiding lake monsters. Without them, I would have no third novel to my name, and I'll never forget that.

Thank you, Alison Dasho. It's impossible to tell you how much our conversations about how to solve the problem like the mines meant to me. You gave me a lifeline before I realized I was drowning, and without it, I could never have told the story that needed to be this book. I find you astonishingly talented as an editor but mind-blowingly awesome as a human being. I could not have done this without you.

Gordon Warnock, you are such a constant force of reassurance in my life. Our messages and conversations take away the doubts and fear that sometimes threaten to overwhelm me. I didn't realize grounding and centering me was part of your job description, but it is an amazing part of your skill set.

Faith Black Ross, you are an insightful, inspiring editor. It's not often that editorial notes make me laugh in delight, but yours did. This book is sharper and softer because of you. Thank you.

Jon F., you made this book so much better and created copyediting conditions that were an incredible amount of fun, which makes other authors look at me like I'm crazy when I tell them about it. I bet you both hate and love the previous sentence, WHICH I worked hard to make real good. Feel free to correct it.

Kellie and Robin, I am in debt to your incredible eyes and ears during the proofread on this one. I wrote the first draft in six weeks (on deadline), and there were echoes of echoes of echoes in some sections. I'm so grateful that you caught them so this book reads the way I hoped it would.

Lake Union team, Alicia Clancy, Gabe Dumpit, Laura Barrett, and Danielle Marshall, I have loved working with you over the course of each and every book. I always thought Seattle was a rad city, but my time there is exponentially better now that I get to spend part of it with you.

BookSparks, Crystal Patriarche, Taylor Brightwell, Keely Platte, and Madison Ostrander, I have been blown away by your strengths and talents. Thank you for encouraging me to do things I never believed possible and for giving me a voice in the world beyond those of my characters.

Ben Greenberg, when you kissed me on a midnight street thirteen years ago, I knew something amazing had begun, but I had no idea it would lead us here. You are my true partner in life, love, work, and family. Every part of my life is better because you are by my side.

Thompson and Eve, someday you will read this and realize that your mother contains multitudes, like each of you do. I love you both with all my heart.

Morgan Cowie, I am in awe of you always. You are cool as hell, beautiful in every way, and fierce as a guinea pig who hasn't had a carrot in a while. I love you and yours, the esteemed and phenomenal Marc Hollin, and the irresistibly awesome Jasper and Emmerich.

Kim Slater, Nate Nash and Miss Olivia, Kate Rose, John Bennett, Miss Abbey, and Mr. George, you are embedded in my life and my heart forever, and I'm grateful for our chosen family.

Thank you to Natasha, Griffin, Siryn, and Phoenix. Your courage, huge hearts, and beautiful hope make the world a better place. Our stories are what we leave behind, and I'm so proud of the way you are writing and living yours.

Tasha, Julie, Danielle, Kelly and Carlo, Christine, Shauna and Ian, Charlene and Steve, Mel and Jamie, Celia and Dave, Jenna and Mike, Grant and Alison, Daniel and Nancy and Georgia Stubbe, I think you are all rad and I love our friendship.

To the amazing crew at Andina Brewing who have been such an incredible network of support, knowledge, and teamwork for both Ben and me. Andy and Rocio and Mel and Brent, you are good people doing awesome things in the world, and I'm so glad we know you.

Thank you to the Stellas: Deborah Wade, Tatiana Lee, and Jan Redford, and to our gifted and committed namesake, Stella Harvey. Our meetings push me to create, give me space to learn, and allow me access to the behind the scenes of the incredible work you do.

Thank you to the MasterMind, Karen Dodd, Mahtab Narsimhan, Sonia Garrett, and Caroline (Rae Knightley), for keeping me accountable, honest, inspired, and supported. True friends and good people raise each other up, and I'm grateful for the opportunity to celebrate your amazing writing and for the foundation of strength you give to mine.

Thank you to my family: Ava Perraton, Deryl Cowie, Darlene Cowie, Joan Jacobsen, Chris Cowie, Donna Cowie, Auntie Carla, Helen and Myron Smith, Auntie Linda, Uncle Dale, Cousin Sherri, Auntie Carla, Natasha, Siryn, Phoenix and Griffin, Linda and Ulrich, and Lee.

Big props to the dazzling team at Sister in National Crime-West, Charlotte Morganti, Karen Abramson, Karen Dodd, and Marcelle Dube! I am proud to stand with you and create the intricate professional and personal network we have.

Thank you to the unwavering, hilarious, astonishing, and deeply relied-upon support of my talented fellow Lake Union authors, including Kerry Lonsdale, Suzy Krause, Nicole J. Persun, Steena Holmes, Nicole Robertson Meier, Catherine McKenzie, Emily Carpenter, Libby Hawker, Elizabeth Blackwell, Kim Taylor Blakemore, and Imogen Clark.

Enormous thanks to the wider community of authors I have been welcomed into, including Robyn Harding, Shannon Kirk, Loreth Anne White, Blake Crouch, Bryan Gruley, Linda Joffe Hull, Keir Graff, D. M. Pulley, Christina MacDonald, Andrew Pyper, Samantha Bailey, Marisa Stapley, Angie Kim, Carl Vonderau, and A. J. Devlin.

I am also in debt to another incredible author whom I never had the honor of meeting, Michelle McNamara. Her posthumously published book *I'll Be Gone in the Dark* was the best book I read in 2019 and the best true crime book I have read in my life. I thought the fictional town bordering Loss Lake was eerie and fascinating enough to bear her name and I hope she would have felt the same way.

My deepest gratitude to the makers of *PJ Masks*, *Teen Titans Go!*, and *Sugar Rush*. Your contribution to working parents everywhere is monumental and must be recognized. This book could not have been completed without your creative accomplishments, and I salute you.

Finally, because this is my book and not yours, I bow down to Trixie Mattel and Yekaterina Petrovna Zamolodchicova, who are the best companions for the moments in between thoughts that beg for distraction. Trixie, your belief in yourself and your work gives me hope for this broken-down dreamer. And Katya, I would be so honored if my dad used that name.

READER GROUP QUESTIONS FOR AMBER COWIE'S *LOSS LAKE*

1. Mallory seeks to leave her grief behind by uprooting herself from Vancouver and moving to a brand-new community. Her mother suggests her decision is rash and rushed. Given the complexities of her loss, what are the complications surrounding her decision to move? Does it seem that her decision is a good one?

2. The town of McNamara is tight-knit and insular. Its citizens have long relationships with each other but still seem welcoming to a newcomer like Mallory. What makes Mallory feel safe in McNamara? What makes her feel insecure?

3. In a place as remote and socially cohesive as McNamara, stories about a town's history and an individual's character can become self-reinforcing. Are there any assumptions in McNamara that seem unusual or dubious that everyone accepts as fact? Was Mallory's judgment about any events or individuals influenced by these larger beliefs?

4. Mallory learns of several unnerving elements about McNamara and her own property after moving. Could you live in a home where someone had died as Sean did? Or beside a lake that had been the site of many deaths and drownings? Is Mallory able to reconcile herself with it?

5. Mallory states that she is more attracted to Joel than she was to her husband. What draws Mallory to Joel? What attracts Joel to Mallory?

6. Mallory's thoughts are not always clear, even to herself. There are gaps in her memory, and she isn't always capable of showing the people in her life and the readers of the story the truth about her actions (e.g., the end of Graham's life, her last interaction with Cynthia, her true reason for coming to Loss Lake). Is Mallory a sympathetic character?

7. Monsters have served as symbols in many different cultures, and several are referenced within this novel as examples of proper behavior. The monster of Loss Lake seems to represent something different to each character. What does it mean for Logan and Betty? Joel and Jonathan? Mallory? Why does Joel use the wendigo as a parallel? Why did Frederich pick the Minotaur?

ABOUT THE AUTHOR

Photo © 2019 Ben Greenberg

Amber Cowie is a novelist and freelance writer living in a small town on the west coast of British Columbia. Her work has appeared on CrimeReads and in the *New York Times* and *Salon,* among other publications. She is the author of *Raven Lane* and the number one Kindle bestseller *Rapid Falls,* which was also a runner-up in the Whistler Independent Book Awards. Amber serves as a board member of her local chapter of Sisters in Crime, and she holds an undergraduate degree from the University of Victoria. She is a mother of two and a reader of many who likes skiing, running, and writing stories that make her internet search history unnerving. For more information, visit www.ambercowie.com.